Crime Song

Praise for Crime Song

...since ....is one of the best dialogue hounds in
the business, Marr is blessed with some terrific street
talk.' Marilyn Stasio, *New York Times Book Review*

'David Swinson is one of the most exciting new voices
to come along in crime fiction in this decade, and *Crime
Song* is Exhibit A of his remarkable talent. Swinson's
writing is heartfelt, powerful, and authentic, and
Frank Marr is as fully rendered as any detective
in recent memory.' Michael Koryta

'So convincing . . . Compulsively readable.'
Jack Batten, *Toronto Star*

'Former DC detective Swinson knows his stuff . . . His
second in the Frank Marr series features sharp prose,
spot-on dialogue, and a protagonist as complicated and
unlikely as he is appealing. Fans of gritty crime fiction
will want to add Swinson to their reading lists.' *Booklist*

'A veteran detective, David Swinson knows DC's secrets and
it shows in this killer noir, so authentic it'll make you get
up and lock your doors. *Crime Song* is even better than the
fantastic *The Second Girl*, and Swinson writes with a refreshing,
understated realness. This is right up there with Richard Price
and *The Wire*.' Matthew Quirk, author of *Dead Man Switch*

Crime
Song

David Swinson

MULHOLLAND
BOOKS

HODDER

First published in Great Britain in 2017 by Mulholland Books
An imprint of Hodder & Stoughton
An Hachette UK company

This paperback edition published in 2019

1

A CIP catalogue record for this title is available from the British Library

Paperback ISBN 978 1 473 61821 3
eBook ISBN 978 1 473 61819 0

Printed and bound in Great Britain by Clays Ltd, Elcograf S.p.A.

Hodder & Stoughton policy is to use papers that are natural, renewable
and recyclable products and made from wood grown in sustainable
forests. The logging and manufacturing processes are expected to
conform to the environmental regulations of the country of origin.

Hodder & Stoughton Ltd
Carmelite House
50 Victoria Embankment
London EC4Y 0DZ

www.hodder.co.uk

For Linda Schwendiman

*She loved a good mystery, and God unveiled for her
the greatest mystery of all*

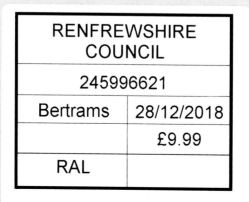

Luck is a very thin wire between survival and disaster, and not many people can keep their balance on it.

—Hunter S. Thompson

Crime Song

ONE

I tried self-restraint once. Not on purpose. Caught a bad virus. Put me down for a bit. When I got better I continued not using, but after a couple days I came back, preferring high spirits and liking myself again over a state of near comatoseness and self-loathing.

That's the memory that comes to mind when I think about what I have left of my stash. I can't get it outta my head. It'd be an incredible supply for the mere social user, and it might even last someone months, but it certainly isn't enough for the devoted.

Like me.

So in part, that's what has kept me working this case after I learned what my cousin Jeffrey Baldwin got himself into. I've been tailing and surveilling him off and on for over a week now.

Jeffrey's mom, Linda, still lives in the same small town outside Akron, Ohio. Last time we talked I was a detective at Narcotics Branch, but we lost contact when I was sent into retirement.

4 • David Swinson

Didn't return her calls. It was on me, not her. She didn't give up trying for a long time.

Then when she called me last week, I answered. She talked like we'd been keeping in touch all this time, told me she hadn't heard from Jeffrey in days and he was skipping classes at George Washington University last semester so now he has to attend summer school to catch up. Said he got in with a bad crowd in his senior year of high school in Ohio, and she's worried he's found another bad crowd to pull him down again. She thought I was still a cop and could help. I told her I was a PI now and maybe I could. No fee, though, I insisted. The least I could do in return for not keeping in touch and because she'd been there for me as a kid after my mom died.

I hate to admit it, but Aunt Linda was right. I have enough to give her, but for my own selfish reasons, I need to go further. That stash of mine ain't gonna grow on its own.

Last Thursday I followed Jeffrey to the same spot I'm headed to now—Spotlight, a trendy nightclub on Connecticut Avenue. Mostly college kids, but they get a few locals from the area, including some who look like players. Real players, not wannabes like my cousin. It didn't take me more than a few minutes to figure out the action going on.

Jeffrey would do some little deals there on the sly, quarter and half grams, a dime of weed, but only occasionally and nothing that would draw attention. Most of his dealings were with other students, outside the nightclub.

He'd meet up at the club with one of the local boys who'd re-up him for the weekend. I don't think the local is a supplier, but he'll lead me to whoever is. Eventually. Another benefit, but I'm not ready to go that far just yet. I'll get a quick hit out of Jeffrey before I tell his mom, though. It'll be like I'm doing her a service anyway. Maybe teach him a life lesson along the way.

I find a nice spot to park on Connecticut. I've got a good view of the front entrance, and there's a large tree at the curb with a trunk that gives me good concealment.

I drive a newish-model Volvo with nice tint, so I'm not worried about the pedestrian traffic, even without the tree and its large trunk. These people aren't gonna pay much attention to me.

I honed my skills conducting surveillance when I was on the department working 7D Vice, then later as a detective. You wouldn't get away with what I'm doing here in most of those locations, and most of the time you'd have one or more partners to watch your back.

I need a boost, so I grab my prescription-pill container out of my left pants pocket. It has fifty capsules that I packed tightly with cocaine. Two capsules make for a nice line—or, in this case, pile. I twist one of the capsules open and squeeze the powder out of each half onto the back of my hand. After I look around, let a couple pedestrians pass, I take a snort, twist the capsules back together, and repeat the process. Light a cigarette after.

It'll never be like the first time, but the initial wave is still nice. Also takes more than it used to, mostly when I'm home alone.

The sunset isn't so sudden during the summer months. It just softens into nighttime. This area is well lit, too: large office buildings, restaurants, and retail stores.

I notice Jeffrey. It's just after nine. Right on schedule. Not like working some of the street ops from back in the day. Can't depend on those drug boys worth shit. At least he's reliable. He's wearing designer jeans and a stylish black slim-cut sport coat over a gray V-neck T-shirt.

Fucking kid. What happened to you?

Fuckin' me. What the hell am I doing? Just go tell Aunt Linda and leave it, maybe have a talk with him after. In my mind he's still just a small round-faced boy.

I watch him enter, then I give myself another bump and exit the car. I flick my cigarette to the gutter, put my suit jacket on to conceal my sidearm, straighten it out so it falls nicely over my shirt collar, then make my way to the front entrance.

Two

An older cop in a cheap suit is working the door tonight. He greets me with an upward tilt of his head. I don't know him. He's not one of the regulars who work this part-time gig. He's a big man, mid- to late fifties, but I wouldn't ever fuck with him. He looks like he hits the gym almost every day.

The music's loud, though not as uncomfortably loud as it'll get when the DJ hits the mixing board with that techno-electronic shit and scratches vinyl on his turntables. Scratch vinyl? Good God. I should be long gone by then.

Jeffrey's standing at the bar nursing a beer. Everyone seems well dressed. Trendy. Black leather booths set in darker areas for those special moments. The area around the bar is backlit against gold to highlight the liquor bottles on the shelves. Two bartenders working—one male and one female. She's wearing a bra like it's an eighties fashion statement.

It's early enough for me to find a seat at the edge of the bar, where it's darkest. I've got a couple of hours before the in crowd starts to show. I order a double Jameson Caskmates 'cause the bartender measures the shit out, and an ounce and half is nothin' but a sip for me.

I notice Jeffrey over my left shoulder still nursing his beer when I'm surprised by a question: "Just saw ya last week, Frankie boy. You becoming a regular here?"

Willy Jasper is leaning on the edge of the bar between me and an empty stool. He's a master patrol officer out of the First District and runs the part-time here. It's an unsanctioned off-duty job, 'cause cops can't work as bouncers at a club.

Who am I to care?

Jasper's not wearing a suit tonight, so I'm assuming he's not here to work.

"Willy, hey. Just finishing up that security gig, that building down the street. What's up with you? I thought they had a dress code here. Or are you working undercover?" I ask with a bit of a smile.

"Undercover. Shit. I'm on my way to work midnight shift. Stopped by to check in on my boy first. Then I saw you at the bar here all by your lonesome and thought I'd drop by."

The bartender in the bra shows up for Jasper.

"Hi, sweetie," he says.

"Hey, there, Willy. Can I get you something?"

"Just a soda."

She shoots him a smile before she turns.

"Yeah, you got a good gig here," I tell him.

I casually look over my shoulder to make sure Jeffrey's still there.

He is.

"I can hook you up if you want. Money's good, and I can use the extra manpower. Chief's got us working all kinds of mandatory OT shit. Hard for me to fill up some of the hours here."

"I keep myself busy enough, and I'm not pressed for money

right now. But you never know what the future holds. I'll keep it in mind. Thanks."

The bartender returns with his soda.

"Thanks, hon," Jasper says with a smile. "And give my boy here another of whatever he's drinking on my tab, would ya?"

"'Preciate it, Jasper." I lift my glass toward him, and he clinks his glass of soda against mine.

He throws me a peculiar half smile after.

"But seriously," he says after sipping his soda. "Big boy Wyatt Morris over there at the door is retired, like you. He's been working with me for a few years. We go back. In fact, he was my training officer."

"No shit? Yeah, I noticed him. Looks like he keeps in shape for his age."

"Ex-military and straight to DC police after. Retired outta ERT."

I down the rest and trade the bartender the empty for another. Looks like she gave me a good pour this time.

"Job comes with benefits, too, huh?" I take a drink.

"Naw, man, I ain't tapping that," he tells me.

"I meant the drinks."

He belts out a screwy laugh. "Oh, yeah. They take care of ya here."

I casually look toward Jeffrey again.

Jasper looks at the time on his big wristwatch.

"I gotta roll. Still have to hit the locker room and change up before roll call."

"Be safe, Jasper."

"Likewise, brother. Drop by again sometime. I'm always here Fridays, Saturdays."

"I'll be sure to do that."

He walks back to the front, talks with his boy for a moment, then rolls out.

With any luck, after tonight I won't have to come to this place again. My hangouts are the spots that never change, like Shelly's and Rebellion DC. They don't cater to crowds who expect the next trend. Or, thankfully, play this fucking music. I'm just hoping my cousin gets this shit done before the DJ hits the stage.

"You a cop, too?" the bartender with the bra asks.

She's leaning over the other side of the bar facing me. Maybe a little too close.

"No. Not anymore."

"You look too young to be retired."

"Moved on is all."

"So what do you do, then?"

"I like to drink. Occasionally sleep," I say straight-faced, with a tone that I hope expresses lack of interest.

She shoots me a cute smile, and with little effort she slips away to help another customer.

There was a time in my life I might've been interested, pursued it with enthusiasm. See if she really liked me or was just making a flirty attempt at getting a bigger tip. But no, I'm too fixed on a certain lifestyle, one that I can't jeopardize. And Leslie Costello is a major part of that lifestyle. Last thing I want to do is fuck it up with her. You don't get that many chances in life.

Third drink in, more people showing up, and Jeffrey is still at the corner of the bar, but now nursing a martini. It's been around forty-five minutes, and he hasn't budged.

Few minutes later, a young kid wearing a white T-shirt with an abstract cannabis leaf design on the front seems to bounce through the entrance. His baggy dark blue jeans hang a bit too low, and his dreadlocks fall to his shoulders. It's not the same kid as before, when I was here last Thursday, but I note Jeffrey clocking him.

At the bar, they share some kind of special handshake. They

talk for a second, then Jeffrey gets the attention of the male tender and orders something. The tender draws a glass of beer from the tap, slides it to Dreadlocks. Jeffrey pays the tab, and the two walk to a corner booth in a quieter area of the club.

For an experienced guy like me, the exchange is obvious and quick. Jeffrey stuffs something into the left inner pocket of his sport coat—something that seems too large to fit there. He stands afterward and walks to the men's room.

Dreadlocks picks up his beer and walks toward a group of girls near the DJ booth. A couple of them smile as he approaches.

I could follow him into the restroom. It'd be easy. So easy I even find myself giving it serious thought. He'd know who I am. That'd make taking the shit off of him easier. What's he gonna do? It'd scare the shit outta him, but then maybe we'd hug after. Fuck me. I know what he's got, and I know he's going into the restroom to check it out. At most he'll share a half a gram with a couple of cute girls, but that's about it. He'll go home, probably shove what he got in a shoe box, and hide it somewhere close to his bed. I'll snatch it up after he goes to his morning classes. After I give his mom everything I know, she'll kick his ass into the military or some shit like that—I hope.

I down the rest of my drink, then signal the bra queen for the tab.

"It's taken care of," she says kindly.

"Thank Willy for me, then."

I drop a twenty on the counter. She smiles.

I go home, see if I can find some sleep.

THREE

First thing I do when I get home is go check my stash wall. I admit I'm getting increasingly paranoid, but for some reason being aware of it makes it feel less like a weakness. It's become obsessive, I guess, a stupid little ritual. Otherwise I don't feel safe. Seeing the neat little wall in its place, I feel my heart lift. It's like magical thinking in reverse.

There's a small room just before the entrance to my kitchen. Inside is the HVAC system for the house as well as a washer and dryer. I unlatch a phantom hinge that allows me to open the molding along the outer edge of the drywall. It's like a tall, thin secret door. I slide the drywall that's against the right side of the washer out along its hinges to open the enclosed area.

Inside there are several shelves affixed to two-by-fours.

I got rid of the weapons I've picked up along the way, 'cause I'm sure they had bodies on them. I still carry, but I'm covered under my retirement and 218, so mine's legal. Will a certain assistant chief at the department try to fuck me out of my weapon? Maybe. But then maybe he forgot about old Frank and I'm just being twitchy.

I also have a shelf where I store several large baggies of weed; four pill containers, the labels torn off, containing Oxy, Vicodin, Valium, and Klonopin, none of which is prescribed for me; another shelf that holds a little more than twenty grand in cash, stacked and secured with rubber bands; and a baggie that contains around an ounce of good powder. That's what's left—an ounce.

Who knows if I'll get anything out of Jeffrey's apartment? So I gotta slow down a bit on what blow I have left. My body says I gotta slow down, too. Just have to start cutting back to certain times of the day, never while working. Unless it's an emergency. Most of the time it is. That's why I have to do the quick hit on my little cousin's place and have a plan for what comes after. Planning these ops and then executing them can often take up more of my time than my real job as a PI. But that, along with my scanty pension and whatever work Leslie Costello throws my way, pays the bills.

I'm not getting much work from Leslie, though. It's taken a while, 'cause I've known her for a long time, but we've finally settled into a relationship of sorts. It's something cozy and fun for now. But I don't think she feels comfortable with bossing me or having to pay me for my PI services. I don't mind. I actually like it.

After I've had my time with the bank, I slide the wall back, secure it.

Upstairs, I grab two 1mg Klonopin pills out of a container I keep in my pocket and down them with a nice shot of Jameson.

I set my iPhone on the coffee table in case Leslie calls, think about putting an old Johnny Cash record or maybe the Cowboy Junkies' *The Trinity Session* on the turntable. I light up a smoke instead and bide my time reclining on the sofa. After a bit, the Klonopin flows. It helps ease the tension and my cravings with it.

FOUR

Daylight is sudden. Trying to surprise me by creeping behind the top edge of the curtains. Pretty sure I found sleep. Unusual because of the amount of blow I put through my system. I check the time on my phone: 7:00 a.m. Damn!

No time for a shower, just a quick change of clothing. I throw on a newly pressed shirt and the suit from last night, but no tie. I snort up a couple of lines. Almost feel human again. I check the vial to make sure I'm supplied, then secure my holster and the pouch holding two magazines to my belt, grab my backpack containing my essential items, and head out the front door. I lock it, check it, then check it again.

I have a little time to kill before Jeffrey goes to his class, so I head to the diner on 18th Street in Adams Morgan for a couple cups of coffee and a quick bite.

When I'm done, I drive to Jeffrey's little English-basement apartment on N Street. Don't see his car. I drive around twice looking for a legal parking spot. Find one around the corner on 22nd. He'll have left for classes by now.

It ain't cheap renting in this area. GW ain't cheap, either. Aunt Linda must've done well for herself, especially after the divorce. It's too bad about Jeffrey, but I'll snatch him up eventually. Try to talk some sense into him. But first I'm sure he'll be good for at least a couple of ounces, maybe more. That's only pocket shit for me, but I'll take what I can get at this point.

He's too easy, really. All these expensive homes, with their heavy landscaping, make for perfect targets. I have to wonder how many of these spots have already been hit. One more won't matter. Doubtful if Jeffrey will even report it. After I get done in there I'm sure that'll be the last thing on his mind.

I walk down the steps to his front door like I got a reason for being there. I take the tactical gloves out of a side pocket of the backpack and slip them on. Ring the doorbell. After a minute, ring it again, followed by a couple of knocks on one of the door's square glass panes. I look behind me and up the steps. Clear. The brick walls on either side of me are concealment enough. The front door looks simple—probably just need a screwdriver to pry it open, or, better yet, I could smash out one of the door's glass panes.

I grab a hand towel and a screwdriver out of the middle compartment of my pack, fold up the towel, and cover a corner pane on the door. Using the butt end of the screwdriver, I hit the towel toward the bottom, smashing the glass inward. Only sound comes from inside when the glass breaks on the floor. I reach in and unlatch the door, open it, step in, and lock it behind me. I stand still by the front door for a moment to survey the scene. To listen.

Looks like it was furnished by the owners, not a kid Jeffrey's age. The small living room opens to a tiny kitchen separated from the living room by a wooden breakfast counter and three stools. A love seat flanked by two mission-style end tables is against the wall ahead of me. There's a coffee table in front of it and an armchair to the side. A sixty-inch flat-screen television, along with an Xbox and several stacks of Xbox games, sits on another coffee table across from the sofa. A short hallway to the right of the kitchen leads to two doors on the left and one at the end of the hall, which is probably his bedroom. I scan the ceiling and the walls, including the entryway where I'm standing. Nothing that looks like surveil-lance. Don't expect it, but you never know, especially when the occupant is a rich white kid dealing drugs. My little cousin: damn.

It's messy, but the kind of messiness you'd expect from a kid his age living on his own—worn clothing hanging over the sofa; sneakers everywhere; couple of empty containers of Chinese takeout with plastic forks still in them; microbrew beer bottles on the coffee table and breakfast counter. Not close to looking or even smelling like some of the spots I've hit over the years, both in my current position and when I was on the job ex-ecuting actual search warrants.

When I've taken in enough I walk down the hall toward his bed-room. I always start in the bedroom. That's where I usually find what I'm looking for. Most of these boys like to keep the shit close.

The bedroom is messier than the living room. No family pho-tos. Something happened there; probably the divorce. I look under the bed, lift the mattress, but don't find anything. Find a couple of joints in an ashtray on the nightstand beside his bed. I put them in my shirt pocket. I search the drawers, then go to the closet. After a thorough search of the bedroom I return to the liv-ing room area and the small kitchen. I find some paraphernalia in a cabinet beside the stove—little Ziploc bags for quarter and half grams, a scale with residue on it, cutting agents, and that's fuck-ing about it. It pisses me off. I mean, who am I to judge? But shit,

I don't deal, and I certainly wouldn't want to put my lifestyle on someone else, especially Jeffrey. It ain't for everyone.

The apartment is so small it doesn't take long. I've spent too much time in here already. He either took the shit with him or hooked up at the club and didn't come home at all. Fucking waste of my time. Fuck.

I roll out. Figure I'll go back home and write this thing up for Aunt Linda. I got what she wants—or, rather, what she doesn't want. I'll give her some comfort and say I'll talk to him, scare him, even. I know how to use fear, and with any luck Jeffrey's not so far gone that it won't work.

FIVE

When I make the turn onto 12th I see several marked and unmarked units as well as an ambulance. Couple of local news media vans, too, with cameras already set up on tripods. Looks like a bad scene, and it's near my house. Shit, I'm high. Now I have to take an illegal spot at the corner. And fuck, I gotta walk through all that to get to my house. If I can get to my house. They got the yellow tape up, connected to a fence a couple homes down from mine and stretching across the sidewalk to a utility pole. One of the cruisers, I notice, is cruiser 1.

The damn chief.

A few neighbors are out. Worried faces all around.

When I get half a block up I'm more than startled to see the house they're moving through is mine.

Fuck!

I got my pack full with shit I don't want to be found, and I probably smell like weed.

I light a cigarette. Puff the smoke down so it folds around my clothes.

What good is that?

Did they finally hit me, and that's a search warrant?

I think about going back to my car, taking off. At the least drop the pack off in my car. Taking off sounds better, though.

I'm frozen. I never freeze.

One of the officers notices me. I know him. Hal Lloyd. He's an old-timer outta 3D. He waves me toward him, then signals a detective close by and points me out to him.

I think I just got fucked.

Cameras pan toward me.

So much for taking off.

I acknowledge him, and after a couple more puffs of the cigarette I slowly make my way over there, still considering the possibility of running.

How stupid is that? Fucking cameras got me on the local news now.

"That's my house. What the hell's going on here, Lloyd?" I ask.

"Hey, Frankie. I'll let the detective here advise you about that," he says while lifting the tape so I can duck under and enter.

The young detective is there to greet me. No cuffs out, so maybe…

"Detective Joe Hurley." He introduces himself and extends his hand to shake.

I accept.

"What happened?" I ask with more than a bit of trepidation.

"Let's talk at your house. Let me get the detective on the scene."

When they don't answer, then it's not gonna be good.

"You're a detective," I tell him.

"I'm on a burglary-fencing task force downtown. I'm not the lead on this."

"My house was burglarized?"

"Let's find Detective Millhoff."

When they don't answer...

"Millhoff? I know him. He's Homicide."

"He's inside your house" is all he says.

The chief is standing beside his number two man, Deputy Chief Garrett Wightman, who is on his cell. I have a history with Wightman, and it's not good. What the fuck is going on? Am I done? They got something on me and hit my house?

The chief turns to take notice of me, but there's no reaction. He just lets the detective walk me to my stoop.

I snuff my cigarette out on the sidewalk. Heart's racing. I need a drink.

I notice Wightman again. He's off his cell. Looks at me hard. Not with the Wightman half smile that he likes to give to those who are about to get fucked, so maybe...

Six

My house is a crime scene.

I'm in the hallway but can see to my living room. It's been ransacked. Sofa cushions are turned over; end-table drawers are open and the contents spilled out.

Search warrant or burglary?

Hurley steps away toward my kitchen to find Millhoff. He walks past the laundry room, where my stash wall is. Doesn't look that way when he passes. *A good sign?* It's a small room, so even from here I'd notice movement inside. But maybe they already cleared it. Can't take not knowing.

I'm not in handcuffs, but a rookie in uniform is stationed at the front door behind me. Seems at ease as I stand there alone.

Millhoff walks out of the kitchen, followed by Hurley. He doesn't gaze in the laundry room, either. Millhoff has latex gloves on. He's wearing khakis and an untucked navy-blue polo shirt with MPDC HOMICIDE BRANCH embroidered in gold on the breast. I go back with Millhoff. He's good people. Handled a drive-by shooting I got caught up in about a year back when I was working a missing-girl case. A patrol officer got killed on that one. I was damn lucky. Most of that crew they arrested will be lucky if they ever see the light of day. The cop who got killed was found to be dirty. Of course that was based on information I leaked to a certain FBI agent. Didn't hear much about that part on the news. Go figure. You didn't hear anything about my early retirement on the news, either.

"Frank" is how he greets me.

Doesn't take off the latex gloves to shake.

"What the hell is going on here, Timmy?" I ask.

I look in my living room.

"That wasn't us," he says like he knows I'm worried.

"You saying my house got hit?" I ask Millhoff.

"It looks that way. Where you been?"

"Working a job early this morning, then breakfast. So why the hell you here? And for that matter, why the two chiefs outside just for a burglary?"

My stash wall.

"Can we talk in your living room?"

That was a question.

"Yeah."

They follow me into the living room.

Wires are hanging out of a hole in the wall where the flat-screen once was. Worst of all, the stereo equipment, including the old turntable and vinyl collection, most of which belonged to my mother, gone, along with my CD collection. Who'd steal vinyl? The laptop's also missing from the coffee table.

"Shit," I say.

Lot of activity in the kitchen. I try to get a glimpse. I got a strong feeling about what's in there. The air has a nauseating sweet odor to it. I'm all too familiar with that smell.

Hurley lifts a couple of the cushions off the floor and places them back on the sofa. I sit on the edge so I can look toward the kitchen. Millhoff takes the armchair.

I light a smoke, offer one to Millhoff and Hurley.

Shake their heads.

"You have a roommate, Frankie?"

What kinda question is that?

"No, of course not. I live alone. You got a body in my kitchen," I say, not ask.

"Yes, we do."

"Police-involved shooting? The burglar?" I ask, assuming it was a burglary in progress that went bad.

"Not police-involved," Millhoff says.

What the hell, then?

I feel uncomfortable as shit sitting there, high as I am. Racing heart and negative adrenalin is making it worse. My head like a hare trying to outrace a pack of wolves.

"You were working these last couple of hours?" Millhoff asks again.

"What?"

"What the fuck, Frank? I gotta ask. You know that."

"What you gotta do is tell me what happened in my house."

"All right. Was going to have to do this part anyway. May as well now." He stands. "I'm going to need to see if you can identify the body."

"Fuck," I say more like an exhale of air.

Please, not my stash wall.

I need to know.

I snuff out my smoke and follow Millhoff through the dining room and into the kitchen. Another detective is there, but I don't know him.

A body on the floor.

My back door busted inward, splintered frame.

A white male.

On his back.

It's Jeffrey. My cousin. My legs buckle a bit, feeling like I'm about to fall out.

"Frank?" Millhoff sounds concerned.

Holy fuck!

His shirt's rich with blood. A fresh color at the chest with an area near his waist that has pooled. Looks like strawberry Jell-O without the film coating. And this was the smell in my home—a lingering, disagreeably sweet odor. My cousin's.

I drop to my knee.

"You okay, Frank?" Millhoff asks.

I don't respond.

Death is in his dull eyes—a frozen, forsaken stare, as if taken by surprise. He's wearing the same clothes he wore last night at the club. Jacket's still on. Same V-neck T-shirt, but his blood has turned it a darker shade of gray. I wanna put my hand on his head, feel him. He can't be dead.

"What in the fuck—"

"Frank, you know this guy?"

But still—my stash wall.

SEVEN

H e's my cousin. Jeffrey Baldwin," I say. "It doesn't make sense."

His face an older version of the five-year-old kid's. I wanna take his hand.

"I thought you said you didn't have anyone staying with you," Millhoff says.

"I don't. That's why this doesn't make sense."

"Did he have a key?"

I don't answer. I just shake my head, like I'm starting to lose it. Fading away. I have to turn away from him. Can't look at him like this.

"Let's talk in the living room," Millhoff says.

Still have enough sense to be worried about my stash.

How could I think about that right now?

I purposefully walk toward the hall. They don't stop me. I watch my steps, though, make sure I don't trample evidence that might be on the kitchen floor.

When I enter the narrow hallway I casually look in the laundry room as I pass.

It's all good.

Wall still intact.

Fuck. I'm so relieved I even get the chills. For a brief moment I feel fine, but then reality slaps me in the face.

Jeffrey. Dead. On my kitchen floor.

I light another cigarette when I get back to the sofa.

This time Hurley sits at the other end. Millhoff on the armchair again. I'm having a tough time. Feeling a bit sick to my stomach, even.

"Did he have a key to your house?" Millhoff asks again.

"No, of course not."

"Why 'of course not'?"

"'Cause he's the case I've been working. For his mother. My aunt. He didn't know."

Did he know?

"Last time he saw me he was about fourteen years old."

"So where exactly have you been the past couple of hours?" Millhoff asks.

"Driving around the GW campus looking for him."

"He was missing?"

"No. His mother wanted me to watch him. That's all. Report back if he was up to no good. He was. Why the fuck is he dead in my house? It makes no sense. We never met after he moved here. Never even talked. Everything was surveillance. Nothing close. I don't understand this shit."

"But aren't they on summer break?" Millhoff asks.

"He was in summer school."

"What's his address?" Millhoff asks.

I give it to him, and he writes it in his notebook. He goes on his radio.

"Carlson, you on?"

Carlson's response is filtered through the radio. "Go ahead, Timmy."

"I have an address for the decedent when you're ready to copy."

"Go on."

After he gives it to him, Carlson returns with, "I'll get some patrol guys down there to secure it."

Fuck me.

But I know they won't find anything they can connect to me. I'm no amateur.

"What was the kid into?" Millhoff continues.

"Jeffrey knew I was a cop here. Maybe he found out where I live, came here for help. Or maybe I fucked up and he made me. Came over and he was followed. But it was just petty shit he was into."

"Frank, what was he into?"

"Um—have you notified his mother yet?" I ask.

"No. We didn't even know who he was until you identified him."

"No ID on his body?"

"Nothing. Clean. His mother live in the area?"

"No. Ohio. I forget the town, but I have numbers."

"We'll have to notify her through their local jurisdiction. Not on the phone, but I'll still need those numbers. So what was he into?" Millhoff tries again.

Last thing I want to do is hinder a homicide investigation.

"GW student pretending to be a player; nothing but low-level shit. Deals small quantities of cocaine, weed. Nothing else. Damn."

"And you found all this out how?" Millhoff asks.

I like Millhoff, but that question pisses me off.

"You forgetting what I did when I was on the job?"

"No. You were one of the best narcotics detectives in the city.

I still gotta ask, though. There has to be some connection that brought him here."

"Yes, and I don't mean to sound hostile. It just...I don't...I don't understand this."

"Are you sure he didn't know you were following him?" Millhoff asks.

"Right now I'm not sure of anything. But I've never been burned before."

"Anybody else know about you watching him and what he was up to?"

"Leslie Costello knew I was watching him but not what he was up to."

"Former cop Costello turned defense attorney?"

"Yes. We go out on occasion. Talk about work."

"We'll need to talk to her."

"There's no connection there, but do what you gotta do."

"Anyone else you can think of you may have talked to?"

"No," I say. "I was coming home to write it up for his mother and give her a call after."

"You were coming straight from the GW area?" he asks.

"Yeah. His car wasn't there, so I figured he finally went to a class."

"Approximately what time in the morning did you leave your home?" Hurley asks.

"Maybe oh-seven-hundred. Wanted to try to catch him leaving his place and going to class. Like I said, the car wasn't there, so I stuck around for a bit. I'm guessing patrol got dispatched for sound of gunshots here."

"Yeah," Millhoff advises.

"With what I saw outside, including the media and in here, it had to be close to an hour ago, maybe less. Right?"

"Something like that." Millhoff is vague.

"Neighbors see anything?"

"Got our boys canvassing now."

I start thinking like a cop again.

"The back alley is narrow as shit. Hardly fit in one car. Couple of the homes rear of mine are three stories. Might want to have that street canvassed, too."

"We're on it, Frank."

"His car, too," I say as I pull the notebook out of my back pants pocket.

Leafing through it, I find the entry I made when I first made his car, including the tag. I hand it over to Millhoff. He copies the information into his notebook. He seems to hesitate before handing it back to me.

"Can I keep this? Make copies and return it?" he asks.

"Fuck no. That's about all the notes I took on him, anyway. It wasn't the kind of case that involved a lot of note taking."

I have nothing to hide in there. I'm not stupid enough to take notes about what I do outside my legit work, so I add, "Go ahead and look through it if you want. I certainly don't want to impede your investigation, but I'm not giving it up to you."

It pisses me off when he takes me up on it and looks through it briefly. Fucking doesn't trust me. He hands the notebook back. I slip it back in my pocket.

"Thanks, Frankie," he says. "Rizzi!" he calls out toward the kitchen.

"Yeah" from the kitchen, then a young plainclothes officer appears.

"This is the info on the decedent's car. Get a couple of patrol guys to canvass the area, all right?"

"Copy that."

After Rizzi writes everything down in his notebook, he exits the front door.

"Did you identify where he was getting his drugs?" Hurley asks.

"Huh? No. No, that wasn't part of it. But I did see him get re-upped a couple of times. A trendy dance club on Connecticut every Thursday night."

"Last night, then?" asks Hurley.

"Yeah, last night."

"What trendy club?"

"Spotlight."

"You were there last night?" Now it's Millhoff asking.

"Yes. Look in his breast pocket. He should have a baggie of cocaine or something."

"He's clean. Remember I said he was clean. No ID, keys, nothing," Millhoff says.

"The kid your cousin met with—you think he could've made you?" Hurley asks.

"No. Too much going on in the club, and it's not like I was in his face. In fact I was talking to Willy Jasper from 1D."

"I know Jasper. He's a good FTO," Hurley says.

"Yeah, and I don't want to get him fucked up, because he's got one of those part-times at the club. And you know how Wightman can be."

"I could care less about the part-time. Hell, I work one. Does he know your cousin?" Millhoff asks.

"Why would he know my cousin?"

"Because he's working part-time as an officer in the club where your cousin was dealing drugs."

"That's something you'd have to ask Jasper. But I doubt it."

"Why were you looking for Jeffrey this morning?" Now Hurley.

"I told you. His mother wanted to know when he was cutting classes. I know he had one this morning, though."

"Obviously he wasn't there?"

"What, we repeating questions now?" I say, a bit hyped.

No answer from either of them.

"By the way, those look to be the same clothes he was wearing last night," I add, then "Fuck, fuck, fuck…" like I thought it instead of said it.

"What?" Millhoff asks.

"What do you mean, 'What?'"

"You just said 'fuck, fuck, fuck' like you realized something."

"What? No, it's just…" I try to keep my heart from hammering too loud. "There's got to be something I'm missing."

"Well, let's work through it, then," Millhoff advises.

"Did you follow him out after he re-upped?" Hurley asks.

"No. I only wanted to see him do that shit, and I was out of there. Can't stand the music."

"Would you be able to recognize the guy who brought him the drugs if you saw him again?"

"Yeah, pretty sure I can."

"Describe him for me."

"Medium complexion, early twenties, maybe five eight, dreads down to his shoulders. He was wearing a T-shirt with a marijuana-leaf design on it. There's a female bartender who was working. She served him a couple of times. Maybe she knows him."

"You know her name?"

"No, but she was the only female bartender working when I was there. First time I was surveilling him, though, he stayed until closing. Left alone."

"What times were you there?"

"Around nineteen thirty to around twenty-three hundred hours."

My mind, still riding on coke, keeps moving.

"What was he shot with?" I ask.

"We don't have that yet," Millhoff says, and I know he's not telling the truth.

"I have a .38 I keep upstairs in my nightstand drawer. You'll wanna go check if it's there."

Hurley stands.

"I'll check it out. Be right back," he says.

"You know how it looks, Frank," Millhoff says after Hurley leaves. "For all we know you were gone because you were disposing of your own property. You confronted your cousin about what he was doing, and it went real bad."

"Fuck you, Tim."

"And you made it look like a burglary."

"He is my cousin, but if I was the shooter I'd sure as hell do a better job at making it look otherwise. The body certainly wouldn't be in my kitchen. So again, fuck you."

"Take it easy, Frank. You know I had to go there, just like I have to go here."

"What's that?"

"Don't leave town."

"Fuck you twice."

He smiles, but it's the kinda smile you make when you understand.

"Don't waste too much time on me or you'll never solve it, 'cause next time it'll be more than a 'fuck you.'"

"That a threat?"

"A bitch-slap threat."

He smiles again, differently this time.

EIGHT

There's gotta be an answer.

I try hard to relax myself on the sofa, take slow, deep breaths, without drawing attention to how high I am.

"I'll need an inventory of what's been stolen," Hurley tells me. "When we get finished here, I'll do a walk-through with you."

I bow my head, cup my chin in my hand. I feel sick. I never feel this way when working, but this is my home. My own damn family.

"Frank, we're going to have to test you for gunpowder residue. Rule you out. And your fingerprints, because they're obviously going to be all over your house and we need to rule those out, too," Millhoff tells me.

"I don't have a problem with that," I respond because I knew that was something Millhoff would ask, and they won't find my fingerprints at Jeffrey's house. "You have to let me know when you notify his mom so I can call her, all right?"

"Of course."

I stare at the wires hanging out of the wall and the vacant

area on the dusty entertainment console where the CDs and my mom's vinyl collection and turntable used to be. The thought that it is or was all in the possession of some bottom-feeder sets my blood hot. And there's Jeffrey.

I kick the coffee table with the sole of my foot, sending it across the room to land legs up ahead of the fireplace, surprising the hell outta Millhoff and a couple officers in the hallway. Two detectives enter from the kitchen, guns drawn at a tucked position.

Millhoff waves them off.

"Didn't mean to do that. Sorry."

"Understandable," Millhoff says. "Understandable. You'll have to come to VCU. Give a formal statement."

"Yeah, I know."

NINE

A patrol unit located Jeffrey's car parked on W, about a block away. They got guys in his house, too. I heard it come over Hurley's radio that it's a burglary. Shit. I just made the investigation more complicated for these guys.

My mind is skipping, tripping over itself. I need a Klonopin. I need two, but Hurley and I are doing the walk-through.

Everything's a mess. Same way I'd do it if I were the burglar.

In my bedroom the drawers have been pulled out, dumped on the floor. Clothing, personal items, and papers tossed into a pile.

I move around the bed to the nightstand. The drawer and its contents also on the floor. No gun. Back downstairs, I sit on the living room sofa with Hurley. Millhoff is now outside, probably getting Jeffrey's vehicle towed. I have a preliminary list of what I know to be stolen. The revolver's serial number is on a concealed-carry permit in my wallet; I note the make, model, caliber, and serial number along with my rounds. I also note approximately two hundred assorted vinyl albums and a few of their titles; approximately three hundred assorted music CDs, also with a few of their titles; one old-model Technics turntable (no serial number); two Polk shelf speakers; a sixty-inch Samsung smart TV; a Samsung laptop (serial number unknown). Approximately three years old. I got the main stuff.

"Might discover more later," I tell Hurley.

"Let me know."

He hands me a card with his cell on it.

"I'm usually always working," he says.

"I gotta tell you, I don't like feeling like a victim. What pisses me off most is the turntable and the records. I inherited about sixty percent of the vinyl from my mother. And the turntable. She used to listen to all her records on that thing."

He looks at me funny. "Sorry to hear that."

"Thanks. I was a little kid when she died. Long fucking time ago."

Jeffrey's fallen body pops into my head, like he's reminding me from beyond that he should be the focus, not the fucking records.

"But then there's Jeffrey. There's gotta be something I missed, something I didn't see."

"We both know Millhoff is one of the best, and personally, I'm pretty good at what I do. We'll figure it out."

"What task force you on?" I ask.

"We call it narco-fencing. It's funded by the feds. We have the biggest burglary-closure rate in the nation. It's all about that one burglar you get, and then working him up the ladder. Damn—crack houses, organized fencing operations, even mom-and-pop ops. Burglary is the nexus to all crimes, really. The .38 might be a tough one, though. It's in the wind. Doubtful we'll ever get that back unless we get lucky on a search warrant or find it on a body."

"I hope it won't come to that—the body, I mean."

"Used records and CDs are pretty easy. Those items aren't

easily traded for narcotics. Burglars usually go to pawn shops or secondhand dealers and get the cash. That's easy enough to check on. Their computers are linked to our database so we can monitor them."

"I know that."

"Yeah. Unless they purchase the stolen items under the table."

"But you can still do a spot check—just show up. I'll make a list of most of the titles, some of them pretty obscure. I can also identify some of them based on the scribbles on the covers. I made those when I was a kid."

He looks at the preliminary list I made.

"Sorry about the handwriting."

He looks it over.

"Yeah. Some of these titles are unique. Your mother listened to Fugazi?"

"No. That's me."

"Well, I'm more of a classic rock kinda guy, so I don't know a lot of these bands. But they're distinctive, so the odds are almost nonexistent that there'd be another collection with the exact titles in it, especially if there's a place that bought them soon after your burglary. I mean, you have Johnny Cash, the Carpenters mixed with bands I never heard of. Bad Brains...Dropkick Murphys? What are you into, man? And then, damn—Bread?"

"One of my mother's, like most of the others, but more sentimental to me. As far as that other shit, what can I say? I grew up in DC back when the 9:30 Club was cool and Fort Reno was the spot."

"I gotcha. And I'll work it in, brother," he tells me. "Don't get your hopes up. You know the odds."

"I'll keep the hope, even though I know the odds."

Then there's Jeffrey again.

"So you'll work the property side and Millhoff the homicide?"

"Yeah. That's why they have me here. And I have to tell you this because I have a feeling you're not the type of guy who's going to sit around and wait on us. Don't get yourself caught up with anything that'll interfere with a homicide investigation."

"I'm good at what I do, too."

"I realize that, and just like I can't tell a regular victim that he can't hire a PI, I can't order you to sit back. So if you do follow through with something, you make sure to keep me posted, especially if you get a lead. You can easily get yourself in trouble on this one. When you see the chief's outside your door? You know it's high priority. And Wightman will fuck you to no end, trust me."

Trust me when I say I know that, but I don't say it.

"No worries."

When we finish, Hurley gets a tech to test for gunpowder residue and take my fingerprints. Negative, but that doesn't mean shit. I know they're gonna look at me as a possible suspect. They have to.

Starting to drift. I light another cigarette. Need something more than nicotine.

"My downstairs bathroom isn't a crime scene, is it? I wanna wash this shit off my hands."

"This whole house is a crime scene, but they've already cleared your hallway bathroom."

I set the cigarette in the ashtray, grab my pack, and go to the bathroom to get what I need, which is more than washing my hands.

TEN

I got back from VCU late. A no-sleep night. Basically the same questions, but they wanted everything recorded. Millhoff got hard on me, asked me about the smell on me. I understand.

Now I got this here.

Cleaning up. The only job cops aren't required to do.

Before I get to work on the blood-soaked kitchen floor, I grab my cell to call Aunt Linda.

She answers on the first ring.

"Yes," she says, but the way she says it is enough for me to know she's been crying for a while.

"Linda, I'm sorry. I don't know what to say except I'm going to find out who's responsible."

"Who's responsible? Who's responsible? Frank, you can talk to our lawyer about who is responsible."

"What?"

"I called you because I had no one else to call. How could you not be responsible?"

"You have to know I—"

"I should have known better than to trust you," she sobs. "You're just like your father."

"What?"

"Don't call here anymore, Frank."

She disconnects.

"Shit."

What did she mean by that? My father? I never even knew my father. Or does she mean my stepfather?

I want to throw the phone but realize I need it. I wanna break something.

I snort a hefty pile of coke instead.

Lawyer? Why the hell not?

I put my latex gloves on, fill a bucket of water with too much bleach mixed in, and pick up a rag from a bunch of old rags I got out of the backyard shed. Never had to clean up blood before. Well, my own on occasion, but never spilled like this.

My cell's been ringing off the hook. Mostly from Leslie and Al Luna, but there are a couple other numbers I don't recognize. Luna was my partner at Narcotics Branch when I was on the job, and he's about the only one I keep in touch with now and still call a friend.

I also did a quick fix on the door. It'll have to be replaced. I boarded it up with two-by-fours I had lying around. It's more secure now than it was before. Maybe I should leave it that way. I rarely use the back door.

I toss the soaked rag in a heavyweight trash bag, pick up a clean one, and let it soak up the bleach water and then scrub again. Most of it is soaked up. The grout will have to be scrubbed. I feel sick. All I can see is his face as a five-year-old, a puffy black eye, and a snicker because he was so proud of it.

My doorbell rings. Startles me.

I drop the nearly blood-soaked rag in the bucket, peel off the latex gloves, and toss them in the garbage bag. I grab my gun from the kitchen counter.

Gun tucked to my side, I peek through the peephole. It's dark out, but my porch light is on. It's Leslie and Luna. I open the door.

Leslie is still in her work clothes, light gray pantsuit with flared cuffs. That usually means she was in court. Luna is dressed down, probably straight from work, too.

"What the hell, Frankie?" Luna belts out.

"Are you okay?" Leslie asks. "We've been calling all day. I finally called Al, and we met up here."

"I'm sorry. Come in."

I close the door behind them, dead-bolt it.

They see me holding the gun.

"You okay?"

I can only stare back at them.

"Saw your house on the news," Luna says. "I drove here earlier, but they wouldn't let me in."

"It's a mess in here. I need a drink," I say. "Can I get you something?"

"I'll have some of what you're going to have." Luna nods his head to the dining room.

"Have a seat," I tell them, then set my gun on the end table and walk into the dining room to find a couple of glasses. I pour more than a double in each.

Leslie is sitting on the middle of the sofa and Luna on the armchair. I hand him his drink, then sit next to Leslie.

"Obviously Detective Millhoff didn't talk to you yet."

"Millhoff? Why would he want to talk to me?" Leslie asks.

"Shouldn't have even said anything, but when he asked if I talked to anyone about a case I was working, I told him you. He's going to call to confirm information is all."

"What case?"

"The one involving my cousin at GW."

"Does he have something to do with this?" she asks with concern.

"He was found dead on my kitchen floor. Shot."

"Oh, my God. What happened?"

"I don't have a clue. It doesn't make any sense."

"Frankie, I'm so sorry," Leslie says.

She places her hand gently on my knee.

"I'm at my wit's end here. Seems like a burglary gone bad, but I just don't know. I followed him over the course of several days, sometimes for hours. I don't believe in coincidence, especially when the odds are a million to one. There has to be a connection. I'm fucking losing my mind trying to figure this out."

I know how it looks.

"I know this doesn't look good for me," I say.

"It's some fucked-up shit, but Millhoff's good people. He'll work it through," Luna says.

"Yeah, good people, but it's a high-profile case that the chief's going to want a quick closure on. When the pressure's hot, I've seen Homicide take down people on nothin' but circumstantial evidence before, and that's sure as hell not about to be me."

"Tell me you had nothing to do with this, Frankie," Leslie says with concern.

I look at her directly. She's stunning, even with her face etched with worry.

"Are you kidding me? Leslie, of course not. I didn't murder my cousin."

"You got an alibi, right?" Luna asks after a sip of whiskey.

"Shut the fuck up, Luna. I don't need an alibi, but I got one."

It's a pretty soft alibi, but I don't want them to panic, especially Leslie.

"Well, you don't talk to the police anymore without me being present," she says.

"I don't need a lawyer, Leslie. This is some weird shit here, but I had nothing to do with it. I called his mom earlier. Won't have anything to do with me, like she thinks I was responsible for his death."

Maybe I was.

"She's family," Luna says. "She'll come around."

"I don't know if there's any coming around this shit," I say, more to myself than to her.

"You need to talk to her face-to-face," Leslie tells me. "She'll have to come to DC—you know…the body."

I shake my head at the thought of her having to identify his body.

"Yeah, maybe you're right."

Luna downs the double shot without any effort.

He stands, bends toward me, places the palm of his hand on my shoulder. Gives it a friendly squeeze. "Call me tomorrow, Frank. I got to go close shop. I'm acting sergeant this evening."

"Chew some gum," I tell him, because his breath smells of whiskey.

"Right. I'll look into this shit on my end, see what I can find out. I'll get your cousin's info from my boy. Don't worry. And you need anything, you call."

"Thanks." I stand up to let him out.

We walk to the door and do a brotherly shoulder half hug.

"Thanks, man. Sorry I didn't get to you earlier."

"No worries."

I lock the door when he leaves.

Leslie's sipping some of my whiskey.

"You want a glass?"

"I just wanted a sip."

Before I can sit she says, "Let me take you to dinner, then maybe you should come stay with me."

Sounds damn good except for the dinner part. I don't want to be seen anywhere.

"How about we call for Chinese takeout when we get to your house?" I ask.

"Even better. I'll drive. You want to get some things together?"

"Get out of these clothes is all, but I need to take care of something in the kitchen. You mind waiting here, sip my whiskey?"

She smiles and takes a delicate sip. I smile back, grab my backpack from the floor, and head to the kitchen to tie up that trash bag and clean up what I can.

I'm used to seeing all my vinyl and CDs stacked together as I walk out of the living room. Damn. This fucking crime-infested city. I'm gonna catch the fuck who killed Jeffrey, maybe get my shit back in the process. Fucking crackhead burglars. Murderers.

ELEVEN

I hate sitting outside when it's so hot and humid. Doesn't bother Leslie a bit.

"You sure you can handle it?" she asks beside me on her front stoop.

"I'll suffer for you."

A glass of wine or two will be fine out here, but certainly not hot Chinese food. I might pass the fuck out.

"Millhoff is treating me like a suspect," I say outta nowhere.

"You're not guilty of anything, so you don't have to worry."

"Leslie. Come on. You know how these things can play."

"You can't believe that, Frankie, and you know I'm here if you need me."

"I know you are."

"You need to call your Aunt Linda, try to talk to her again."

"Yeah, I know. But like I said, it didn't go so well the first time."

"I'm sorry."

"Aunt Linda. She's much younger than my mom was. Had to

be something like nineteen when my mom died, but she was always there for me. Stayed at my stepdad's house here in DC for a while. Looked after me."

I turn to Leslie, not that I expect her to say anything. I just look. She smiles, but it's not just a smile. It's like radiating warmth for my insides.

"I was about five. Linda married much later in life. Funny—when she got divorced Jeffrey was around five. I was there for him, too. Watched over him. I don't want her to think what she must be thinking. That I'm responsible—or worse."

"She's grieving, but it sounds like there's a lot of love between the two of you. Good history, too."

"I don't know why I lost touch."

Yes, I do.

"Give her time. It's a difficult situation for her. For you."

"And I can't make sense of it. My fucking brain's all tangled up."

"Are you sure he didn't know where you lived?"

"Yes. No, actually. Even if he did, it still wouldn't make sense. I mean, he just happened to walk into a burglary in progress? What are the chances of that?"

She scoots closer and wraps her arm around me. I put my hand on her thigh, gently caress it.

Jeffrey's face suddenly pops into my head. For some reason, I see him when he had a black eye and I was the one who gave it to him.

"What?" Leslie asks.

I look at her. "What do you mean, 'What?'"

"You just smiled."

"Didn't realize."

"Do you want to talk about it?"

"Just strange. Outta nowhere, this image of Jeffrey pops into my head. It was during that time just after Aunt Linda's divorce, when he was five years old. I gave him his first black eye. We were playing catch, and the softball tipped off his mitt. Smacked him hard in the right eye. Told him a bit later that it was a nice shiner. Didn't even cry until he looked in the mirror and saw his puffed-up purplish black eye. Aunt Linda got real pissed, but we laughed about it later, 'cause after all the crying, Jeffrey seemed proud of it. Fuck."

Leslie rubs my back.

"He was a good boy. I shouldn't have taken the surveillance as far as I did. Once I knew what he was into I shoulda just talked to him."

"When was the last time you two talked?"

"Couple years before I retired, so maybe seven years? Drove there for Thanksgiving. He was fourteen."

"It's not your fault, you know."

I can't reply to that, 'cause I think it is.

We sit quietly, and her hand caressing my shoulder almost takes me away from these thoughts.

I notice a guy walking on the other side of the street.

"Dude walking this way across the street is looking for a car to hit," I say, trying to keep my mind from going back there.

"Oh, really? Based on your years of experience or just profiling?"

"Obviously both."

"Looks like a normal man walking home to me."

"You've lost your cop sense. Watch him."

She does while sipping her Pinot.

"Look how he's walking close to the curb, head turning ever so slightly to look inside the cars as he passes."

When the man gets closer, he notices us on the steps.

"See? Now it's blown for him. Not looking in the cars any-more, just trying to walk normally."

He passes, but it's too dark to get a good view, so I can't make out if he looks like a crackhead.

"Go on, now, move on outta here, find another block to hit," I say too low for him to hear.

Leslie shakes it off.

"What about that woman over there?" she asks.

A woman appears at the corner, talking on her phone. She crosses the street to our side, walking our way.

"Clueless. Not aware of her surroundings. She's a victim."

"I talk on my cell when I'm walking. A lot. I've never been robbed."

"Two things. You walk like you belong, and you can take care of yourself. Same way I know a bad guy when I see him."

The young lady walks past, gives us a nice smile.

We both smile back, and Leslie adds a wave.

"Victim," I say.

I sip the wine, look at Leslie. Her heavy hair is pulled back in a ponytail. Her lips are closed, but she always looks like she has a bit of a smile. Unaffected. So pretty. I want to kiss her on the cheek. I do. She turns, shoots me a real smile, then leans over to give me a quick peck on the lips.

I notice a marked cruiser turning the corner, slowly driving the block our direction. The driver's-side window is facing us. Gets closer, and I notice he's a 10-99 unit. The window down with his arm hanging out like he's enjoying the thick humidity. He slows down even more as he passes.

Leslies waves, and I shoot him a thumbs-up.

He just turns slightly toward us, gives us an odd, flat glare, speeds up, and takes the next right.

"That's rude," Leslie says.

"Maybe, but you gotta give him a break. It's tough being a cop now, not knowing who's out to get you, destroy your life."

The delivery guy arrives after a few minutes. We go inside, find a mindless action-adventure movie on cable, eat, and drink more wine.

I know she's worried. Hell, I'm worried. I should be more concerned with finding out who killed Jeffrey. But here's the thing I can't get my head around: Why was Jeffrey murdered in my house? Someone knows we're connected. Someone's pushing a pin into me.

Sure, Leslie wants to talk about it, but she knows me well enough to know I'm not gonna talk about it now. Right now, I want my focus to be on her. Tomorrow—well, that's a fucking new day.

When I wake up beside her in the morning, I realize I didn't do any blow the whole night. I slept soundly. Her company kept me from craving, kept me from worrying.

Twelve

Before stepping out of my car I scan the area, check for news-people or anything suspicious. When I get to my porch, I stand and listen before unlocking the door, like I'm worried that whoever murdered Jeffrey will come back.

I lock the door behind me, sit on the sofa, and light a smoke.

I check the Fox 5 app on my iPhone for the news.

Jeffrey's mother is already in town. It's a top story. I drop the phone on the end table and lean back on the sofa, try to rest my eyes.

It's a decent half hour before panic sets in—being hit with the realization that I'll run out of blow before I can find more. This is not a pleasant place to be. Last thing I wanna do is rush into something and get caught up in a situation I might not be able to talk my way out of or even walk my way out of. Busting into Jeffrey's apartment like that is a good example of acting with-out fully thinking it through. Who knows how bad I fucked it for Millhoff? I actually feel sick about it, but what can I do except let it take its crooked course? I'm not worried about the burglary leading to me. In fact that's the last thing I'm worried about. I'm more worried about the homicide investigation and, even more important, having to fucking re-up. There is too much going on around me, though. I was on the fucking news. I don't need this, especially now.

In the kitchen I recoil, thinking I see Jeffrey there again, wrecked on the floor with blood all over him. I did this, some-how. I brought this.

THIRTEEN

I allow myself a very small bump—no thought, no effort. Yes, elevation, and a certain…reassurance. There it is. But it can only feel that way when you know there's more to come. I have more. But I need more.

I gotta get my mind off this. Think about the case.

I hop in the car and make my way to a record store I used to frequent. The owner sells some old vinyl and CDs, but mostly new. I hope he's smart enough, and decent enough, to buy from the right people. He always seemed straight up. But you never know. I could've been buying stolen shit from him for all I know. I'm sure Hurley will get around to checking out the record store, too. Maybe he already has, but I need to do something or I'll just sit around here and burn through my stash. Fucking can't have that. Where would I be then?

Probably up to something stupid.

One thing I know about burglaries—the motivation is mostly crack, sometimes heroin. I know that world well. Worked narcotics most of my career on the department. That'd be about fourteen out of seventeen years. It made me the man I am today. Damn if that doesn't make me smile, but only for a second. It's ironic, because that's when I started using again, and of course eventually got caught. Then coerced into early retirement. The good thing is, only the ones who forced me into early retirement know the backstory. That spared a lot of friendships, like Luna's, and the relationship I still have with most of the members of the department. And then there's Leslie, the most important one of all. God help me if I ever lose her.

It's not even a five-minute drive from my house. Finding a parking spot takes longer. Would have been quicker if I had walked from home. I eventually find a legal spot about a block away.

Some of the old row houses along the U Street corridor have been converted into trendy shops. The record store is located in an English basement below one of those spots, a two-story clothing store that caters to the anorexic.

Down two short flights of stairs, and I open a door to a small rectangular space riddled with bins filled with vinyl and, along the left wall, one large bin stacked with CDs. A song I can't remember the name of by the Screaming Trees is playing in the background. Reminds me of Leslie for some reason. She likes them. Me, too. The music is at a moderate level, but it's begging for more volume. Every bit of wall space is taken up by posters and small gig flyers, both current and from back in the eighties, when I was a kid and into the scene.

There's a young kid, maybe in his teens, at a bin containing R & B CDs. He's wearing an overly large T-shirt and baggy jeans. Oscar, the owner, is standing behind a glass counter looking at what appears to be an order sheet. He breaks away from it, turns his spindly body toward me, almost an about-face but a little more lurchlike.

"What's up?" he says, obviously not remembering my name but still saying it in a tone that suggests familiarity.

"Dropped by to ask you something. You got a minute?"

"Sure."

He sets the papers on the counter. Beneath it are band stickers, buttons, and pins.

"How's business?" I ask him.

"Store's slow, but nothing to complain about. I do most of my business online, so all is good."

"Whatever keeps the doors open, right?"

"You got that right."

"Listen, man. My house got burglarized couple of days ago—"

"Sorry to hear that."

"Yeah, well, they took my whole vinyl collection, a lot of which I bought from you, and my CDs, too. I thought since you sell used records, maybe you'd keep a lookout for them. I know most of these burglars try to turn the property over fast for a quick buck."

"Yeah, they do, and I don't mind helping you out, but I don't buy what I think might be stolen. Most of the used records here I find at garage or estate sales. If someone comes in off the street, he has to have a driver's license or some form of real ID. Not that fake shit. Excuse the language."

"Doesn't bother me."

I try to scan the area behind the counter. There are crates with records in them, some new and some that look used, but nothing I can make out as belonging to me. I notice the kid looking our way, then moving to look at another row of music.

"I hate to say it because it feels like profiling, but I know drug addicts when I see them, and they usually have ID that looks like they got it made at Staples or on someone's home computer. I always send 'em off. I think the word got out that

I'm not the place for that. Last guy tried it was over a month ago."

I pull a piece of paper out of the inner pocket of my suit jacket, unfold it, and hand it to him.

"Nevertheless, here's a list of all the titles I can remember. It's pretty diverse, as you can see, and so an easy collection to note. Lot of the older records belonged to my deceased mother."

"Hell."

"Yeah, so it's, ah…it means something. Probably too late now, but if anyone does come in with a collection like this, do me a solid and buy it. I'll reimburse you for everything, including your time."

I again catch the kid through the corner of my eye. He seems a little too interested in what we're saying.

"I'll keep a lookout for you," the owner says while looking at the titles. "But like I said, anything we buy from someone off the street—someone legit, that is—we have to keep a record of for the police. That's another reason I don't do it anymore. It's too much of a hassle."

"Any other places you know of that buy and sell used vinyl and CDs?"

"Sure. Two pawn shops down the street, probably. You also might want to check out some of the thrift stores around here. I don't know the names."

"Appreciate it."

"Sorry for your loss, man."

And I wonder if he means my mother or my music. Doesn't even know about my cousin. I smile.

Before I head out, I check some of the records in the "Used" bin, including those under *B* for Bread.

Nothing.

I look over to the kid and decide to casually approach.

I glance down at the bin of CDs he's shuffling through. He turns to me but doesn't seem nervous. Tough-looking kid.

I notice a Funkadelic CD and take it out.

"These guys are great. I used to have *Maggot Brain*," I tell him without looking at him.

"What the fuck?" he says like I insulted him.

"*Maggot Brain*'s the name of their CD. Great shit. You should listen."

"I don't fuckin' know you."

"You know any other spots around here that sell used vinyl?"

He looks at me hard, up and down, giving me that familiar glare like he knows I'm a cop.

Once a cop, always a cop.

He backs up, then suddenly yanks at the bin of CDs, which crashes onto my leg.

"Fuck!"

I step forward, and he pulls down another bin, CDs spilling to the floor and over my shoes—the kid's already bolted out the door.

"What in the hell?" Oscar yells as I take off.

FOURTEEN

I trip over the few stairs right outside the door. He's already made it up to the sidewalk.

At street level I see him hoofing it toward 14th. Fucking fast. No way I'll catch him, especially wearing a suit and in this heat. I'll drop within half a block.

I run to my car.

By the time I start it and get it around he's out of sight. I'd see him if he was still running on U, so I'm thinking he made that left on 14th. I drive there as fast as the cars ahead of me allow, which isn't fast enough.

I signal to make a left on 14th, creep into the intersection so I can see south on 14th, and sure enough, there he is, near the corner of 14th and Wallach Place. He's looking back, taking a breath because he sprinted all the way there.

He strides east on Wallach. I'm thinking he bolted 'cause he's either holding or there's a warrant on him and he thinks I'm the police.

I want to see where he goes. Might be good for something.

I make the left and gun the engine to Wallach.

"Damn."

I forgot it's one way going westbound.

I see him. He's walking. Casually.

Car honks behind me.

He looks over his shoulder, but he's about half a block up the road and doesn't make me. Car honks again.

"Fuck off!" I yell, like the honking ass is going to hear me.

There's a couple of cuts in Wallach that he might take or just walk through to 13th. Wallach is a long, narrow road, so I'm betting on the cuts. I drive south on 14th to T, the next street down, and when traffic eases I make a quick left. I slow down toward the cut that extends from T to Wallach.

He's walking, looks like he's coming this way. There's a car behind me, so I can't back up. I pull forward and park behind a car that puts the rear of my car partway into the cut he's walking. I turn the engine off and recline the seat. I adjust the rearview so I can see from my position.

He steps out of the cut, looks both ways, and walks behind my car to cross the street.

I watch him cross, get ready to enter the next alley, heading south. I start thinking this ain't nothin' but a waste of my time. I open the door and step out, close it quietly, walk to the rear of my car, then cross the street. I manage to get right up on him, and by the time he turns his head it's too late, because I grab him tight from behind by the neck of his T-shirt.

He struggles but doesn't fight.

"What the fuck! You got no cause," he squeaks out.

"What the hell you run from me for? I was being polite."

"Didn't do nothin'! You got no cause to stop me. Fucking let me go."

"What you holding? I know that's why you ran."

He struggles and squirms and worms his way out of his double-XL T-shirt. His skinny chest; wide, angular shoulders. His pants are almost below his ass. He pulls them up and runs in the alley.

"Shit. C'mon, now, little man."

I see a small group of people has gathered at the corner. Couple of them have their iPhones out.

"Oh, that's fucking great," I say to myself.

But like a hungry dog I turn back to my prey and run after him.

I chase him through the alley to the next street.

He runs east, toward 13th, but even holding his pants up with his right hand he's still like an antelope. I ain't no cheetah, especially in the heat. I've already run a block, and my shirt's soaked through. Fuck it.

He looks back when he hits 13th. I swear he's mocking me 'cause he walks at a slow pace when he crosses to the other side, looking my way.

I toss his T-shirt in the gutter. Fucking little young punk.

What the hell was I even chasing this kid for?

I make my way back to the car. I need a shower and a change of clothing. After that I'm going to call Hurley, ask him about the secondhand dealers that my boy, Record Store Oscar, told me about.

FIFTEEN

Hurley was at a witness conference when I called him earlier, but he suggested meeting at the Fraternal Order of Police lodge. It's on 4th Street, about a block from the US attorney's office. I used to be a frequent flyer in this spot. Long time ago. Back when I had court almost every day.

Couple of young uniforms are standing on the sidewalk just before the glass double-door front entry. I've already worked up a bit of a sweat on the short walk here. Seeing them standing there talking in this humidity makes me want to sweat more. Don't know how they can be out here chatting it up and put up with the discomfort that comes with trapped sweat under those Kevlar vests. Conditioning, I guess. Personally, I never got used to it.

Just before I ring the buzzer to announce myself, I hear one of them say, "How can they tell me without any notice that I got to work twelve hours? How do they get away with that shit?"

"That is some bullshit," the other responds.

"Well, my witness conference just got a lot longer. I'll be

parking my ass at the Nickel for the remainder. Fuck those protesters."

I chuckle to myself. *The Nickel*. That's the US attorney's office, 'cause the address is 555. I used to call it the Triple Nickel.

"Ching-ching, baby. That's how you have to look at it," the other says.

I push the button for the intercom, announce myself.

I pull the door open when I hear the lock click, walk up a short flight of stairs, then make a right through an open door to the restaurant and bar. Fortunately, it's not that crowded. They've cleaned it up. Looks more like a regular commercial establishment than the dingy old hiding spot it once was. The tough, scratchy-voiced waitress who used to work behind the bar and at the tables seems to have been replaced by a younger, friendlier woman.

A couple of old-timers, more than likely retired, sit on stools, upper halves bent over the wooden bar, propping themselves up with an elbow while nursing something mixed. Their faces weather-worn, with smiles like "those were the days." Same framed photos, maybe a couple of new ones, hanging on the walls. Lot of history there.

I see Hurley sitting alone at a table by the window drinking soda from a straw. Fresh-looking male and female uniform officers a couple tables in front of his sip coffee out of white mugs. The young girl's cute. Both of them glance over as I make my way to Hurley, probably wondering what unit I'm from. Or maybe they saw me on the news.

I shake hands with Hurley and take the chair across from him.

"I just got here a second ago," he says and raises his hand to summon the waitress.

"So you hungry?" he asks.

What do I say to that? No, I'm not. I never am, but I gotta play the part.

"This humidity fucks up my system, but I can manage something."

I grab the menu.

The cute waitress shows up.

"I'll have the FOP club and another soda, please."

I give the menu a quick look-over. Definitely not the same menu.

"Shit, the Kojak? You serve a lollipop with that?" I ask the waitress with a smile.

"Tootsie Pop," she says.

"Damn, the Columbo? What happened to this place?"

"Trust me, it's an improvement," Hurley says.

"I'll also have the FOP club. Water and coffee, too."

"Self-serve coffee right over there," she says, pointing to the wall across from me, where there's a table, stacks of mugs, and a couple of full coffeepots. Some things never change.

"Thanks," I say.

"Will that be all, gentlemen?"

I nod.

"Yeah, sweetie. Thanks," Hurley says, shooting her a goofy smile.

I pull my chair out to stand. "Be right back."

I walk to the table and pour myself a cup of coffee, then return to sit.

"So I went to this record store I used to frequent." I sit back down. "It's on U Street, near where I live."

He looks at me with interest. I decide to leave out the kid that bolted out of the store, 'cause what good would it do for me?

"You know anything about that spot?"

"Sure, and the owner there plays by the rules," Hurley says.

"Happy to hear that. He told me about some secondhand dealers who might not play by the rules, though."

"I'm on that, too. First thing I did was check the pawn data-base. Couple CDs here and there, but nothing like your collection. Checked out a few laptops and some stereo equipment, but it was negative."

"You gonna hit those secondhand dealers soon?"

"Once I finish up with this witness conference. Should be done tomorrow."

"Witness conference have anything to do with the homicide?"

"No. Something else my unit was involved in. A narco-fencing case. But we have a lot of pressure with the homicide. You ever call your cousin's parents?"

"They're divorced. I talked to his mother" is all I say.

"Well, it might be best to stay clear, buddy. She has it in her head that you're to blame."

"She's my aunt," I tell him like he insulted me. "We were close for a lot of years."

"I didn't mean to suggest anything by that."

"I know." Sip some coffee. "Fuck, I taught him how to swim. Aunt Linda has a pool at their house in Ohio. I took a couple weeks' leave from the department after she got divorced to be with him. He was more like my little brother than a cousin. Gotta tell ya, there were moments when I was surveilling him that I wanted to break off and try to pull him outta all that shit. Maybe that's all he needed."

"You can't question yourself like this, what you should've done. Probably wouldn't have made a difference. You know that."

"He wasn't a criminal, Joe."

He doesn't respond.

"Fuck. I gotta get out from under this," I say and realize how it sounds.

"Well, hopefully we'll get to the bottom of it soon."

"Hopefully?"

"Frank, listen. The case we just wrapped up took a *year*. I was surprised they didn't pull the plug on it months ago. They sure as hell would have now because of this case. I don't want to be stuck on this. I like my world of burglary, not bodies." He looks like he realizes how that sounds. "I'm sorry. It's your cousin. I didn't mean for it to sound like that."

"No worries. Anything on that kid at the club, the one with the dreadlocks?"

"We're working all the leads, Frank."

For obvious reasons he's keeping me out of the loop. For all I know they already picked him up and he's in the box getting drilled by Millhoff. I leave it alone.

Hurley seems like he cares and loves the job. That's rare these days, especially with all the shit the guys go through both departmentally and with the general population. Sometimes when you're dealing with cases that involve robbery, burglary, or narcotics, a whole new level of crime can come out of one arrest. Organizations like MPDC don't like that kind of thinking because it usually involves a long-term investigation, which is a dirty combination of words. It's a wrap-it-up culture now. It's about numbers, about procedure. Think outside the box, and you'll end up being like the redheaded stepchild. Come to think of it, Hurley has reddish-blond hair.

I know how difficult burglary cases are to close. It's even harder to recover whatever was stolen. Hurley seems to have mastered it. That alone gives me hope.

Sandwiches finally arrive. Another thing that hasn't changed. If you're gonna eat here, you'd better make sure you have the time. It doesn't matter if it's crowded or if there are just a few people, like now. The orders come slow.

I take a bite of the sandwich. It's good, but I've got serious cotton mouth and no appetite, making it hard to swallow. I drink water, lots of it. Force it down, just like I'll use a few pills to force myself to sleep. Gotta try to live normal somehow.

"I'll check the database again for those secondhand dealers, see if anything shows up. Still might be too early. We depend on the shopkeepers to enter the items, and you know how that can be."

"Yeah. Most of them are nothing but legalized fencing operations."

"You got that right. They serve a purpose, though—for us, I mean."

"No problem with me stopping in some pawn shops or other record stores, right?"

"Of course not, but if you see what you suspect is yours, call me. Don't talk to them. I'll stop by, and if it's good to go I'll put a police hold on it."

"And none of this fucking getting lost at Property Division, right?"

"It is going to be a bit different because it involves a homicide. Usually I just take a few photos of the property and get you to sign a release form and it's yours. I'll see what I can do, though—I mean, if we ever get to that point."

"I got faith in you, my new best friend."

"Ha! You'd better readjust that thinking." And he finishes off one of the sandwich's quarters.

"Thinking about it now, I might even have someone else's stolen shit in my collection."

"Most of the secondhand guys are all right. Mostly it's the pawn shops and those rickety old corner thrift stores that make it hard on us." He holds back on taking another bite, looks over at me like something's been on his mind. "But seriously, Frankie, what's with this PI shit? The work you did at Narcotics Branch? You could've been a consultant somewhere, one of those guys who interviews employees for major corporations or something like that. Six-figure shit."

"Sounds like too much work to me. It's not a bad gig, what I do. I work what I want when I want, and I'm not one of those dopey PIs who work for drug-dealing mopes and try to get them out of jail."

"That's good to hear. I'd hate having to consider you my enemy."

I can't respond to that.

Sixteen

Leslie is an early-morning person. It takes me a couple hours to fall asleep. Even then, I'm in and out of it. My sleep cycle is damaged. We don't sleep together often enough for me to get used to all the damn noise she makes while getting ready for work. The light seeping through the open master bathroom door is enough to wake me. She uses an electric toothbrush, and the vibrating sound gets into your head like cicadas.

There's no place for silence anymore. You can stuff your ears with top-of-the-line earplugs, and the noise'll still find its way in. Or maybe it's always been there.

I try to avoid using first thing in the morning, especially when I'm with Leslie. I could probably sneak a bump while she's in the bathroom, but I don't want to get into that routine. Even home alone, I control the urge until after my morning grapefruit and coffee—sometimes even through lunch.

Leslie walks into the bedroom. She's wearing black bikini underwear. I pretend to be sleeping, manage to use the covers for concealment. She bends slightly to open a top dresser drawer, finds a bra, and puts it on. Damn. What the hell did I do to deserve someone like her?

I pretend I'm just waking up.

"You can sleep in if you want. Just lock the door from the inside."

"No. You should always double-lock it."

"I have an extra key somewhere. The kitchen, I think."

"Sure we're ready for that?" I ask with my best smile.

"Not if I come home one evening and find you lounging on my sofa."

"Uninvited? Don't you worry. I'm not creepy that way."

"I know. That's why I'll give you a key. And no, it doesn't mean anything more."

It's a step in the right direction is what I want to say. Instead, "There's still responsibility attached to it."

"Be responsible, then."

I slip my underwear on, then my socks, head to the bathroom to take a piss. I close the door, and after I piss I flush the toilet to muffle the sound of blowing my nose. Hard. The usual thick greenish-yellow mucus mixed with a bit of blood plops out and into the tissue. Like expelling a lump of crusty Jell-O. I flush that, too.

"Are you all right?" I hear her ask from behind the door.

"Damn sinus infection again. It comes with the weather."

"Then you'll need antibiotics."

"It's not that bad yet."

I wash my hands and splash cold water on my face and in my nostrils.

Back in the bedroom.

She's fully dressed now.

"You want coffee?" she asks.

"Sure."

I get dressed, and she offers me a cup. We sit and drink our coffee quietly.

On the way home, she's heavy on my mind, with some anxiety mixed up and in it. That's new. I need more coffee, maybe a Klonopin or two.

When I get home I devour a grapefruit and have more coffee. I start thinking about what I can do, and I get nothing. I keep getting flashes of Jeffrey, bloody on my kitchen floor. He had his hand on his gut, I remember now, see his hand clear. All bloody.

Fucking almost noon.

I'm going to need to get some work soon, but I can't even think about that right now. My finances are okay. My paltry retirement is transferred directly to the police credit union, and I deposit my legit work payments in that account, too. Most of that money takes care of the mortgage, utilities, Internet, and phone. Stash cash for the day-to-day stuff. Yeah, I'm good, but I also need to find a place to hit soon 'cause I gotta stay good with that shit, too. Finding Jeffrey's coke connection, Dreadlocks, will be a good lead, not only for a good hit but also for Jeffrey's murder. It's a slippery slope, 'cause Millhoff'll be looking for him, too—or, like I've said before, maybe he's already found him. It's still worth a shot.

Seventeen

The music, if you can call it that; the trendy crowd; the DJ bent over the turntables, his long hair whipping air. Not music. Just noise.

I got here early enough to get a good seat at the bar with a view of the entrance, where a well-dressed, fresh-faced guy, probably rookie, is working the door. Jasper's on duty working the streets. The bartender remembers me, pours nice. I'm thankful for that right now, having to cope with this shit. Three hours now. Already on my fourth whiskey. Nursing it this time.

There's a lot of people here, so I keep my focus on the entrance.

I notice a young buck walk in. He's wearing the typical baggy jeans, an oversize T-shirt, and expensive sneakers. A lot of dudes in here are dressed the same way, but what piques my interest is that he stands on his toes, stretching to look over the crowd near the DJ, where the booths are. He walks through the crowd to the same booth that Jeffrey and Dreadlocks sat in last time I was here.

A couple of girls with a couple of guys. Look like college kids.

They scoot together to make room for him. He knocks knuckles with the dudes. One of the girls offers him a sip of her drink. He accepts. They talk for a bit, and I start to lose interest, look back to the front entrance area, then back to them.

Boy with the fancy sneakers stretches over the table, fingers closed over his palm, and he hands it to one of the other guys like a shake. But it's obvious. The guy across the table checks it out, slips it in his pants pocket, and slides some bills across the table for the young boy. He pockets the cash without counting, takes another sip of the girl's drink, and stands.

Not even a minute after, he's approached by someone else. They walk toward the back, where the restrooms are.

For the next half hour or so he stays busy like this. One exchange after the other, but when he's approached by another young girl he shrugs his shoulders and shakes his head, then says something to her, and she nods.

He makes his way through the crowd toward the entrance and leaves. I quickly drop a few bills on the counter, much more than I owe, and follow.

By the time I get to the top of the stairs, where the young rookie in a suit is standing, he's down the stairs and opening the door to walk out.

He's turning the corner toward the rear of the club.

I get to the corner and see him walk into the small parking lot at the rear of the building. I hustle, just in case he's gonna hop in a car, but I stop before the entrance to the parking lot and cross the street like I'm walking to my car. I smell weed in the air. When I get to the sidewalk on the other side I gaze across to the parking lot, notice him talking to another guy. Not much light back there, but the guy he's talking to looks a lot like Dreadlocks.

EIGHTEEN

Dreadlocks opens the passenger-side door of an old-model black two-door coupe. A Mazda, I think. He gets in, closes the door, and hands something to the boy. Fancy Sneakers just re-upped. I walk out of view and cross the street back to the club side, lean against the wall at the corner, and light a smoke.

The kid appears from the parking lot, walks by without giving me a glance, turns, and enters the club. He leaves me the scent of stinky weed.

I walk to the parking lot, where Dreadlocks is leaning against the rear of the coupe, smoking a blunt.

He looks at me, maybe thinking I work at the club, 'cause he doesn't budge. But when I casually step up to him he straightens.

"Weed be legal in this city now," he tells me, like he makes me for a cop.

"I'm not the police. I don't give a shit."

"Yeah, right, you ain't the police," he says with a smirk. He hands the blunt over. I accept. He smiles awkwardly at first, then raises his eyebrows when I take a nice drag, hold for a while, and exhale in his direction.

"Shee-it, I still think you're the police." Smiling.

I hand the blunt back to him. "Naw, not anymore." I take out my wallet and show him my badge. "Retired."

"Do I know you or somethin'?"

"No."

"Well, if you be steppin' up here expectin' to get somethin', then I don't do that kinda shit. I'm just about ready to go into the club is all."

"I can get my own weed if I want. Don't need nothin' from you."

"Then what the fuck you steppin' like you know me?"

"'Cause in a way I do."

"Fuck off, yo. Don't know you for shit. You a fag or somethin'?"

That makes me smile.

"No, not that, either. Just want to talk to you about someone we both know."

He takes a drag, then exhales, blowing the smoke in my face like a challenge. I don't let it faze me, 'cause I don't want to go hard on him. I knew the moment I walked up to him that wouldn't work.

"Would you have been that brave if my badge didn't say 'retired'?"

He just huffs.

"Jeffrey. He was a white college kid. You supplied him with blow. In this club here."

"Step on outta here, fool."

He steps sideways a bit, like he's positioning himself 'cause he's carrying.

I throw the right side of my suit jacket back, sorta like a gun-slinger, to let him see what I carry.

He sees and lifts his shirt to expose his belly and the small of his back.

"I ain't carryin' nothin' like that."

I let the coat slide over my holster again. "I'm gonna be straight up with you 'cause I know nothing else would work. My girl is best friends with Jeffrey's mom. She got in touch with my girl because she was worried about Jeffrey and knew I used to be a cop and could maybe help."

"I told you I don't know who the fuck you're talkin' about."

"I saw you serve Jeffrey in the club last Thursday. Blow. It was so fucking obvious it's silly."

"Fuck this shit, man," he says and sets the remainder of the blunt on the trunk of the car. "Rest is yours if you want it." He starts to walk away.

"You the one who killed him? Jeffrey?"

He turns back to me. Looks startled. Not the kind of look I thought I'd see.

"The fuck you say?"

"You heard right."

"He kilt?"

Okay, now.

I grab the blunt and take another drag. It's good shit. I stretch my hand out to offer it back to him. He steps up and accepts. Takes another quick hit.

"Yeah," I say. "And judging by the look on your face, I'm guessin' you didn't know."

"For real? You ain't playin' me?"

"It's for real."

"Fuck" is all he says, then the last hit, and he flicks the blunt to the pavement. A few sparks spring out of it, are lifted, but die out fast. "Naw, I didn't know. He got robbed or some shit like that?"

"I don't know. Like I said, I'm not the police anymore."

"You always the police, just without the power."

"You're right there. And I did call a couple of friends, but it's a sensitive case, and they won't even talk to me about it. I know how he was found, though. Maybe a burglary gone bad. Like I said, I've been watching him for his mom. He never knew I was watchin'. And I haven't given the police anything about you yet."

"Fuck that! I ain't have nothin' do with that shit. I liked Jiffy."

"Jeff."

"I know it's Jeff, but I call him Jiffy."

Says that like he's still alive.

"Why?"

"Fuck, I don't know. It just come out that way one day, and I liked it so it stuck."

Fuckin' Jiffy.

"What'd he call you?"

He hesitates. "Ray."

Nineteen

Ray's leaning back on the rear of his car again. I offer him a cigarette.

"Naw. I don't smoke."

Got some sense.

"Jiffy piss off anyone you know?"

"Naw, man. People liked him. He was funny."

"Funny?"

"Wisecrackin', but not the type that make you want to bitch-slap him. Just funny. Make you smile."

"Did he use?"

"Use what?"

"Give me a fuckin' break."

Smiles like he was playing me. "On occasion, I guess, like most of us. But it wasn't somethin' that ruled him. You say maybe it was a burglary?"

"Yeah, but don't know for sure. Why?"

"Fuck, you know how I do, so I'm gonna be straight with you, too."

"'Preciate that."

"But you keep my name outta this shit, a'right?"

"Okay."

"Because of what I do, I know me some burglars."

I want to ask about the records and CDs and the stereo, play it like that shit was stolen from Jeffrey, but he's probably been in Jeffrey's apartment, so I can't chance it. He had a flat-screen and some CDs, though. Probably had a laptop, too.

"They wouldn't let me in his apartment," I begin, "but I could see through the door. There was a table that looked like it had a flat-screen on it, couple CDs on the floor. I know that's common shit, but you know a burglar who was trying to unload some music, a flat-screen, and maybe a laptop? I'm pretty sure Jiffy had a laptop, being a college kid and all."

"Most of the thieves here always hit that shit. Not a lot of them brave enough to kill somebody. Crackheads usually just run the fuck away. I know me one, though, might be crazy enough. Least I seen him with a gun before."

"He got a name?"

"Fuck, nobody on the streets gotta full name. He did have a part name. Gibbons, Givens, some shit like that."

"What does he look like?"

"A fucking crackhead. Skinny."

"White guy, black, what?"

"Black dude. Keep his hair nice and tight, not all fucked up like most fiends. And he's smart, too."

"Oh, yeah? What areas does he hit?"

"Fuck, he's all over the place."

"What kinda gun you seen him with?"

"Some kinda nine."

"Did this Gibbons or Givens ever have cause to get with Jiffy?"

"Not that I know."

"Did he ever hang at the club?"

"The crackhead?"

"Yeah."

"Fuck no. He'd never be allowed in that club."

"What was he doing with the gun he had?"

"Showin' it off. Take a lot to scare me away, but that boy did. I rolled on outta there. He actin' like he fuckin' gonna shoot somebody."

"So he get his crack from you?"

"I ain't gotta tell you again."

"When was the last time?"

"When he was waving that gun around. He got what he need, and like I said, I rolled out. Ain't seen him since."

"He go anywhere else to buy his shit?"

"Yeah, he gotta main place, but I don't know where."

He's lying. They all know the competition.

"He drive a car?"

"Hell, no. Man, that's about all I know. Fuck, damn sorry to hear about Jiffy. Fucking good dude. Smart as shit, but never act like he was better because of it."

"Yeah. Sounds like he was a good boy."

"Yeah. Damn."

"You hang here often, so maybe I can try to get with you again in a couple days to see if you heard anything?"

"Yeah, but never fucking in front of no one. You still got cop all over you. Especially that expensive suit you wearin'."

"I got me a part-time gig as a security consultant, so I got to dress the part, right?"

"A'right, then."

"Let me pay you for your time?"

"Fuck no. I don't need your money like I'm snitchin'."

"Okay." And I walk away, but turn to shoot him a nod and memorize the tag on his car.

"Remember to keep me outta this shit. And watch out for that Gibbon. He ain't right."

I nod. Sorta feel bad afterward. I like him.

TWENTY

The phone wakes me up. I scramble for it on the nightstand beside my bed.

Hurley. I was going to call him today.

"What's up, Joe?" I answer.

"May have located some of your property."

"No shit! That was fast."

"Yeah, especially when the suspect makes it easy. I'm at Thrift World, a secondhand dealer not far from your house. You available to stop by?"

"Hell, yes."

I find a pen and an old receipt on the nightstand. I turn the receipt over so I can write on it.

"Go ahead."

I write down the address he gives me.

"I'll be right there."

"Copy that."

I disconnect.

"Damn!" I say happily to myself.

TWENTY-ONE

Thrift World is a two-story redbrick row house connected to two more colorfully painted row houses on either side of it. It's located off 9th Street, Northwest, on a small block that seems to be struggling, either to separate itself from the new trendy U Street corridor or hoping to find its place there. It's only a few blocks from my house and not even a block from the 9:30 Club. Parking's not a problem. I pull to the curb behind Hurley's unmarked cruiser.

This neighborhood looks the way I remember it, which isn't a good thing. Back when I was at NSID we used to hit this block and the surrounding blocks on a regular basis with buy busts. Mostly heroin. Certainly isn't rolling like it was back in the day, but still, I wouldn't trust leaving my car unattended for too long, even if it is parked behind a detective's cruiser.

I check the outdoor temperature on the dash before I step out. Ninety-eight degrees. That, along with the extreme humidity, makes it feel like a mucky hundred and ten.

Hurley's inside waiting for me. No one else is in the store

except for a young short guy in his midtwenties riddled with tattoos. He's leaning against a gold-trimmed glass counter and has a scowl that I've seen countless times when someone thinks he's being harassed. This is probably one of the locations where people would plot their moves back in the day when we had all the IMF protesting going on. Maybe even filled baggies with their own piss to throw at the police standing the line. I don't even know this guy and I've already judged him.

Looks like he sells a few records, which he keeps in bins along a back wall, but he has a lot more CDs. Gotta be hundreds of them. He has old stereo equipment, too, along with a few bikes, small pieces of furniture, a couple of racks of clothing—leather jackets, flannel—and a lot of odds and ends, collectibles.

I greet Hurley with a handshake.

"Everything is behind the counter," he says.

I follow him. The protester reluctantly steps aside to let us invade his space. I get a heavy waft of skunk weed when I pass him, like it's stuck to his clothing and he's sweating THC.

I take a look.

Son of a bitch. My stereo equipment. Fucking son of a bitch. It's sitting right here in front of me. Oh, I'm pissed, but it's a sorta happy mad.

"Yeah, this is my shit."

"Everything you put on your list is in there," Hurley says. "No vinyl or CDs, though. I took a look around because, as you know, I don't need a search warrant." He stares directly at the storekeeper after saying that. "Didn't see anything that matches the description of your other property."

"I told you, Officer, he didn't come in with any vinyl or CDs, just this stuff."

"No laptop, either?" Hurley asks.

"No."

Now I want to slap him silly.

As I turn to face Hurley and Stinky Boy, I notice the cover of *The Best of Bread* tacked to the wall above a cash register. Mounted beside it is the record, broken in half.

It's like I've been violated again.

"You broke my Bread," I tell the owner directly.

He seems baffled at first, then realizes.

He drops his head like he knows he just got fucked twice.

I look at it more closely.

"That's mine. My mother made those little doodles on the cover's corner."

"So where is the rest of the vinyl and the CDs?" Hurley asks.

"Okay, I swear I only bought this one. For fifty cents."

"Why would he only bring in one?"

"He said he had more and just wanted to know how much he could get before lugging it in here. It wasn't enough to make it worth his while."

"So why'd you have to go and mount it on the wall like that?" I ask.

"Dude, I—I just don't like Bread," he says with a shrug.

"Dude?" I return. "Fuck, you ain't got no heart."

A little over the top, maybe, but still. I don't have to look to know that Hurley probably rolled his eyes.

"Can I take it off?" I ask Hurley.

"Let me take a couple of pictures first, and then I'll take it off."

He snaps a couple of photos with a small digital camera. He slips on some latex gloves.

"We're going to see if we can get prints off all this."

"So that means I'm not going to see it for a while."

"Sorry about that. I'll keep everything safe."

Hurley walks over, pulls the tacks out of the cover, and peels the vinyl off the wall. He used double-sided adhesive tape, so some of the wall paint tears off with it. He sets the broken vinyl and covers near the turntable.

"So what's the story here?" I ask Hurley.

"Like I told you the other day, secondhand dealers and pawn shops have to log in whatever they buy off the street, including information about who they bought it from. I was looking through the database we have and noticed that young Mr. Wendland here purchased stereo equipment on the same day you reported the burglary."

Stinky Wendland turns his head away from us, toward the ground, looking like he wants to spit.

"Did you get a name?"

"Yes, and no record. I'm sure it was a fake ID."

"His identification looked good to me, Detective," Wendland says.

"Yeah, they always do," Hurley returns.

Wendland turns back to the ground.

Hurley motions for me to step away from the counter. Talk privately.

"Just a matter of procedure: you know anybody by the name of Graham Biddy?" Hurley asks me.

Damn. I thought it would be the dude Ray gave up, Givens. Maybe this Biddy just sold my property for him, or maybe they worked together.

"Fuck no. Nor did I give him permission to break into my home, kill my cousin, steal my property, then sell some of the shit here."

"You beat me to it," Hurley says.

"I know the line of questioning."

"But let's not jump to conclusions. We don't know if this guy's the shooter."

"Okay. So what now?"

"Simple. I take a picture of your property, put it all in the trunk of my cruiser, and I'll make sure Crime Scene is gentle and kind."

He snaps his pics, and after Hurley gives me latex gloves, I help him carry everything to his car and put it in the trunk.

We return to the store, and Hurley proceeds to light Wendland up for several violations. His lips tighten, and he's shaking his head ever so slightly. Makes me smile.

Hurley's phone rings. He looks at the screen.

"I'd better take this," he says, and he answers. "Really? Yes, of course, Sarge. Heading there now...maybe fifteen minutes. Copy." He disconnects, looks at me. "Damn."

"What's up?"

"I have to roll on something. I'll get back to you soon."

Must be important, 'cause I gotta wonder if Hurley did the right thing leaving me here alone with Wendland.

He starts to walk away. I suddenly remember.

"Wait—before you go."

He stops by the front door, out of earshot for Wendland.

I approach him. "I got some good info for you."

"About what?"

"I was able to get some good info on that kid who served Jeffrey at the club. The one with dreadlocks."

"Yeah?"

I take out my wallet and remove a torn piece of paper from it, hand it to Hurley.

"Ray, and a tag number? How the hell did you get this?"

"Same way you and Millhoff would've, but I did it first."

"Damn, Frank. We told you to stay the hell out of this."

"Don't go worrying yourself. I didn't fuck anything up. I saw him outside the club and got a friend of mine who works security a couple buildings over to approach him. He's an ex-cop, so he knows how to handle himself and how to play these mopes."

"Thanks. We'll follow up on it for sure, but I have to go."

He opens the door, turns to me, and says, "Don't work this anymore, all right?"

"Go or you'll be late."

He shakes his head and hurries to his car. I return to the counter.

TWENTY-TWO

A nything else I can help you with?" Stinky asks.

"Yes. Did Detective Hurley mention to you who I am?"

"No. Why would he?"

"Well, the only difference between me and him is I'm retired. But you know…"

I show him my badge.

"I spent most of my career as a detective at the Narcotics Branch. Had a pretty good reputation, actually, and still have a lot of friends on the department."

"Okay."

"Now I'm a private investigator, so the good thing is, for me, I can get away with a lot more than my good friend Detective Hurley can."

"That sounds like a threat."

"Well, dude, sort of. Maybe. I'm not sure yet."

"I think maybe you should leave now."

"I think maybe I'm going to ask you a few questions, and you're going to answer them."

"I told the detective everything I know. You got your property back. Now you're harassing me."

"So call the police."

"Listen, you got your stuff back, and I lost money on the deal because I don't get reimbursed. Not to mention all these violations I'm going to have to pay now."

"So you're the victim here?" I'm thinking of Jeffrey, but I don't mention him.

"I didn't mean it like that."

"Tell me what you told Detective Hurley."

"I don't have to tell you anything."

"Do you get a lot of return customers? 'Cause damn, you got some attitude. Or is it just the police you have a problem with?"

He doesn't answer.

"Don't worry. Even though I've been known to have anger issues, I won't let that happen here. My girl's a lawyer, and I'd rather make this a civil matter and tie your ass up in court for the next year. We can go that route, but I don't think you can afford it. Or you can just answer a couple questions, help me find the rest of my stolen property. The music collection means a lot to me. Damn important. So there. Now you know why I'm so pissed off."

He doesn't know what to say.

"Couple questions, and I'm outta here for good. Whaddya say? I'll even talk to Hurley, see if he'll cut you a break on the fines."

"That's bullshit, and you know it."

"No, it's the truth. With what I do for a living I gotta be a man of my word. Word gets out I can't be trusted, and it's bad for business."

"Like I said, I told him everything I know, but if you need to hear it for yourself, then I guess that's all right."

"Some of these things Hurley already told me, too, but I'm going to ask anyway."

Odd turn of his head to the right and up, like "Get on with it already."

"This Biddy guy come in often?"

He hesitates.

"Listen. Detective Hurley already has a list of all the transactions this guy's made with you. I just want to hear it from you."

"Couple times a week."

"Does he come in alone?"

"Yeah."

"How the hell did he manage to carry all this equipment in here?"

"He made a couple of trips."

"So he kept a car parked outside?"

"No. He had a cab waiting for him."

"A cab?"

"Yeah. The cabbie waits for him, then they leave."

"Does Biddy sit in the front or the back of the cab?"

"Huh? Backseat, I think."

"Does the cab driver ever help him take stuff out?"

"No. He just sits in the front seat and pops the trunk."

"You ever help him?"

"Uh...no?"

"Do you know the cab number?"

"No. Why would I?"

"Describe the cab for me."

"Indie cab. Black with white letters on the front. An older model, like the old cop cars you guys used to drive. Some of you still do."

"What does the cab driver look like?"

"I don't know, man. He's just an older black guy."

"Give me a description of Biddy."

"I don't—African American, tall and skinny."

"Complexion, age, hair..."

"Medium complexion, I guess, maybe early thirties. Short hair."

"You tell Detective Hurley all this?"

"I didn't get a chance to. He was asking me a bunch of questions, then you came in, and he stopped questioning me."

It takes a lot to surprise me, even a burglar who has a cab pick him up and lets him pack stolen goods into the trunk, then transports him to a fence. It's only one more story to add to the list of heartbreak and terror and betrayal. Now the question is, do I tell Hurley? It is my life on the line, after all.

Twenty-Three

I have a plan.

Wendland gave me good information after all that. What I need to do now is sit on Thrift World and wait for a cab that fits Wendland's description to drop off Biddy or some other burglar. According to Wendland, they come by on a fairly regular basis, but not always on the same days. If Hurley and Millhoff find out I'm holding on to this info for myself, I don't know what they'll do. But I'm not going to just sit back. Besides, if they start working it, who knows how long it'll take? Like I said, and will probably keep saying, it's my life in the fucking grinder here.

Jeffrey again.

His, too. I can't forget that.

I can get away with a lot more than the police can. Plain and simple. At least this is what I tell myself. I'll start tomorrow when the store opens, at 10:00 a.m.

I wonder, too, if Wendland does a little more than just weed. Based on the odor radiating from his body, the weed's gotta be good. I'm thinking, even hoping, he might be into blow, but I doubt it. His type usually smokes morning, noon, and night.

I stay parked for a while, keeping an eye on the store. I pull out a capsule from a vial in my pants pocket, twist the capsule open, and squeeze the contents onto the back of my left hand. I scan the area, then snort it up.

TWENTY-FOUR

More coffee, with a couple of grapefruit, a scalding shower, and then dressing down for surveillance. I grab my backpack and stuff a large plastic bottle of water in the pouch on the side.

I drive back to Thrift World and find a good spot on a side street that faces west and most of the block the store is on. I'm far enough away not to be made. That's why I have palm-size binos. I got about twenty minutes before he opens.

I slide the car seat back and recline to my usual comfortable position. Everything I need within arm's reach. Have to keep the car running, though, or I'd die of heat exhaustion. It's gonna be another hot and humid day. But the heat is good, 'cause my car won't spew exhaust like it would in the cold months. Honestly, no one's going to think much of me parked here anyway. I'm not in the type of car cops use, and I know Vice isn't hitting this area that much anymore. They're stuck on more important details, like standing on corners in uniform and serving lemonade under an umbrella.

A little after ten, a young white chick unlocks the front door to Thrift World. I peer through my binos. She's fairly attractive in a grimy sort of way. She has long dreads and wears a V-neck white T-shirt and short shorts. Her nose is pierced, and she's got a lot of ink. She enters and closes the door behind her.

The hot coffee I bought on the way is cooling down. I grab a bottle of Jameson out of my pack and pour a couple shots' worth in the paper cup.

After a long sip I exhale with contentment. Gotta keep yourself content.

In the couple of hours that follow I only notice a handful of people entering, but they look like regular customers. Today might not be the day for the other kinda business. Buying stolen shit might be reserved for those days Wendland is working. Who knows at this point? It's only the first day, and this spot sure as hell doesn't look like a fencing operation. Maybe mom-and-pop, but nothing major.

The day's a bust. Night encroaches. The interior of the store darkens a bit. The front light over the door and interior back lights go on. A couple of minutes later she exits and locks up.

I watch her as she walks around the corner. I follow.

When I get to the corner, she's heading toward 9th Street. I ease up to let her make that turn, then I drive to the corner. She walks into a place I know well. The Velvet Lounge. Used to be a cool hangout, probably still is, but I haven't been there in years. I'm thinking I want a drink, but then maybe that's not such a good idea, especially if Wendland is meeting her there. I won't take the chance. Drinking alone at home is what I'd rather do anyway. That I do enjoy.

I park the car on the corner of 12th and W, just barely legal. I make sure everything is secured in my pack and exit. Tap the key fob to lock it up and walk. There is something soothing about the cicadas at this time of the evening, when the sun begins to set, like gentle waves seeping into the sand after they hit the shore.

I hear the rumble of a car's big engine behind me, and when I turn I notice the marked patrol cruiser easing up to the curb and stopping. It's gotta be someone I know. But then the emergency lights go on and the driver's-side spotlight is directed at my face, blinding me, so I have to look down and shield my eyes.

What the fuck is this?

I'm thinking it's all over, but then I realize no, it's just one vehicle. If it had to do with the homicide, they sure as hell wouldn't come at me with one patrol car. I hear the car door open.

"Please place the backpack slowly on the ground behind you."

"What the hell is this about?" I ask with authority.

I move my head away from the direct light, shield it with my right hand so it doesn't blind me so much. I see a young officer, looks like he's fresh out of the academy, standing behind the open passenger door of the cruiser with his gun pointed at me. The strobing lights catch my attention, but only for a millisecond.

Fuck, I love those lights.

"I want to see your hands."

"They're right here and empty, Officer. Tell me what's going on. My house is right down the street."

"Turn around and lace your fingers over your head. Slowly step backwards toward the car."

"I'm a retired DC police detective. Check my wallet."

I hear him mumbling something to the driver.

"Now!" he commands.

I don't think now is the time to tell him I'm armed. I slowly raise my hands over my head and lace my fingers.

"Now slowly walk back toward me until I say stop."

I'm not about to argue with this fucking rookie, so I obey.

"You're making a big mistake, Officer. I know most of the officials at 3D. Who is your supervisor?"

"Stop there!"

I hear him talking to the driver again.

"My name is Frank Marr. I know Fulton. He's a captain at 3D. Hit him up on the radio."

More talking.

Then: "Now get on your knees."

Fuckin' shit.

"You have me mistaken for someone else. Have the driver step out. I probably know him."

I hear the driver say something unintelligible.

"On your knees, sir."

I go to my knees, reluctantly, but not so reluctantly that he has to ask me twice. I hear him approaching, then he grabs my laced-together fingers resting on my head and squeezes them together. Something I used to do. A lot. He pats me down.

"Gun!" he calls out to the driver. Odd, because I don't hear the driver step out, unless he was very quiet. He should be backing this rookie up.

"Take it easy. I told you I'm a retired DC cop. I have all my creds in my wallet, right rear pants pocket."

"I'm doing this for your protection and mine until we figure this thing out, okay?"

He pushes me forward so I'm kissing the sidewalk. He's got strength. He takes my right wrist and cuffs it, swings my arm back until I wince in pain. He cuffs me, rolls me to my left side, and pulls out the gun.

"I got a gun here!" he yells again.

Still no word.

"Reach into my right rear pants pocket. You'll find my credentials, including my H.R. two-eighteen permit to carry."

I feel him take out my wallet.

"Damn," he mumbles. "Sir, you match the description of a suspect in an armed robbery that just occurred. I see you have a badge and credentials, but you can easily obtain those online."

"Officer, why isn't your partner out here assisting you if I'm a suspected armed robber? He should be here with you."

He pats me down thoroughly, finding my medicine vial with the capsules that don't contain medicine.

"Careful with that. I need that medication."

He sets it on the ground beside my keys, then takes my 9mm mags and cigarettes.

"Don't move."

I turn my head and can just barely see him as he places the gun on the hood of the car and talks to whoever is inside.

The driver's-side door opens. The spotlight washes out his face. He moves toward me and in front of the spotlight so his large body blocks the direct light.

"Fuck," I say because I recognize him.

Jasper.

"Damn, Frankie. What the fuck are you doing down there? Uncuff him, rookie," he says.

He's in uniform. MASTER PATROL OFFICER embroidered on the right shoulder.

The rookie obeys.

"I'm sorry, sir. I was just doing what I was told."

I push myself to my knees, grab my stuff, and stand.

"You this kid's FTO?" I ask.

"Yeah. Sorry about this shit, man."

"What the fuck is this, Willy? You would've recognized me right away. Why did you let me go through that shit? Your rookie here mighta shot me."

"No, sir," the rookie says. "Not unless you pulled your weapon on me."

I give him a hard glare, nothing more.

"I didn't have my glasses on, Frank, and you did match the description."

"You know how many times I used that bogus line to stop people? I can't count. And I'm certain I don't fit the profile of any of the suspects committing robberies around here."

"What can I say?"

"You heard when I told this officer here my name, right?"

"No. I didn't catch that."

The rookie looks at Jasper, eyes wide, but doesn't say anything. He knows better.

"What's with sending this young officer out alone? You never do that shit."

"I teach 'em right. Let's not take this to another level, Frank. We always been good, right?"

I look straight at the rookie, back to him.

"What are you doing in 3D anyway? You're a bit outta your district."

"We were grabbing some dinner on Fourteenth, that police-friendly El Salvadoran place. Thought I'd get him familiar with the Third. Real coincidence it was you we ran into, but thanks for participating in the training," he says, trying to joke. "Stop by the club. Drinks'll be on the house for the trouble my rookie caused you."

I can tell the rookie looks worried, like I might complain or something.

"I don't care what your FTO tells you. Never walk up to a suspect alone, without backup, especially if he's a suspected armed robber. The both of us were getting fucked by your training officer."

"All right, Frank. Drop it. I was right there. He had backup, and I honestly didn't know it was you."

This is horseshit, but I don't know him well enough to know whether this was meant to be some kinda joke he was playing on me or the rookie here.

I don't want to escalate this, so I say, "No harm. Just got my clothes a little dirty. Advise your rookie that I'm not the type to complain. He seems spooked. And I will take you up on those drinks."

"You hear that?" he tells him. "Frank Marr is straight up. Always was. Was also one of the best narcotics detectives on the department a few years before you came on. Why you retired early, I'll never know."

"That's where I'd like to go, sir," the rookie tells me.

I look at him like, *What the fuck?*

"I mean Narcotics and Special Investigations Division or Vice," he says.

I just nod. "You wanna give me my gun back? I gotta get home."

Jasper tilts his big chin, and the rookie grabs the gun from the hood of the car, where it shouldn't've been, and hands it back, muzzle toward the ground. I holster it.

"You boys be safe," I say.

"Sorry for the fucking confusion, Marr," Jasper says with a smile so broad he's squinting his eyes.

"Never apologize," I tell him, then turn to walk home.

Twenty-Five

That scene was seriously weird. Something really off about that whole situation. Dangerous, though it felt like they were both playing roles.

I'm being paranoid.

No, I'm not.

The last thing I look like is a robbery suspect. I might have a little scruff, but other than that I'm a clean-cut guy. Not to mention my nice jeans and Nat Nast shirt. Maybe a bank robber, but not a common street robber. What the fuck? But seriously, the Nast shirt alone is unique in design and color. Who'd be stupid enough to rob someone wearing this shirt?

Takes some kinda dope to play a joke like that on his rookie. Takes an idiot to play it on me. Even those I know well on the department, like Luna or Millhoff, wouldn't pull something like that. Hell, maybe Jasper was telling the truth; I'd really like to think he's just an idiot FTO.

I go to bed early, fall in and out of sleep for most of the night. When I wake up again, it's not even 7:00 a.m. Fuck it, I'm up.

I loaf around, get a call for a job, some guy who needs an employee checked out for possible embezzlement. Said he heard about me through another client. I turn it down. "Unfortunately, I'll be committed for at least two weeks," I tell him. "Call back then if you don't find anyone else."

I check my iPhone for the local news, see if there's anything new. Jeffrey's mom is all over the place. I need to stay off this thing. It's just gonna drive me crazy. I half expect Millhoff and company to kick my door in any day. How crazy is that? And then last night. I still can't shake what happened. And no, I'll never admit that it scared the living shit outta me. Hell, no.

I figure, as hard as it is, I'm gonna try to burn that feeling out of my system. I drop to do my push-ups, then the crunches. But for some reason, I just feel more pissed off when I'm done.

Twenty-Six

The majority of burglars in DC are crackheads, and the one thing I know about crackheads is that they're predictable. They have a habit bound by routine and, after a while, by superstition. They stick to their regular spots and the people they have grown to trust. That goes for where they sell the stolen goods or trade them for drugs, where they have to go afterward to buy the crack and smoke it, and sometimes who they will smoke it with.

The amount of burglaries a crackhead has to commit on a daily basis depends on how big the habit is. I've debriefed guys who were smoking over eight hundred bucks a day. That's at least three or four solid burglaries a day. My house would be a good hit because of the laptop, the flat-screen, and especially the gun. The laptop is old, so not worth more than fifty bucks on the street. The TV is good for about a buck fifty. The gun, back when I was working—they'd go for three to six hundred on the street, depending on the model. Mine's a revolver, but a nice one. It should get three bills or more.

But like I've said a few times before, it's easier to control your habit when you've got a stash at home. I'm talking cocaine for the most part. But whereas coke is a demon, crack is the devil—once you start smoking you never stop. That's what most of the guys and gals I debriefed have told me. That's what separates people like me from them, except when the stash has run out. We gotta get more. I've never let myself get to that point.

Wendland opens the store. Wearing the same damn clothing from the last time I saw him. Wouldn't surprise me if he lied and my flat-screen and laptop are at his home right now. He doesn't seem like the gun type, so I doubt he has that.

I crack the window and light a smoke. Another humid day, so it'll be another day of surveillance and burning gasoline.

Not even an hour, four cigarettes, and two bumps later, a black old-model Crown Vic cab pulls up to the curb in front of the location. It matches the description Wendland gave me. I write down the tag number in a notebook.

"Here we go," I mumble to myself. I especially like when I'm right.

I grab my binos. A tall skinny man shouldering a bulging knapsack slides out of the rear passenger side. Looks a little scraggly to be Biddy—hair not so trim—but maybe he's had a rough couple of nights. On the other hand, if Wendland was truthful with his description, I don't think hair would grow that fast, even on a crackhead.

The vehicle's trunk pops open as he makes his way behind it. It looks like a small flat-screen and what might be a large suitcase are loaded in the trunk. I grab a digital camera with a long lens from my backpack. I start snapping pictures of the driver through the closed driver's-side window and of the scruffy guy pulling out the flat-screen and carrying it to the front door. He returns to grab the large suitcase, struggles to get it out, and when he does he wheels it over to set it beside the TV.

He opens the door, but before he can enter Wendland appears inside and looks like he's blocking him.

Wendland shakes his head and points back to the cab, like he's refusing to take him in. After dealing with Hurley, and maybe a bit of me, Wendland is smart enough not to buy anything that might be stolen—for a little while, anyway.

The dude raises his hands in the air and mouths something that I'm sure has the word *fucking* in it. They go back and forth for a couple of minutes. The scraggly one signals to the cabbie with some inaudible words and a shake of his head. Wendland shuts the door, and that's the last I see of him.

The trunk pops back open, and the fiend wheels the suitcase back, then struggles to lift it and stuff it back into the trunk. He gets the flat-screen in, too, slams the trunk, and returns to open the left rear passenger door and slide in.

I focus with my binos now on the driver. His head is turned back, as they seem to be talking. Can't really make him out. Shortly after, the cab pulls from the curb. I wait a second, then follow.

Twenty-Seven

I'm not sure if that's Graham Biddy in back, but I'm certain that's the cab that dropped him off at Thrift World with my property.

It's before lunch. Traffic is light. That can work for me and against me. I like another vehicle to hide behind occasionally. Ideally you want a couple more cars when you're tailing someone; I don't have that luxury. If you're solo like me, the only thing you have to worry about is keeping the right distance and not letting the suspect see you twice at different locations. Then again, the suspect has to be paying attention. Lot of these knuckleheads don't even think about it.

The cabbie makes his way to U Street, turns left onto 14th, going south. Just before Thomas Circle he hangs a U-turn, slows down, and double-parks in front of a small convenience store. I stay back, pull to the curb next to a hydrant.

The tired-looking brick convenience store is one of the few survivors left on the lower end of 14th Street, and in all likelihood it is not a welcome neighbor. All the other newer buildings, stores, and restaurants around here, with their well-kept exteriors, make the store look toxic, like something that'll eventually eat away and destroy a beautiful coral reef.

Again the passenger exits and pulls out the small flat-screen. He sets it on the pavement between the cab and a parked car. He fiddles with the suitcase, but it doesn't look like he's trying to pull it out. Instead he grabs a laptop from inside, closes the trunk. He cradles the flat-screen with his right hand, walks to the store, opens the door with the hand carrying the laptop, and disappears inside.

The cabbie rolls down his window, takes a puff of a cigarette, exhales out the window. He looks to be in his early sixties. He has a round, friendly face, a well-trimmed beard, salt-and-pepper medium-length hair, and he wears glasses. Looks like a well-seasoned cabbie.

I call Luna using my car's Bluetooth.

"What's up, Frankie?" He greets me right away.

"Are you at your desk?"

"What do you need?"

"Just a little love. Can't I miss my ex–work wife?"

"Fuck you. You're the bitch in this relationship."

"Maybe now, but not then."

"Just give me the name you want me to run and tell me you're not doing anything stupid."

"Actually, a tag, and no, I'm not. I'm working a new gig."

I hate lying all the time. Especially to him.

"Go on."

I give it.

"A cab?"

"Yeah."

"He piss you off or something? Or is this really actual work?"

"Both."

"Doesn't have anything to do with the murder of your cousin, right?"

"Right."

"Hold on," he says.

I hear his fingers working the keyboard.

Seconds later: "I get caught doing this shit for you it could mean my job."

"You keep saying that."

"Ready to copy?"

"Go."

I ready my pen and notebook.

"Robert Diamond, black male, DOB 09/07/45. It's an indie cab that comes back to an address in NE."

He gives me the address.

"No record?"

"Hold on."

More typing.

"He's clean. I can go deeper, but WALES shows no record."

"Naw, that's good enough for me, bro. Appreciate it."

"I know you do, 'cause you got no one else."

"I do, but I love you best."

"All right, now."

"I owe you a lunch."

"Drinks and a cigar at Shelly's."

"Good enough. I'll give you a call when I get through this shit."

"Be safe."

"You, too, brother."

I tap the screen to disconnect.

Robert Diamond. No record. You're gonna be my new friend.

TWENTY-EIGHT

Not even ten minutes inside and the crackhead comes out sipping a bottle of orange soda.

He walks to the rear passenger-side window. Diamond leans toward him. They're across the street and down a bit, but I can make out the cash transaction between the two with my binos. Diamond appears to pocket the money after. The trunk pops open. A few more words between the two, and the mope pulls the suitcase from the cab and walks back into the store. Diamond rolls up his window, and I can tell he's about to pull out. Their deal is done.

I have to make a quick decision, and it doesn't take more than a second to figure Robert Diamond is the one I'm gonna follow. He's an easier mark, with a lot more to lose, and I got a feeling I can break him easier than I can break a violent, possibly dangerous crackhead. Even if the crackhead is Biddy, Diamond will lead me back to him. If I play him right.

I stay a couple of cars behind the cabbie as he drives south on 9th Street. I need to stay back as best I can. The cab is easy to make out from a distance, but I don't want to get too far back and chance getting jammed up in traffic or stuck at a light.

Diamond pulls up to the curb at the southwest corner of 9th and I Streets for a young lady trying to hail him over. She has a purse and a small wheeled carry-on suitcase. She puts it in the rear seat and hops in. Damn. I think about going to the address Luna gave me for him, but then what if it's a bad address? I can't risk losing him. Just have to stick with it.

He drops her off at Union Station. Luckily for me, he doesn't go around the semicircle again and park with the line of cabs waiting to pick up fares. Instead he makes his way to Mass Avenue and to E Street, where he heads west. This might be a long fucking day. I check my fuel level. Three-quarters full. That should do it if that's what it becomes.

TWENTY-NINE

I tailed him into the evening. Nothing but a few fares. Nothing suspicious, but I did get some good intel, especially when I followed him home and confirmed he lives at the address Luna gave me.

Can't take it for granted anymore when I enter my home. My shirt is tucked behind the grip of my gun with my hand firmly on the grip. I close the door behind me. Quietly. Lock it, scan as I move toward the kitchen. All as it should be, but still can't relax. Damn—burglary, murder, who knows why or what they'll do next? Not even ten o'clock, and I'm gonna hit the sack.

Leslie calls a few minutes later. I let it go to message. Don't know why.

I undress in the master bathroom, drop my clothes in the hamper, put on some fresh boxer briefs and my old gray Redskins division-champs T-shirt, and go to bed. I'll force-feed myself in the morning, eat some grapefruit and down a couple of vitamins. That should be good enough to go. Well, that and replenishing my supply, but not with as much as I usually take. Need to conserve.

Thunder's in the distance. Another storm heading our way. I love a good storm. Helps me sleep.

Two in the morning.

Did I sleep?

I think I did, but I don't remember dreaming. Might be a good thing. Means I might've slept deeply, as short as it may have been. As much as I want to, and this body wants to, I can't bother going back to bed. It'll just get me thinking.

After my morning ritual cleansing, I pack up my backpack. I put on my good suit 'cause it makes me feel like a detective again, and I'll need that if I get the chance to chat with Mr. Diamond today.

I do feel like I used to feel back in the day, which really wasn't so long ago, when I had to get up before the sun to execute a search warrant. Everything but the suit. I'd never wear a suit to a search warrant back then, when I was actually a cop. I do on occasion nowadays, but those situations aren't really search warrants, and the suit is more of a disguise than a uniform. Fake armor.

Rain-drenched landscape. What little grass I have in front needs it. Must've been a good storm. The humidity is oddly low. Sky is cleared of clouds, allowing the subtle first light through. The quiet time.

I drive the car around the block to make sure I'm not being followed. I take some back roads, too. Easier to spot a tail that way. No rush hour, so I make it to Diamond's neighborhood quickly. I do a drive-through in the alley at the rear of his house. His cab is there.

It's a tough one to set up on. Would've been easier if he'd parked in front, because then there'd be only one direction he could go. I need to get an eyeball on his car. The only way to do that is to set up in the narrow alley and trust that a neighbor won't complain or, worse, call the police. It's early enough to think I might be okay. And luckily it's not so humid, so I can turn the car off.

The sun is slow to rise behind me, but when it does it's beaming.

Seven in the morning.

You'd think he'd get out there by now. Rush hour beginning, burglars starting their rounds casing the neighborhoods.

Don't know when I'll get another chance, so I look around me, squeeze the contents of two capsules on the back of my hand, and snort once, then again. It's a good one. I usually don't do it this early, but I felt the need. It takes a couple more sniffs to break the rest through, and there it is again. Damn. It's great when you have good shit, before they get a chance to step on it a couple of times. Mine flaked off a nice cloudy-white rock. Slight bluish tint if you look closely. Mighty fine hit. Maybe because it's early and the sun is behind me, rising just right.

Now it's 8:00 a.m., and he's backing out. He's going to head in the other direction, where the street dead-ends, and he'll have to make a right back onto 4th. I back out of the cut and onto 4th just before he comes into view. Slowly I follow. He turns left at the next street. Back to Northwest. My neighborhood.

Damn if he doesn't make a right on 11th heading toward Florida Avenue, which is just around the corner from my house. The Florida Avenue Grill stands on the southwest corner, tucked beside a large all-glass structure like a tiny neglected monument. Across the street from it is the Howard University campus police building. I know a few of those guys. A lot of them retired MPD working as campus investigators now. Left on Florida to 12th, and another left is the street my house is on. He parks on 11th, ahead of a bus stop and on the same side as the Howard police building. I drive past him. He doesn't take notice. Through my rearview mirror I can see that he's walking north. I find an illegal parking space a short distance down from the Grill, near an entrance to Howard security. I still have a good view of the entrance to the Grill. I recline my seat all the way down and turn off the engine.

It's a long block, but I notice him crossing to the west side of 11th, then going into the Grill.

Fucking son of a bitch. Right around the corner from my house. Is he going in there for coffee or to shoot the shit with some boys over breakfast before he rolls out to aid and abet?

This is what's called playing it by ear. Could be good. Could be bad. Most of the time it's worked out for me. I put my old police patch on the dash so the Howard boys or one of my own won't give me a ticket.

It's starting to get hot, so I turn the car back on and crank the air. I put my seat back to its original position, step out of the car, walk around to the front passenger side, set my backpack on the floor behind the seat, and hop in. I light a smoke and get ready to catch a cab.

About forty-five minutes later I see him exit. He walks slowly toward his car, and I exit my car not far behind him. There's more traffic now. Cars passing. A couple of people coming up on his side from Florida Ave., but they cross the street to continue north on 11th. He's not paying much attention to this side. I shoulder my pack, walk at a fast pace toward his cab.

I get to the rear of his cab and turn around to see him walking across the street toward the driver's-side door.

I walk to the driver's side of his cab as he takes his keys out to unlock it. It's an old model, so he doesn't have a key fob. He looks at me, not worried, probably just wondering why a man in a nice suit is standing in the street next to his cab.

"Mr. Diamond," I say.

THIRTY

"Do I know you, sir?" he asks with a kind smile. Not an image of this man I expected to see.

As a PI and a retired cop, I'm breaking one of the biggest rules I can break, but still, I pull out my wallet and flash my badge, trying to do it so fast that he can't take notice of RETIRED etched above DETECTIVE. I can easily get my license revoked doing this kinda shit, but I've been lucky playing it so far. And fuck, I break rules. I do.

He withdraws his smile. Guess he didn't see the RETIRED part.

"Did I do something wrong here, Officer?"

Not the question to ask if you didn't do anything wrong.

"Yes. But nothing we can't work out." And I immediately regret saying that, but it just came out, so now I have to go with it.

"What's this all about? I ain't done nothin'."

"Well, I don't know about that, Mr. Diamond."

What the fuck? My mouth's quicker than——

"What are you talkin' about? I ain't done nothin', nothin' at all. And I'm parked in a legal spot."

"It's not today we have to talk about."

"I'm an honest, hardworking man. I never been arrested. What's this about?"

"I'm sure you're hardworking. And I know your record is clean. There is a possibility it can stay that way, but that'll depend on how you wanna play this."

"Play this? I don't know what the hell you talking about. I got fares I got to pick up. I'm a working man. And what the hell you doin' standing next to my car, anyway? You been here waiting for me?"

"I'll be straight with you. I followed you from your home on Fourth Street."

"What?"

His old hands start shaking, and he panics and struggles to put the key in the lock to open the door, but his hand is trembling too much. I almost worry he's gonna have a heart attack.

"Slow down there, Mr. Diamond. Give me your keys. I'll open the door for you."

"Hell, no. You got some kinda warrant? I want to know what this here is about."

"I'll open the door for you. We can sit and talk in your car."

He pauses like he's considering it, but then he faces me, keys dangling in his trembling right hand.

"What kinda line of questioning is this? You want to talk to me in my car? What kinda police do that?"

"The kind who can help you if you help them. And I'd like to keep this private, but if you want I'll call a marked unit, and we can talk at the Third District."

If he calls my bluff, I'll have to call a unit. Millhoff will come in, and I'll have to give up everything I know. Piss him off, and this old man'll probably lawyer up. I know that's how it'll play out, so don't call it, old man.

"I'm a hardworking man. I don't know what the hell you're talking about."

He's just playing the game now. Okay.

I snatch the keys out of his hand. He steps back, startled, like he's going to scream for help.

A car slows to pass him. I notice the driver turn to look at me, passing me slowly. No threat, just a concerned citizen.

"Step to the front of your car or you're gonna get run over."

For some reason, he obeys the command. Maybe I got my real police tone back.

I unlock the door and open it.

"See, I opened the door for you."

He just stands there, on the other side of the open door, mouth gaping.

In my experience, an innocent man would either demand a supervisor or get on his cell and call the cops himself. He wouldn't take this shit. Bad guys aren't afraid of the police anymore. That I know for sure. Especially getting the keys snatched out of his hand the way I did. He knows what this is about, but I don't think he's much of a bad guy. I can tell he's mulling things over in his head, thinking something like maybe one of his burglary boys got arrested and rolled on him.

He's wearing a tucked-in short-sleeved shirt with no bulges, and he's fucking too old for an ankle holster 'cause he probably can't even touch his toes, but I still don't wanna take a chance.

"You got a gun or any kind of weapon under that seat or anywhere in the car?"

"Lord, no."

"Well, for your safety and mine I'm just gonna check under your seat. And you're no match for me, Mr. Diamond, so don't get stupid."

"I ain't got no gun, and I ain't stupid."

While keeping an eye on him I reach my right hand in, feel around the floor under the seat. I stand and reach further in to open the center console. Nothing.

I move back, extend my arm to the open door, and say, "Why don't you have a seat, Mr. Diamond?"

He sits down in the front seat, looks up to me.

"What about my keys?"

"I'll give them to you once I hop in the front."

He shakes his head. Lips tighten. He shuts the door. I walk around the rear of the vehicle, keeping an eye on his movements. I unlock the front passenger door, sit, and shut the door.

"Starting to get real humid," I say while handing his keys back to him. "How about you start this up and get the air going? Then I'll tell you what this is all about."

THIRTY-ONE

He keeps a clean cab, which is interesting. With the air on it cools down nicely. A plug-in deodorizer sticks out where the car lighter should be. Smells like cinnamon. His ashtray is clean, so I'll be polite and won't even ask about smoking. There's thick Plexiglas with a slide-open window that separates him from the passengers in back. Doubtful it's bulletproof.

His hands are on his lap.

"You keep a nice cab."

"Been doing this for thirty-three years. Always kept a nice cab. You never told me your name, Officer."

"Frank Marr, and I'm going to start by being straight and tight because I don't want to waste my time or your gas. I got you good, so in order for this deal to work between us I need you to work with me."

"Wha—"

"Don't even go there, because here's what you stand to lose: you'll get a warrant for your arrest. You'll get your cab seized because you used it during the commission of several felonies. It'll get impounded as evidence. What are you, late sixties?" I ask before he can respond.

"Seventy-two."

"You look good for seventy-two."

He looks at me like I'm crazy.

"You married?"

A moment.

"My wife passed."

"I'm sorry."

"No, you ain't."

"You don't know me. Just tell me what I need to know. What about kids?"

"All due respect, Officer—"

"Investigator will do."

"Investigator. All due respect, why you need to know all that?"

"I like to know the kind of man I'm dealing with."

"I got a son. He's in the military."

"What branch?"

"Army. He overseas somewhere."

"You must be proud."

Nods.

"So you're at that age when you stand to lose a lot, maybe everything. If your health is good, you're not counting the years yet. But in prison you do. Not to mention your son. So here's what I have. I got you solid on several burglaries. There's also an accessory to homicide."

"What? You fucking crazy. Get out of my car!"

"That'd be a mistake. You should let me finish."

"I don't know what you're talkin' about. Homicide?"

"Even though you weren't the one breaking into the homes, and even though you didn't kill anyone, you aided and abetted those who did, like Graham Biddy and this other dude, Givens."

My head's not in the game right now; too long since my last bump. But I get the reaction I like. That sudden intoxicated look: he feels like his insides just dropped to the pit of his stomach. We'll see if I fucked it up.

"I mean, really? Transporting them right from the site of the homicide to the fence who bought the stolen goods? Not to mention chauffeuring one or both of them to a hit? Never would have dreamed it. These are serious charges, because you'll get hit with several counts of burglary two, along with conspiracy, trafficking in stolen property, and accessory to murder. Some serious shit."

"No, sir, you can't do that. I don't aid and abet nobody. I don't know nothin' about any murder. I just pick up people and take them where they want to go. I don't conspire with them about breakin' into other people's homes. I'd never have anything to do with killin' someone."

"You pick up crackheads, let them put merchandise—flat-screens, laptops, music, and on and on—into the trunk of your cab. I got photos. I got witnesses. And like I said, you don't have to break in to pick up the same charge."

"Hell, I don't know what they doin'. For all I know they moving."

That's what I want to hear.

"Yeah, moving stolen property. And it doesn't look like you're in the legitimate moving business. The Taxicab Commission might have something to say about that."

Bows his head this time.

"I mean, Thrift World and that mom-and-pop convenience store on Fourteenth? You were at both of those spots the other day. I have photos to prove it. Shows everything." I don't allow him to answer. "Don't play me for a fool or you don't got any kind of chance here. I'll walk out right now."

"How come I ain't locked up, then? You say you got all that on me."

"So you don't deny it. Good."

"I never said that. You puttin' words in my mouth now."

"You're not locked up because I choose not to have you locked up. If I believed for a second that you were a murderer we wouldn't be having this conversation. I need your help."

"Like I said, I ain't stupid, and I never heard of the police working deals like this. Sitting here like you are, no partner or other cops around."

"That's because I do things a bit different. Got a different set of rules. For instance, I'm actually working a different case, and that's the one I need your help with. I could care less about all these other burglaries, but I know a detective who does. He's the lead detective for burglaries in the city. I can call him here, too, if you want, but he's by the book, and you'll get hit with everything. No kinda deal like I'm going to make. I'm just looking to pick up Graham Biddy and Givens."

I'm starting to think I didn't play this right. I gave up the homicide and the suspects much too soon. I'm off with my interrogation skills. Haven't had the cause to do it for a while. He's gotta know something about Jeffrey's murder.

"You're thinking too much, and you don't want to take that kind of chance. I can get Biddy on my own, but it'll just take a bit more time. And the other detective working the case, he'll get you right away, 'cause I'll pass off all the evidence I got on you to him. It's an easy out for you. You just show me where Biddy took certain property, then help me find him and Givens."

"I don't know anyone by the name of Givens."

He's lying. It's the way he paused, even if it was for a second, before he said "Givens." I don't want to push it, 'cause I might lose him.

"Biddy, then. You find him for me, I'll let you slide."

"Why would you do that?"

"I told you. I'm different. I care. I believe you're a decent man who just got caught up with the wrong people. I mean, it's gotta be hard being an independent cabbie in this city."

"Sure, no denying that."

"You got it good. Self-employed. Good-looking little house. You own it?"

"Yeah."

"Don't jeopardize all you've worked for."

"It's just hard nowadays. You got that Uber business jackin' you and then the Taxicab Commission making it even harder to earn a living as an independent."

"I truly can understand that. I personally don't like Uber. Don't trust them, but I'm old-fashioned that way."

"Old-fashioned? Shit, you're too young to be old-fashioned."

I chuckle in my head.

"How much do you make on a good day, not including what those mopes give you?"

It doesn't take him long.

"I'm lucky to pocket a hundred bucks after a ten-hour day and expenses."

"How much extra do you make picking these guys up and taking them where they have to go?"

He's hesitant.

"Is it worth getting locked up, losing your cab, and going to jail for? For what, a few more bucks?"

"Naw, it ain't."

My phone rings. I pull it out of the suit jacket's inner pocket. *Shit.*

It's Hurley.

"What's up, partner?" I answer. "No, I can't right now. On

an interview. Yeah, I do have to work. No kidding? Really? Shit. Okay. Around two o'clock. A little hard to talk right now. Right. Sounds good, man. You got it. Bye." I disconnect, slip it back into my inner pocket.

Fuck, they found my .38.

I turn to Diamond.

"That was Detective Hurley. Seems he recovered some interesting property related to the burglary I'm working. Good for me, not really good for you."

"You playing me or somethin'?"

"This is where the conversation ends, and you're either with me or you're fucked."

"You playin' me. I know what you all do."

"Mr. Diamond, I've told you more than I would've told anyone else in your position. Don't ask me why, 'cause I fucking don't know. I got you picking up burglars who put stolen goods in the trunk of your car. I got you taking them to fences, like that spot on Fourteenth by Thomas Circle. I got them paying you after they sell the goods." I stop just in case I've gone too far. Don't mention the murder again. He might shut down. "All I'm going to say now is you can get yourself out of this and work with me here."

"How do I know you're tellin' the truth?"

"You don't. You don't. But I am. For whatever that's worth. You don't get far in my line of work if you fuck people over. Word eventually gets out, then my name's worth shit."

I pull out my wallet from my back pocket, open it, making sure he can see the edge of the badge shine just right, and I count out ten twenties. After I slip my wallet back in the pocket I hand it over to him.

"This is to show good faith. That's double a hard day's work for you."

He looks at it, looks worried, like I'm offering him a bribe.

"It's for real. I'm not playing you."

"What kinda damn investigator are you?"

"The kind you want as a friend."

He takes it. A gentle manner.

"What you want me to do, then?"

Thirty-Two

I need you to take me to the location where Biddy beds down. Also, I wanna know where he buys his drugs."

He looks down, then out the window. I'm assuming it's at nothing in particular. He just needs a second or two.

Turns to me and says, "Yeah, I can do that."

"And whatever other fencing locations he sells property to."

"I only know of the two. The ones you already mentioned."

"You remember a place he hit right around the corner here? He came out with a couple hundred record albums and CDs, a flat-screen, and stereo equipment."

There he goes with that fucking guilty head drop. Then he's got another expression. Fearful.

"Talk to me," I tell him.

He's hesitant.

Then he looks at me direct.

"I just wait where they tell me to wait. Nothing more. You understand?"

"Yes, but then there's that whole aiding-and-abetting thing. You go down just like the one who did it. It doesn't have to be that way, though, 'cause you can lead me to the one responsible. It'll go a long way for you, especially if it leads to who was responsible for what went on inside that house."

See what he says to that last bit.

"I just sit in this here car. That's all."

"Like I told you, I know, otherwise we wouldn't be having this conversation."

"He took everything to Thrift World, but they only bought the stereo equipment. The rest of the stuff he sold to the store on Fourteenth Street."

"Okay, I already know about the stereo equipment, so you're telling the truth. I appreciate that."

"All right."

"Did the convenience store buy the gun that was stolen from that house, too?"

"I don't know nothin' about a gun."

"The convenience store bought everything else, though?"

"Well, the boy didn't come back out with anything."

"But that shit's old. Why would they want that?"

"Lord if I know."

"What time did you take Biddy there to hit the house?"

"I can't remember. Early morning, though."

I have a feeling he knows what happened in my house, and now he's scared. Shit, for all I know, he's the shooter and I'm totally off my game, but I have a stronger feeling he's not capable of something like that. I want to go easy on this.

"Let's roll, then," I say.

"You mean you want to do this now?"

"Yeah, of course. That was a substantial fare I gave you."

"I thought you said that was in good faith."

"Yeah, but it doesn't come without some good faith on your part."

"Damn. All right. But can you at least sit yourself in the back like a regular customer? Looks too suspicious having you in the front like that."

"That I can understand."

I look at the keys in his ignition, think about taking them until I get in back. I decide not to, 'cause I have to show trust, even though I trust him for nothing.

"You pull away on me when I step out, I'll personally be kicking in the door to your house."

"How many times I gotta keep tellin' you I ain't stupid?"

I shoot him an ever-so-slight smile. He'll get nothing more.

I slide open the Plexiglas window between the seats and step out of the car, but before I close the front door I open the rear door. When it opens, I shut the front door and hop in back. I roll down my window to see if I have control of it.

"Show me where he buys his drugs first."

"Drugs?"

"Give me a break. Take me to where Biddy buys his drugs."

He drives.

We get to the 1300 block of Riggs, Northwest, where he slowly passes and points out a two-story connected home. I get the address and write it down in my pocket notebook. I never got any intel about the house back when I was working narcotics, and I had an excellent source for this area. They're all, like, million-dollar homes now.

"I don't want them to see me here," he says.

"Don't worry. No one's gonna see you. Just drive to the next spot."

Riggs is a one-way street, so he drives west to 14th. After a couple of minutes, with traffic getting heavy, he makes a left on

14th and then a right on R Street, one block down. Again he drives slowly and points out a multistory apartment building. This block I am definitely familiar with. It was hoppin' a few years back. I copy the address.

"I don't know what floor, but he stays at that building. I think with a woman, or maybe his mother."

"Make this right on Fifteenth, and drive by the store on Fourteenth so I can make sure we're talking about the same place."

He makes a right and drives back around to 14th, where he makes another right. Once we pass Rhode Island Avenue, he points out the same convenience store I sat on the other day.

"Good," I tell him. "Now let's find a private spot to talk for a minute, then that'll be it for today."

"You talkin' more of this shit?"

"Let's just get through this here first, okay? In fact just head back to the area of Eleventh and W and find a parking space. I can get out from there after we're done."

"What the hell did I get myself into?" he mumbles.

"Big mess, but nothing we can't fix together. Right?"

I see him look at me through the rearview, tighten his lips again.

Diamond finds a parking place on 11th near the spot he was in before. I stay in the backseat but lean forward a bit to better talk to him through the slot portion in the Plexiglas window.

"The place on Riggs—what does Biddy purchase there?"

"Hell, I ain't into drugs. I don't mess with all that."

"I'm not saying you do, but we both know Biddy does. What does he buy?"

"Mostly crack, but I know he's got himself some heron on occasion."

Heron. I haven't heard that in a while.

"He's on heroin, too?"

"I never seen him use it. Don't allow it in my cab. I just know he talked about getting some there."

"Are these young guys, old guys, what?"

"You mean on Riggs?"

"Yes."

"Two young punks who think they're tougher than they are."

"You ever see any of them with guns?"

"Hell, no."

"They do a lot of business out of that house?"

"I assume so. One day Biddy spent over four bills there for crack."

"Did Biddy just walk up to the door?"

"No. No, sir. Can't do that. Had to call beforehand, then he'd meet one of the young ones in the alley behind the house."

"You take any other of the boys there?"

"Shee-it."

"Not anything I'll write down. I just need to know the extent of their business."

"Yeah, and I can tell you they rollin' big-time."

Oh, yeah. I love hearing that.

"You know their names?"

"No. I don't know them like that."

"Any of the boys you bring here ever mention a nickname, anything like that?"

"Not that I can recollect."

"So here's the deal. I'm going to hold on to everything I got you on, and I'm not going to write it up or let the detective assigned to all these cases know about you. If I'm gonna do that, you're going to have to stay away from transporting those boys around."

"All right."

"So what are you going to say if one of them calls?"

"That I got a fare, something like that."

"I'm gonna trade cell numbers. You're going to call me right after one of those boys calls you, especially Biddy."

"If you go snatch them up like that, they gonna know I set them up."

"No, it won't be like that. I've done this sort of thing more times than I can remember, and they won't have a clue. Don't worry about that."

Shakes his head slow.

"I mean it, Diamond. The only way you're gonna work this off is doing what I tell you. Then you'll be free of this shit. I'm also going to pay you a buck fifty a day for the next couple of days."

"One hundred and fifty? What do I got to do for that?"

"Mostly like what we did today. I sit in the back here again, and maybe you show me some other spots."

"I showed you what I know."

"You showed me where Biddy goes. I want to know where all of them get their drugs, 'cause narcotics is mostly my line of work. Getting the property back, too, of course, and maybe solve a murder along the way."

"Shee-it. I told you I don't know nothin' about a murder."

I don't respond to that. Instead I say, "You don't know where I might have eyes, so I catch you doing something you shouldn't be doing, everything is off, no deal, and you'll have a warrant for your arrest."

"Don't have to worry about that."

"So when Biddy or one of the other boys calls you, he uses a cell phone."

"I'm assumin' so."

"It's always the same number?"

"Biddy's is, but not always everyone else."

"Give me Biddy's number."

"You ain't gonna call him?"

"Now you're thinking I'm stupid. I'm going to see where the number goes to, that's all," I lie, because it's not easy like a landline. It'll take a subpoena to get that from the provider. I certainly can't do that.

I pull my phone out.

"Let me get it," I say.

I tap the icon for Notes as he pulls his older smartphone out of his right front pants pocket. Searches his contacts, then calls out the number for me.

"Now you call my phone from yours."

He's reluctant, but he obeys. I give him my number, and he taps it in. Couple seconds later my phone rings.

"I'm going to save you in my contacts. You do the same."

He does.

"Put my name in your cell as Fagin," I tell him.

"That your real name?"

"Yes."

He taps it in.

"I'm going to go now, but tell me this: Why didn't you get a call from any of those burglars today?"

"I don't always get a call. Sometimes it's in the early morning. Sometimes in the evening. Sometimes not at all, 'cause most of the time they can haul their goods in a backpack."

"So you get a call when they get a big hit?"

"Yeah."

"You know what to do then, right?"

"Call you if they call."

"Call me the second after you disconnect with them."

"I got it."

"Unless I hear from you first, I'm gonna give you a call tomorrow in the early afternoon to come pick me up. I'll give you the corner to drive to and hail you down when I see you."

"Just like a regular fare, huh?"

"No. The buck fifty kind."

THIRTY-THREE

Once I get home I change, pull out a cigarette, and wait for Hurley to show. He wanted to meet me at two o'clock, but after thinking about it, I decided I didn't want to go to headquarters, run into the news or, worse, walk in and don't walk out, so I called him when I got home and told him to come here.

He shows up. Right on time. Tim Millhoff, too.

I open the door.

Hurley is shouldering an old tan canvas briefcase. His sweat is already seeping through the underarms of his orange Tommy Bahama shirt. "It's suffocating out there," I say. "Come in."

I close the door behind them, shake their hands.

They follow me into the living room.

They notice the wires still hanging out of the wall.

"Have a seat."

Millhoff sits on the sofa. Hurley unshoulders his case and sits toward the middle. Guess they're allowing me the hot seat.

"You guys want something cold to drink? Or coffee?"

"I'm good," Millhoff says.

"Me, too."

I plop down on the armchair.

"So tell me about my .38."

"Even though the serial numbers match, and we know the gun belongs to you, I need you to identify it for me," Millhoff says.

"Of course."

Hurley pulls an evidence bag out of his briefcase, opens it so I can look in.

"Definitely mine. I know because of the crack on the grip, and you say the serial numbers match, so..."

Hurley carefully folds the evidence bag and slips it back into his briefcase.

"Where did you find it?"

"Fourteen hundred block of Rhode Island," Millhoff answers. "It was placed on the decedent's chest, Marr. Kind of like the shooter was making some kind of a statement."

"Shit."

"Yeah. I want to show you a photo of the body, see if you know him."

"All right."

Millhoff turns to Hurley, waits for him to take the photo out and hand it to him. Millhoff in turn hands it to me.

"Aw, fuck. No."

It's fucking Ray.

"You know him?"

It's just a medium shot, shoulders up. Bit of blood on the right side of his cheek, like spatter. His eyes are closed. Peaceful.

"Fuck, that's Ray, the kid who served Jeffrey at the club," I say. "The kid I told you about. You never found him?"

"Well, yeah, you just looked at the death photo."

"Don't be an ass, Millhoff. You know what I mean."

"Your reaction made it sound like you know him better than you're letting on."

"No," I lie. "It's just another connection that fucking doesn't make sense."

Did I get him killed by talking to him?

"We tried to find him. The car tag you gave us came back to someone else. She claimed she didn't know him and her tags were stolen," Hurley says.

"But she didn't report it, right?" I ask, already knowing the answer.

"Of course not. We staked out where you said he was hanging, stopped a few people, but he was in the wind."

"What can you tell me about the scene?"

"Not a drive-by," Millhoff begins. "More like face-to-face, and he was caught by surprise. Execution, maybe?"

"Damn. What's his full name?"

"Came up in the system as Eugene Wrayburn. Don't have his juvenile records, but he does have a few PWIDS and a CPWL charge."

I'm thinking I unknowingly got caught up in something else, something big as well as bad. Jeffrey's murder, the burglary, and now this? All of it only seems to tie back to me.

"You said the gun was placed on his chest?"

"Yes."

"Was it used to shoot him?"

Millhoff and Hurley look at each other, like there's more to this.

"What?"

"The bullets that were recovered from your cousin's body were a match to your pistol."

"No!"

"I'm sorry, man."

"Sorry, Frank," Hurley says, too.

Millhoff straightens himself on the sofa, looks at me.

"You're still not thinking I'm a suspect in all this."

"I don't know what to think, Frank. Bodies dropping all around you."

"Fuck you. Tell me what Ray was shot with."

"A .38, but not your gun, unless you have another .38 in the house we should know about."

"Fuck this. No. That mean you gonna come back with a search warrant? Because if it does, I'll save you the trouble and take you around my house so you can see for yourself."

"Appreciate that, and I'll let you know if we want to do that."

"You're wasting your time looking at me."

No answer.

"You compare Wrayburn's prints to the ones you pulled from here?"

"We are," Millhoff says.

"We also showed Wrayburn's photo to that Wendland character at Thrift World, but of course he doesn't know him. Says it isn't the one who goes by Biddy."

"Well, it sounds like you guys will be working some midnight shifts, going clubbing. Ray would do his dealings in the parking lot."

"I'm really looking forward to that," Millhoff says.

I want to tell them about Diamond, but doing so now fucks me six ways worse.

"I can't make sense of this shit," I say more to myself than to them.

"We will," Millhoff says with confidence.

"And if you're silly enough to be thinking I'm a suspect for Wrayburn, then call Leslie, because she's my alibi."

"You kidding me? You're tapping that?"

"Watch your mouth," I snap back.

"Damn, Frankie."

"Shut the fuck up already."

"You were with her all night?" Hurley asks.

I just give him a look.

"I'll take that as a yes."

"How many enemies do you have, Frank?"

"Back in the day or as a PI? And we all got enemies, you know that. But I don't know one who would go through all this shit just to get at me."

"Could you try to make a list anyway?" Hurley asks.

"Fuck, man, can you make a list? I wouldn't know where to begin, all the people I locked up. This here is something else."

"What?" Millhoff asks.

"I didn't say that like I knew what the fuck it is, Timmy. None of this makes sense to me."

"This case is getting pretty damn interesting," Millhoff says.

"Wish it weren't. I like simple," I say.

THIRTY-FOUR

After they leave all I wanna do is hit the bottle and the blow. Bottle's not something I worry about. I have to hit the brakes for the other, though, show some control. It's not like I can go to the corner to re-up. That hustler gets busted, gives me up, and I get sent up the river.

I pour myself a bit of Jameson. Down it in one swig.

Doorbell rings, and I nearly drop the glass.

Who the fuck now?

I get to the door and look through the peephole.

It's Linda. Aunt Linda. Fuck.

I hesitate to open it, I'll admit. Look through the peephole again like I need to make sure.

It's her; she's alone.

I rush back to the living room, take my gun from the end table, slip it under the sofa cushion, then cap the bottle of Jameson, put it on a shelf in the dining room.

I quickly make my way back, look through the peephole again, and after a couple of deep breaths, I open the door.

She's standing there. A slight smile. Her face is puffy, with bags under heavy reddened eyes. She looks so much older than her midsixties. Or is it just the stress?

"Aunt Linda," I almost mumble.

"Hello, Frankie."

"Please come in."

Her eyes look past me toward the interior of my house, then back to me. She loses her smile. "I can't come in."

I realize why but don't say anything. I step on the porch, close the door behind me so it's only slightly ajar.

I should hug her, right?

She wraps her thin arms around my waist before I can decide, begins to sob.

"I'm so sorry, Aunt Linda. I'm so sorry" is all I can think to say.

Never apologize.

Fuck that. I am sorry.

I don't know how long we hold each other, but we do so until she tenderly pulls away.

She sighs and wipes her eyes. "I parked down the street. I had to use my GPS to get here. It's been so long." She looks at the exterior of my house. "It looks like you've done some good work."

"Yes. Last time you were here I was still renovating. It's more like a home now." For some reason I regret saying that.

"I'm sorry for what I said on the phone," she tells me.

How do I respond?

"You don't have to apologize."

"I don't want to stand here. I know it's awfully humid, but can we take a short walk?"

"Of course," I say.

I follow her as she steps off the porch and turns right, toward W. It's a narrow sidewalk, so I move to her side, closer to the curb. Her pace is slow. My mind is fast, so I have to make an effort to walk at her side, not ahead of her.

"Did you drive from Ohio?"

"Yes. It wasn't bad."

"Do you need help with anything? I can drive you back home when you're ready."

She stops to face me. "No. No, but thanks for the offer." She looks down. Seems like she's hesitating. "Why was Jeffrey in your house, Frank?"

First thing that comes to mind is *She's got a wire*. I quickly realize how ridiculous that is.

"I don't know, Linda. I don't. I sincerely wish there was something I could tell you. A reason. But we never had contact. You never told him where I lived, right?"

"No, but he knew you lived around here. He was too young the last time he was at your house, so he wouldn't have remembered."

"The police will figure it out. Detective Millhoff is very good at what he does."

"Just tell me, Frankie, and I'll believe you."

Tell her I'm an idiot and I somehow fucked up? That it's all my fault? 'Cause that's what I believe. Maybe I am guilty. But I sure as hell don't know what I did to get him murdered.

"I had nothing to do with Jeffrey's death. I don't know what brought him to my house."

Tears stream from her eyes again. I take her hand.

She nods. Believes me.

I continue to hold her hand as we walk.

"This is my car," she says, pointing to a Lexus SUV.

"Where are you staying?"

"At the Hilton."

I look away for a moment. Honestly don't know what to say. I'm at a loss.

"You're nothing like your father. I should never have said that."

"I don't know what you mean—"

"Your real father. You're nothing like him. Your mother married young. He wasn't a good man."

"I never knew my real father," I say awkwardly.

"I know. But no child should have had to go through what you went through."

Does she mean my mom's suicide?

"This isn't about me, Aunt Linda."

"We've both suffered such great losses, Frankie. That's why I came here—to see you. We're family. You are the only connection I have left to your mother, my sister. Even Jeffrey." Her eyes tear up, but she smiles. "This humidity is stifling." She steps to her car and unlocks it. Before she sits, she turns to me. "When Jeffrey was a junior in high school he told me that he wanted to go to college in Washington, DC, to be near you." She sits and starts the car.

I notice her push the button to unlock the passenger-side door, hear that familiar, oddly comfortable click as the door lock pops up.

She closes her door, and I walk around and get in.

"He wanted to major in criminal justice."

I shut the door. Air inside already feels good as it hits my face.

"That was his major?"

"No. In his senior year of high school, and after all that trouble he had with drugs, he changed it to business."

"Smart decision." That didn't come out right.

She rests her hand on my knee. It's like a feather. As uncomfortable as it makes me feel, I place my hand over hers.

"Jeffrey was really clumsy when he was a little boy. So were you, by the way. Do you remember I used to take you to the grocery store? Your half brother always wanted to stay home with your stepdad."

So much of that time is a blur. I know she stayed with us for a while, though.

"Yes," I say.

"I'd let you push the grocery cart sometimes, despite how clumsy you were, how many displays you knocked over."

Turns to me with such a comforting smile.

"Are you sure I didn't do that on purpose?"

"I know you didn't, because you felt bad after, just like Jeffrey did."

"Yeah. I do remember he was a bit heavy-footed."

"Couldn't catch a ball, either, could he?"

"No, he sure couldn't." I chuckle.

"Jeffrey used to look forward to your visits so much."

"I looked forward to them, too. Had more time on my hands in my twenties, before I became a cop. I'm sorry for losing touch with the both of you. That never should have happened."

"You were a good influence."

Is she blaming me for losing touch, for him turning bad?

"We'll both make the time now, won't we? We won't lose touch."

"No. We won't."

She takes a deep breath, like it's calming.

"The police will…no, I will. I'll get to the bottom of this, Aunt Linda. I really will."

I want her to believe me. She has to believe me. Fuck, I have to believe me.

"Let's not lose touch again," she says and squeezes my knee.

I don't think she believes me.

Don't say anything.

THIRTY-FIVE

I go through half a bottle of Jameson and I don't even want to know how much blow.

This shit's got me reeling, and I'm not talking the coke and alcohol. It's all too close to home. Literally. My aunt? I don't know what to make of her visit. I don't know what Millhoff and Hurley are thinking at this point, either. I'm afraid to know. Shit. I'm just getting paranoid again.

If Wrayburn was involved in Jeffrey's murder, I'm sure they'll connect him with DNA or some other evidence. But what if he had nothing to do with it and was taken out simply because I talked to him? I gotta find Biddy. He's either the shooter or he's gotta know who is.

I start getting myself so worked up with all this shit, especially Linda's visit, that my stomach starts to churn. I feel like I gotta puke.

I run to the hallway bathroom, lift the toilet seat, and there goes all my Jameson.

Haven't done that in a long while. I rinse my mouth out. Return to the sofa. Light a smoke.

Aunt Linda looked so frail. I don't remember her looking like that. And why did she come here, especially after what she said over the phone? She did apologize for that, though.

Am I all she has now?

That would not be a comforting thought.

I want to hear Leslie's voice. That is comforting. Even better, have her next to me. I'm too fucked up, though, and I'll just do something stupid. I've been known to occasionally get stupid.

I wake up early in the morning and feel oddly refreshed. Maybe there's something to that puking shit. A cleansing. Might have to look into that.

While drinking coffee I start to worry about why I'm not getting a call from Diamond. Maybe he screwed me. What am I thinking? It's like I forgot who I'm dealing with. Criminals, even low-level ones like Diamond, are unpredictable. You can't trust them.

I give him some time, and when that's up, about an hour later, I call him.

He answers on the fourth ring. After a lot of reluctance on his part and a bit of unsubtle persuasion on mine, he agrees to pick me up at 10th and U Streets, just a couple blocks from my house, so I can walk. He says he's not that far from there.

"Northwest corner," I advise him. "About fifteen minutes, then."

He agrees.

I get there in ten.

About another ten minutes later I see what appears to be his cab heading west on U Street, toward me. I hope it's him, because when it's close enough I raise my hand to hail him over.

I recognize the old man through the front windshield as he pulls to the curb.

"Head toward that house on Riggs," I tell him, slipping inside.

"What you gonna do?"

"Take Thirteenth."

"Shee-it." He pulls from the curb.

"You hear anything about a shooting on the fourteen hundred block of Rhode Island a few nights ago?"

"No. I don't watch the news. Too damn depressing. That got anything to do with this? 'Cause that shit ain't worth a hundred and fifty bills."

"No. Don't worry. It's something else," I lie.

"Slow down here," I tell him. There's an alley on the west side of 13th, right before Riggs. Some kind of school on the east side, where Riggs dead-ends.

"Stop here."

"Man, I can't be seen here like this."

"Listen, old man, this ain't the 'hood. You'll be fine. This is the rear of the house you said Biddy buys his drugs from, right?"

"Yeah."

"They meet up right in the rear there?"

"I don't really know. There's a parking lot that belongs to those apartments farther up. I think they meet them up there."

"What makes you think that?"

"'Cause when I drop him off, I seen him walk up the side alley on Riggs that leads to this alley and the parking lot. I never seen him walk from this way before, even if I do sometimes drop him off at the corner there."

"Yeah. This is a tough one."

"What do you mean?"

"Surveillance, Diamond. What makes this job fun."

"You can't have me in this shit. I got rights, and there's gotta be some kinda regulations you're breakin'."

"Oh, hell, yes, there are, but you gotta figure it's worth your freedom, right?"

"I don't know about all this here. Somethin' ain't right."

"Say the word and I'll give Detective Hurley a call right now. I'm not bluffing. You want me to?"

"Man…"

"Listen up. You pick up burglars and haul their stolen goods for them and get shit for it. Plus you risk your livelihood doing it. Plus there's at least one body. Yeah, I'm breaking rules, but you're breaking the law. You're safe with me, and you're gonna make a hell of a lot more money, too."

I give him a second.

"So say the word. I'll make the call, or you just rest easy and make the money."

"Shee-it. How do you wanna do this?"

THIRTY-SIX

It takes a few minutes, but a parking space finally opens up across from the cut. All I need is to see all the way across it. With my binos, I can even make out a bit of the parking lot that Diamond mentioned. I don't have to see any transactions, just players. Their faces.

Diamond turns the NOT IN SERVICE sign on and pulls out a sandwich from a brown paper bag.

"You don't mind if I eat, right?"

"Of course not."

I'm going to have to try to figure out how to get some bumps, especially if we're going to sit here for more than a couple of hours. I've got a few cigarettes laced with cocaine, but that's pretty much worthless. It might get me by, though. I also poured a nice bit of Jameson into a sport bottle.

Unfortunately, I need Diamond with me. He can identify Biddy and some of the other players for me. One of them killed or likely knows who killed Jeffrey. That's the priority here. I'm not gonna lie, though. It's also about getting a good hit. And I'm hoping this house on Riggs is just that hit.

It doesn't take long before we see a rail of a man walking north on the other side of 13th. He's shouldering a backpack that appears to be stuffed.

"You know this crackhead?"

"Huh?"

"The dude across the street, walking this way."

He waits for him to get closer, reclines down in his seat so he won't be noticed.

"No, but still I ain't takin' no chances."

The man makes a right into the cut directly across from us. I tuck down a little and cup my binos in both hands.

He walks slowly past the rear of the house and into the parking lot, where he disappears between cars. Not even a minute later, I see one of the boys Diamond mentioned yesterday exit the rear gate and step in the narrow alley. I get just enough of his face to make him out. Young, maybe early twenties. Pristine old-school tennis shoes, baggy jeans, and a white T-shirt. And it sure as fuck looks like the boy who ran from me at the record store. He was last seen running toward this area, so maybe he was holding. Shit—for all I know, maybe he was getting ready to deliver to Oscar at the record store. Fuck, all these connections.

"Is that one of the boys?"

"Yeah, that's the young one."

"What's his name or nickname?"

"I told you before, I don't know them like that."

"Just testing," I say with a smile.

Baggy Jeans makes his way toward the parking lot and also slips out of sight between the cars. Not even three minutes later he's walking back, cradling a laptop and holding something in the palm of his hand that I can't make out. He enters the rear gate

to his house. Shortly after, the crackhead appears, but he turns right, into the alley cut that leads to Riggs.

His backpack does not seem so full anymore.

I take a swig of Jameson from my sport bottle.

"I need to smoke."

"I don't allow smoking in my cab."

"I'll roll the window down, keep the cigarette outta the car."

"I hate that shit in my cab."

"Twenty-five extra to allow me to smoke. You can air it out when we're done."

"You killin' me, man."

I light one of the cigs laced with coke. It's immediate, but it doesn't last more than a few seconds. I feel a bit with each puff, though, and have to smoke it quick so I don't lose any. Better inside me than lose it to the atmosphere.

I flick it out when I'm done. After a couple of minutes all it does is make me want a hefty pile on the back of my hand.

Another swig of Jameson.

We spend a couple of hours there, and it does seem to be hopping. The two mopes, Younger and Older, take turns. Sometimes they return from the deal with certain property, but most of the time they don't. Just bills, like they're dealing tens and twenties.

Diamond's cell rings a couple of times, but it sounds like he's talking to friends or other cabbies.

Diamond is able to identify a couple of the burglars he drives around, but not Biddy. I'm going to have to come here in my own vehicle and sit on it late, see when they come and go. I gotta go sit on R Street, too, so I ask Diamond to pull out.

"Just a little while and we're done. I won't need you the rest of the day."

He drives to R, and we find an illegal spot to park, far enough away from the building to avoid a problem. The area has changed.

The fourteen hundred block of R is not the same as it was when I was working. Drugs, burglaries, and robberies are still occurring, but not like before. This used to be a real hot spot. We'd get in a foot chase with a suspect who'd run into one of the buildings across the street, and that was it. Gone. Right now, I'm just hoping that Biddy will show. We'll give it a bit, then I'll let ol' Diamond go.

Thirty-Seven

I'm feeling toasty—from the whiskey, not from the heat. It's making me tired, and I'm all out of the cigs I laced with coke. I call it a day.

"Go ahead and drop me off at Tenth and U."

Diamond rolls out, takes a right on 15th.

He drops me off at the same corner. I count him out one hundred and fifty dollars and hand it through the little opening in the Plexiglas window. He counts.

"You said an extra twenty-five for allowing you to smoke those sweet-smelling cigarettes of yours."

I hesitate, because that statement throws me, like he knows what burning coke smells like. I keep it to myself. Give him fifty instead.

"Why the extra?"

"You did good today," I tell him.

"I did nothin' but sit on my ass."

"No. I got some good intel. And you remember to call me if any of your burglary boys gets in touch with you."

"Yeah."

"It's still early enough for you to pick up some good fares. That should make this a really good day for you."

"It should. Do I have to say thank you or some shit like that?"

"Not when it's a mutual understanding."

I grab my backpack, but before I get out I say, "I might call you tomorrow just to check in on you. Always answer."

He nods.

Diamond doesn't hesitate to pull out. I watch him drive to 9th, where he makes a right.

When I get to my porch, I stand and listen before unlocking the door, like I'm worried that whoever murdered Jeffrey will come back.

The first thing I do when I get home is—hell, why even mention it anymore? I've got needs.

I give Leslie a call to let her know I'll be working a late surveillance gig I got hired for but will have my phone on vibrate if she wants to call or text. We get together on most weekends nowadays. This weekend is uncertain. It really depends on what kind of intel I get tonight, if I even can.

"How about we play this weekend by ear?" she says.

"I would like to see you, though. Get out of my house."

"Tomorrow night if you're not doing a real late-night thing."

"Sounds good. I'll talk to you later."

"Be safe with whatever it is you're working. It has nothing to do with your cousin's murder, right?"

"No. Of course not."

"Frankie. I'm worried about you."

"There's nothing to worry about."

"Frank." She sighs. "Talk to you later, then."

"All right."

She disconnects first.

I stretch out on the sofa to close my eyes and allow them rest. I certainly won't get any sleep.

I start to think about my mother for some reason. Never really knew her, but I do remember a little of what she looked like and the music she used to listen to. She loved music. When I was in my teens, about five years after her death, my stepfather finally opened up to me and said it was because of bad depression. That's why she took her life.

When I was on my own, after high school, when I was working for a landscaping company, my stepfather retired and moved south, somewhere in South Carolina now. His pension goes a long way there, I guess. My stepfather didn't wanna lug all those records and the stereo equipment, so he left them for me. My older half brother got married and moved for work to Orange County, California. None of us communicates. An occasional Christmas card from my half brother, but that's about it. I'm actually surprised that neither of them called me about Jeffrey's murder. Maybe they don't know. Dysfunction at its best. I don't expect more, nor do I even want it. We're all comfortably settled in our ways. Less clutter that way. I do have an odd attachment to my mother's records, though, as well as my own records and the stereo equipment. Nothing that I can explain. Even if I could I wouldn't. All I know is I want that shit back. I want to get to whoever killed Jeffrey first, before Millhoff. Didn't think I'd ever see the stereo again, but I did, thanks to Hurley. The odds are very slim that I'll ever see anything else, but the odds are good that I'll find Biddy. Finding people is easy, long as you're smart.

THIRTY-EIGHT

Cicada shells are scattered about, leftover remains of some bird's meal. Their delicate forms gently cling to the trunks of trees. Remnants of the past. The ones that still carry on are louder than normal. Their static-electric cry is everywhere.

Their song stays with me, though, even now in my car with the windows up and the air conditioning low. It's like being in the ear canal of someone who suffers from tinnitus.

Or do I have tinnitus? Fuck.

I love surveillance. It's like a secret space, and if it's done right you can make yourself invisible, mostly to regular citizens. They don't pay attention. Drug boys do. They're the opposite of cops, but they have the same weird ability to spot the other side.

I find a tricky spot on the south side of the 1300 block of Riggs, right across from the cut leading to the alley behind their house. I adjust the rearview so I can see their stoop. If they do leave, I've got all angles except where the alley ends at 13th Street. I'm betting they keep a car on Riggs or in the parking lot behind the apartment buildings west of their house.

I assume my comfortable position in the car. Not what I want, but again I've gotta keep it running for the air. I have everything I need in the seat next to me. Seriously well supplied this time, even water to stay hydrated 'cause of all the liquor I will more than likely consume. I'm good to go for as long as it takes.

The sun sets late, maybe by 7:30. That's almost an hour and a half from now. Lot of young business types live on this block. A lot of them walking. Few look my way.

Several people take the cut throughout the evening. Most of them make their way to the neighboring parking lot, where shortly one of the boys will appear in good cheer.

It's not crazy busy, but they do have regulars. It's enough to pique my interest.

By 9:00 p.m. business seems to stop. Haven't seen the boys for about an hour. I notice a few suspicious types roll in and toward the lot, but no Younger and Older. They're either out of supply or they don't work it after a certain time. I'm hoping for the latter.

A few minutes after 10:00 p.m. I notice movement in my side mirror. The boys step out to the front stoop, lock the door behind them. They seem dressed for a night out. By that I mean their jeans are less raggedy and their sneakers are fresher. Younger shoulders a small backpack. Both of them are wearing oversize T-shirts with abstract patterns on the front that I can't make out.

A car chirps half a block away, headlights flickering on what appears to be a black late-model two-door Honda. Older walks to the driver's side while Younger slips into the passenger seat. I let them pass, readjust my rearview mirror, then wedge myself out. Turn the lights on when they hit the stop sign at 14th and turn left.

I stay a couple of cars behind, thinking they're going to continue south, but they take a right on R. When I make the turn they're halfway down the block. Left on 17th. I start thinking they're headed to the club on Connecticut because it's right around the corner, but they continue, and once they pass K they slow down again. This time like they're trying to find parking. It's a fairly busy night. Lot of nightclubs in this area. I slow down and pull behind a parked car near the Mayflower Hotel. Turn my lights off. Watch the boys head in to one of the nicest joints.

About an hour in, and my cell phone rings.

Luna.

"What's up, bro?" I answer.

"Just checking in on ya."

"Playing my big brother?"

"Yeah. You need a good influence in your life."

"Well, that you are, my friend. All's good here. Working a side gig with a bit of surveillance."

"Well, yeah, I know how much you love that shit. Don't know how you can sit on your ass all that time, though."

"You should know, sitting on that chair at your desk all day."

"At least it reclines. And shit, I do get out on occasion. This gig you're working, though. You sure it isn't something that might interfere with a homicide investigation?"

"Come on, Al," I say so I don't have to lie. "Any news at your end?"

"They got some of our boys assisting with the drug angle."

"You mean at the club?" I ask him with a bit of apprehension.

"I know you know, 'cause I talked to Hurley. That boy found dead on the fourteen hundred block of Rhode Island is a known drug dealer. Couple of the guys here are familiar with him."

Fucking hope it doesn't lead to the house on Riggs.

"You identify any of the other players yet?"

"Not that I heard."

"You keep me in the loop, though, right?"

"Yeah, brother. I gotcha. No worries."

"Thanks, Al."

"Be safe. You need anything, call."

"I will."

Fuck. I'm gonna have to be a little more careful, make sure no one from NSID is on these boys, too. That's all I need.

Thirty-Nine

At around 2:00 a.m., the boys exit the club with a group of other people. They hang out, talking and smoking what appear to be blunts. The two then break off from the others and walk toward their car.

I follow them back the way they came but continue driving when they make that left turn onto Riggs from 13th.

Still wired when I get home. No television to watch, which is probably a good thing, 'cause it just makes me want more coke. I decide on stripping down to my shorts and getting into bed. First I down two Klonopins with a double shot of vodka. But even that isn't enough to take the edge off a restless mind.

So I wait.

I don't know when I fell out, but the buzzing iPhone snaps me up to a sitting position like I got springs in my back.

It's dark, but the phone casts a beacon of light from the nightstand.

Fucking Diamond, and at fucking five in the morning!

"Marr," I answer.

Diamond starts to rattle off something about office burglaries and a bunch of stolen laptops he has to help transport.

"Is it Biddy?" I ask, because that's all I really care about.

He says, "No," and goes off again.

"Calm yourself, Diamond. Start from the beginning. The quick version."

He does.

When he's done I say, "Do not go there. Just sit tight, and I'll take care of it. No. Don't worry about that shit. I'll take care of you. They'll never know. I do this shit all the time. I'll call you when it's done. Sit tight."

If that's possible.

I disconnect, hop out of bed, slip into jeans and a T-shirt. I feel half dead. I secure my magazine pouch and my holstered weapon on the belt, grab the backpack, and rush to the car.

Did I lock the door?

I run back to the house to double-check. It's locked.

"It's locked," I repeat to myself like it'll stick in my head that way. Pathetic.

It only takes me a few minutes to get to the lower end of 11th Street. I drive past the alley Diamond was talking about and notice two guys sitting near a Dumpster, leaning against the wall of a multistory office building. I park at the next corner, where I can still see the opening to the alley. I grab the burner cell phone I keep in my backpack and call 911.

I try my best not to sound like an ex-cop.

The dispatcher answers, "Nine one one, what's your emergency?"

The location is the first thing she needs.

"Two guys in the alley, rear of the seven hundred block of Eleventh Street, Northwest," I begin, and then think, shit, that sounds like a cop talking. "They just broke into an office building and stole a bunch of laptops. They're in the alley now." She asks for a description. "Two guys. I didn't get a close look. I think one is either white or Hispanic and the other one is black. They're sitting there right now. They hid the laptops behind a Dumpster and are acting like they're waiting for someone to pick them up."

She tries to get more information, including stuff about me.

"No, that ain't gonna happen. Just get the police here fast and quiet or they'll lose them. I ain't involving myself."

I hear her dispatch two units to the location, telling them something about "a concerned citizen." I disconnect the cell and pull away from the curb, make a right on 12th to go around the corner. I drive slowly.

It's almost shift change, midnights to day work, so the primary unit on this call probably isn't too happy. This is First District, so it'd be nice if the primary is Jasper. Just a little payback.

By the time I get around to 11th again, I see a unit speeding south on 11th. No lights or siren. The cruiser looks like it's occupied two times. Didn't look like Jasper. I head in that direction as another unmarked unit comes from the other direction.

I turn right again, pass the alley at a slow speed, notice the two guys up against the wall, face-first and legs spread. I make my way back home. It's not my concern whether they find probable cause to lock these boys up. Like I said, I could care less. All I wanted to do is follow through for Diamond so he wouldn't have to pick them up. Now he doesn't.

I call him on my phone.

"Yeah, police got them," I say. "We'll just say it was an anonymous call from a concerned citizen."

I advise him that I appreciate the call and tell him to let me know the second Biddy calls.

I find the same parking spot near home. It's too fucking early, and I'm going to have another long night of surveillance on

Younger and Older. I figure they gotta be good for a little something, maybe more. I'm enthusiastic for something more. I'm not gonna deny my need. My brain's wired that way, 'cause if I run out I'm useless. I've been there, and I don't want to go back. I justify these actions because there's also the possibility that I might get good information outta that house. Something that might lead me to Jeffrey's murderer.

I strip back down to my shorts and hit the sack.

FORTY

I wait for Younger and Older around the same time as last night. This time they step out a little early. Younger lights up a big blunt on the stoop, shares it with Older.

I tail them the same way, but this time they slow to a crawl on 17th before Rhode Island Avenue. They take a right on Rhode Island. I get to the corner just as they're making a U-turn a quarter of the way up the block. I pull up slowly, like I'm gonna turn left, but I notice them park illegally alongside the curb behind some orange construction barrels. I make a left because I don't want to pass them. I pull into the opening of a narrow alley, blocking the sidewalk. A couple of pedestrians give me a dirty look as they have to walk around my car. Not many other folks around this time of night.

I cup my binos and observe them exit the vehicle and walk toward Connecticut Ave. Are they going to the club where Jeffrey used to go?

I back out carefully, letting a couple of cars pass, then I drive slowly behind them. It's a long block, so I have to stay back.

They get to the corner and wait for the WALK sign before crossing Connecticut. I double-park farther back and tap on my hazard lights. I can barely make out the entrance to the club, but I can see enough of the steps to know whether they're about to enter.

They cross, and, sure enough, I notice them walking up the stairs, but I lose sight of them before the front entrance.

Damn. The odds of winning the lottery are better than this shit.

I look around, see if there's anywhere to park so I can get an eyeball on their vehicle. Parking is damn near impossible. I opt to park behind another car, but I'm partially obstructing Saint Matthew's Court, which is more of an alley than a court. I turn my lights off.

Not even fifteen minutes later a cruiser rolls up behind me. Emergency lights go on shortly after. The driver and his partner approach my car. I roll down the window. Driver's handheld Streamlight blinds me. I shield my eyes.

He stays behind, near the rear passenger door of my car, so I have to turn to him. The partner's Streamlight searches the interior of my car.

Driver lowers his light a bit so I can see him, then says, "You're not planning to park here, are you?"

He's a young guy. Fuck, they're all young nowadays. I hardly know anyone anymore.

My suit jacket is off, so I worry about whether my mags and sidearm are visible to him. Don't want another situation like before, or worse.

"I was hoping you officers would let me, just for an hour or so while I stay in the car."

He gives me a look, like maybe I'm drunk or something.

"It's not like that, Officer. I'm a retired DC cop working a part-time security gig for a couple of buildings on Connecticut. They're getting torn up with office burglaries, but you know that."

"You have credentials?"

"Of course. I'm going to reach for my wallet. It's in the inner pocket of my suit jacket on the front seat."

Still doesn't see my weapon. The magazine pouch is too close to the driver's-side door, and I figure the gun is tucked far enough toward my back to stay out of sight.

"Lift your jacket slowly off the backpack and hand it to me," Driver says.

"No problem."

I slowly hand it over to him. He backs up a bit while his partner keeps his Streamlight on me.

"Frank Marr?"

"That's me."

"Your badge says you're a retired detective. You look too young to be retired."

"I left early, after seventeen years."

He moves back toward me, then hands me my suit jacket but keeps the wallet.

"Where were you assigned?"

"NSID."

"Stand by for a second, sir, all right?" Driver says.

He backs up to enter his car. His partner stays. I know Driver's gonna run me, make sure I am who I say I am. No wants. No warrants. No worries.

A couple minutes later he returns and hands my wallet back to me. He gives me his business card with it.

Officer Todd Tyler.

"You get a burglar, shoot me a call and we'll take the arrest," Tyler says.

"Appreciate that. Saves me a lot of trouble having to deal with the dispatcher."

"You take care, Detective Marr."

"Be safe, Officers."

They return to their car, turn off the emergency lights. Partner waves as they pass me.

I look at Driver's card and put it and my wallet back into my suit jacket.

An hour quickly passes. I'm thinking Younger and Older are going to be there late, like last night at the other club. I roll on home. I'm not ready yet. And damn, I forgot to call Leslie.

FORTY-ONE

After a late-morning shower, I dress down again, 'cause the suit makes me look like a cop.

I try to call Leslie. It goes to voice mail.

"I'm sorry I forgot to call you the other day. Need to get my mind off things, so I've been working this other job. Call me. Miss you." I disconnect.

After I get what I need, I walk to 11th and U.

It's hotter, more humid than it was earlier, but it's a short walk. I get there a few minutes early. So does Diamond. He pulls to the corner as if he were waiting for me at the next block.

I tap on the front passenger-side window. He rolls it down.

"This ain't my bank, but it's got an ATM," I tell him, pointing to the bank behind me.

He nods.

I withdraw three hundred, because that's all it will allow.

I walk back and hop in the rear of the cab, set my backpack beside me.

I count out two hundred and hand it to him through the open slot.

"I'll give you the rest when we find Biddy."

"That wasn't the deal."

"I said I need to find Biddy and need your help to do it. You agreed. Besides, how do I know you won't just drive me around to different spots acting like you know where he might be?"

"I ain't about that, and I've already given you good shit."

"I don't know you, Diamond."

"And I don't know you, and I don't think I want to anymore after this is done. So I want you to find him, and then we're through."

"That's a deal, but still, you'll get the remainder if we find him."

"Shit. All right, then." Diamond yields.

He drives off, west on U Street.

"I know where a bunch of them go to smoke their crack. I dropped him off there once. He come and go, but it's a good place to start."

"So why didn't you tell me about this place before?"

"Musta slipped my mind."

I don't say what I'm thinking.

He puts on the left-turn signal when he hits 12th Street, waits until it's clear, and makes a U-turn to head east on U.

"Where is this place?" I ask.

"Old abandoned building on Sixth, just off Florida."

"What makes it so popular that he hoofs it all the way down there to smoke?"

"I can only assume it's because it's gettin' harder to find a safe spot to smoke. All this construction. Everything getting bought up like it is."

"How big's the building?"

"Just takes up a portion of the corner is all."

"Let's see how it looks when we get there."

"What you plan on doing if you see him?"

"Have to play that part by ear, but whatever I do won't burn you, so don't worry."

"Yeah, right."

Old man's starting to get bothersome, and I have a feeling this is gonna be another waste of time.

Traffic is already bad, and it isn't even evening rush hour yet. It takes longer than it should to get there. Diamond's right; there's too much damn construction in this city.

Lot of pedestrians are out, but guys like Biddy know how to walk the streets. They're the ones walking the curb, using the trees, the posts, and the parked cars as cover. It's like they had special training at their own academy. Prison academy.

When Diamond hits 6th Street, he goes south. Damn, he was right. I need to drive around the city more. There was a time not so long ago when I would have counted a dozen abandoned buildings and row houses by the time we hit 6th. Instead it's little coffee shops, restaurants, and boutiques. Homes with well-kept front yards. Prosperity.

"There it is there," he says, directing me with his head.

It's a large two-story detached home. All the windows are boarded up. By the looks of it, crackheads won't have much longer with this place, either. A contractor's sign has been posted in the front yard.

"Make this left so I can get a view of the side and back."

Couple of questionable characters walking side by side on the sidewalk on the S Street side of the house.

"You know those boys there?"

"No."

They cross 6th and continue west on S. Don't know if they just came out of the house or not, but when Diamond makes the turn it appears that the only safe way to gain access is from S Street, at the rear of the house. It's too close to the neighboring house on the 6th Street side. Looking at some of the beautiful homes and landscaping here, I gotta assume I made a good investment with my house. Who fucking knew?

"If you back into the cut up there and come back this way, there's a parking space across Sixth right at the corner."

"Man, you gonna get my ass burned bad. Real bad."

"You'll be parked facing west. If people come out of the house they won't even catch a glimpse of you."

"Unless they make they way cross Sixth on S and pass me."

He's smart. "You worry too fucking much, old man. This how you talked to all those B-and-E dopes when you pulled right up to the house they just got finished busting into?"

"Shee-it" is all he's got to say.

"I think you can handle this, then, huh?"

He drives ahead, backs into the cut, heads west on S, and pulls into the parking place.

"I'm parked illegally."

"If any cops come around, which I doubt, it'll look like you're dropping off a fare."

He rolls down his window and turns the car off.

"You kidding me, Diamond? I'm gonna roast back here."

"Damn. You know how much fuel that burns just parking with the air on?"

"I'll cover the fuel cost, so turn the damn car back on. Shit."

He obeys.

I feel like having a fucking smoke, but I don't want to make this situation more testy than it already is.

I put my pack on my lap, slide to the other side, and stretch out over the seat. It gives me an easier view through the rear window, so I don't have to wake up tomorrow with a stiff neck. I get my binos just in case.

Let's see how this pans out.

FORTY-TWO

It's most certainly a crack house. Not that much traffic inside and out, but I bet the police have been called to it on several occasions because of complaints from some of the neighboring homes. Been sitting on it for over an hour, and I'm fiending, not only for a bump or two but also for a smoke.

A few minutes later I notice a white male and a black male walking together toward the house. They definitely fit the profile—crackheads, I mean. I get Diamond's attention and point them out to him.

"What about those two?"

"I seen them around the neighborhoods, but no one I know."

It's already rush hour, and a lot of vehicles are rolling by. My opinion—Biddy's gonna be a no-show or never was going to show. Another part of me is starting to think I'm being played, period.

"I'm not going to waste any more time on this shit," I say.

"All right, then," he says with a little too much ease.

"I'm also starting to get the impression you're fucking me good."

He looks at me through the rearview mirror, won't even turn to face me. That's how I know I'm right.

"I've worked with a few burglars in my time, and I know how much some of them can smoke on a daily basis. That means a lot of homes they need to break into. I don't understand why he hasn't called you yet."

"I told you he doesn't always call 'cause he doesn't always go for the big items."

"I think he's called you, but I can't figure why you wouldn't tell me unless you're trying to protect him or you're just plain scared. I don't figure you for being scared, so you better fucking give it up or I will surely mess up your life."

"You can smoke a cigarette if you want. Just roll down the window and blow the smoke outta my cab."

What the fuck?

"What kinda answer is that?"

"Figured you need one. Might calm you down."

Now he's being a smartass, thinking he can turn it around.

I sit up and lean toward him so I'm near the back of his head.

"You sure you wanna try me like this, old man?" I tell him.

"You want me to take you to R Street, sit there for a bit?"

"I think we both know that'd be a waste of time, too."

No answer.

"Tell me what's going on, Diamond. I won't give you a second chance."

I can see that he bows his head, looks up again, and gazes through the front windshield, probably at nothing in particular.

"Haven't I been a man of my word with you?" I ask him.

"Yeah, pretty much."

"Pretty much? Fuck you. You're still driving the cab and going home after."

"I ain't stupid, either, so I figure you for either one dirty cop or not one at all."

Damn, he is sharp.

I lean back, pull out my wallet.

"Turn around for me."

He does.

I show him my badge and my creds.

"Can you see it good enough?"

"Yeah, including the identification that says you're retired, but you showed me that before, and I didn't see 'retired' on it, so isn't that against the law, pretending to be the police?"

"I told you before—I'm always the police. But I chose not to tell you that I'm a private investigator now. I can lie. That ain't against the law." That's not quite true. I can lie, but I can't impersonate a cop unless I say I'm a retired cop, so he's right. I'm gonna take a chance that he doesn't know that, though. "I regret lying to you, but I'm being straight with you now. I do have enough evidence for the police to arrest you if I turn it over to my buddy on the burglary squad and the detective in charge of the homicide. Doesn't matter how I obtained the evidence because I'm not working on behalf of the police department, so they'll take it."

"You got me all messed up now. I don't fucking know what to believe or what you want."

"I want to find Biddy. But more than that, I want to find out if Biddy killed my cousin in my fucking kitchen."

"What? Your cousin?"

Head drops.

I had to go there. Personal. It's my only chance to keep him with me.

"You got it, Robert. My cousin. You know now. Something you might not know. The gun he stole—"

"I don't know nothin' about a gun."

"The gun he stole from my house was found on another boy's dead body."

"Fuck no. Robby would never do something like that!"

"Robby?"

"Biddy. His middle name is Robby. I call him that sometimes."

Shit. Biddy is an alias, and Robby is someone—something more—to him. I'm certain of it now. He's protecting him. Probably thinking I'll give up pursuing it after a while.

"On Rhode Island Avenue. That ring a bell?"

He doesn't answer. He knows something.

"I know you feel you can't trust me, but I'm telling you the straight truth. I was thinking all the time that Graham Biddy was a fake name, but now I'm still bettin' he's probably never been arrested before. Just got caught up with smoking crack somehow. I'll tell you this: his time is short. He will get arrested, but I'll turn you in before that happens. They'll find out who Biddy really is, 'cause I know now he's something to you. I don't want to do that, though. That's the truth, Diamond. Really is."

He slowly shakes his head, considering things. Not a good sign.

"What the hell you protecting this guy for? Why would you put yourself in a position like this?"

"He my nephew, and he ain't bad. His mother just fucked him up, and he ain't ever had no dad."

"But you were like his dad."

"Yeah. I been there for him."

"And your son in the army, like Biddy's brother."

Doesn't have to respond to that.

"So he doesn't live on R Street, does he?"

"He don't, no. He ain't no murderer, though."

"But he might know who is."

He just keeps on shaking his head, not knowing what to do.

"I understand now," I say. "If my cousin Jeffrey were still alive, I'd be doing the same thing to help him. But he doesn't have a chance now. He's fucking dead. And like Biddy was more to you than just a nephew, Jeffrey was more to me than just a cousin."

"I'm truly sorry for that, but Biddy would never harm anyone. That ain't no lie, either."

Am I losing my touch? I shouldn't believe him, but I do.

"Let's start with me finding out where he took the rest of my property. The records and the CD collection. The laptop and flat-screen."

"He never been locked up before."

"You can't protect him from that. Crack's a monster, and it don't care."

"He get locked up it'll change him. Like his mother."

"Your sister."

"Yeah."

"If he didn't do the murder but knows who did, the cops will work with him. I'll make sure of that. I got a friend who's a great lawyer."

"He can't go to jail."

"I don't know what to tell you. I'm no social worker. I can just assure you that I will help keep him out of jail."

There he goes with shaking his damn head again.

"You'd give up your livelihood and go to jail for him?"

"Yeah, I probably would."

Didn't want to hear that.

I could beat it outta him, but I have a feeling that wouldn't work, either. Family goes deep, and somehow he feels responsible for how it turned out with his nephew. That gives him strength and an upper hand. I know guys like Diamond. Hell, I'm one of them.

FORTY-THREE

If Biddy hadn't stolen my fucking laptop, I'd run a background check on both him and Diamond through LexisNexis. Thing is, my password is saved on my laptop, and I can't remember it. Fucking ridiculous. Can't ask Leslie. Can't bring her into this mess. I can't go to my buddy Luna, 'cause he'll know I'm working the case, and he won't step out like that, even to help me. Diamond's the only worthy lead I have, but he won't budge. He'd probably take a bullet in the teeth for that nephew of his.

"Take me home, Diamond. You know where I live," I say all of a sudden.

"I'll take you to the corner I picked you up at."

"And you're comfortable with this? Because I am going to give the police everything. They'll get warrants on you and your nephew."

"No. I ain't comfortable with any of this."

"Here's your choices, then—drop me off, and I guarantee you both will get arrested, or let me talk to him, find out what he knows about the murder, find out where he sold my property, and that's the end of it. I won't bother you again, or I can recommend a good defense attorney and you work it out that you or both of you turn yourselves in. It would be to your advantage if you did this before they get warrants. You give everything up, and in my experience you'll probably get some kind of deal, especially if Biddy or you has information about the homicide."

"I got to look after him."

"I figured that much, you risking everything because of him. But I'm at my wit's end here, so make a decision or I'll make it for you and call Detective Hurley right now."

"I gotta find him. Then I'll call you," he says.

"When?"

"Tomorrow morning the latest."

He turns to face me.

"I'm probably a fool for trusting you."

"No, you're not."

He fiddles with something near his lap. I lean forward to get a better look. It's the money I gave him. He tries to hand it to me through the slot.

"I don't feel comfortable taking this until you two meet up."

"Keep it. I trust you," I say without meaning a word of it. I have a sense for these things, and I know now after he tried to give me back the money that he's full of shit. It's something you know after years of dealing with all kinds of people. I'm sure I'll get a call in the morning, but he'll have one excuse or another for why he can't find Biddy.

He slips the money under his lap.

"All right, then" is all he says.

After he drops me off, I watch him drive off. I walk quickly to my car. I still got what I need in my backpack, so the plan is to drive right back to Diamond's house and sit on it for as long as I gotta.

FORTY-FOUR

I don't think taking the side streets made much of a difference as far as time is concerned, but it's always a good policy to do that if you think you're being tailed. I got lucky with a good parking space. It allows me a view of the front entrance of Diamond's house and the cut leading behind it. Whatever route he uses, I'll see his car.

Since I like to keep up with what's going on locally, especially when it concerns me, I tune the car radio to WTOP.

More rain in the forecast. That's always a good thing. After the commercial break, first thing on the local news is about Jeffrey Baldwin.

Shit. I feel for Hurley and Millhoff. It's turned political. Who am I kidding? I feel more for me. What the hell is going to happen? What the hell am I doing?

Maybe I've let myself get too close to Diamond. Revealed too much. Damn—my prints are all over the interior of his cab. Just the thought of being suspected is bad enough. I've been there, and it's not fun.

A couple of cars rolling by catch my attention. They pass slowly. Probably looking for a parking space, though.

Evening settles in, and still nothing. Those cicadas change their song. No lights on in the house. I should be more concerned right about now, but the Klonopin I took earlier is kicking in. Easy. Easy.

Time slows down while you're on surveillance. It's like fishing, being out on the Potomac in that old johnboat I used to have. It's not like surveillance: when I was fishing, it didn't matter whether I caught anything or not. On the river, sitting back with the line out and letting the current do all the work was more than enough.

Headlights beaming through my rear window bring me right back. I slide farther down in my seat, let the car pass.

It's fucking Diamond, and it looks like he has a passenger in the front seat.

He double-parks in front of his house a few cars up and across from where I'm parked. The cab's hazard lights turn on. They exit. I'm betting the passenger is Biddy. He's a skinny young man, but he's well dressed and doesn't look like a typical crackhead. Most likely because he's not homeless and might even shower on occasion.

The young man follows Diamond to the front porch and then into the house, closing the door behind him.

Warm glow filters through curtains on the front window. Shortly after, another light on the second floor.

I focus my attention on that front door for what seems like more than an hour. Then the door opens, and Diamond walks out, followed by the young man, now carrying a medium-size suitcase.

Has to be Biddy. He's been staying there all this time, but now the protective uncle is gonna take him somewhere else. I hope he won't do something stupid after, like take my advice and turn himself in. No, I have a feeling that when he calls me tomorrow he'll come up with something like he can't find Biddy, some shit like that.

I let them make the right turn, then turn my headlights on and speed up to the intersection.

Traffic is light. Hell, it's a Monday night. Diamond's obeying the speed limit, which is a good thing. It allows me to stay farther back and get behind another car when I can. He crosses Constitution Avenue, still heading south on 14th. The Washington Monument's to the right. Obvious he's gonna take the bridge across to Virginia.

He does, but he stays to the right and doesn't hit the HOV lane. Instead he takes the exit for the George Washington Memorial Parkway and National Airport.

He's going to fly him out of town? Fuck that shit.

If I believed in luck I'd be crossing all my fingers and toes right about now. Instead I only believe in survival.

The exit for the airport is a couple of miles away.

When it comes up, I don't see a blinker. He continues on GW toward Old Town, in Alexandria. Thank the Lord for the nighttime. It makes it easier to tail someone.

He slows down as we enter Old Town, and then after a couple of blocks he slows even more and puts on his right turn signal. He's gonna turn into that old motel on the edge of town. I pass him as he enters the parking lot, then make a U-turn at the next traffic light and park illegally across the street from the motel.

The young man, who I now am sure is Biddy, pulls his suitcase out of the trunk and follows his uncle to the motel office. I can't make out anything through the small office window. A few minutes later they both exit, walk along the room doors on the left. I count the doors they pass. They stop at the sixth, and both enter.

I won't know until tomorrow what it is Diamond's trying to pull, but that doesn't matter to me anymore, 'cause I know where the fuck Biddy is.

Shortly after midnight, Diamond exits the room, enters his cab, and makes a left, back onto the GW Parkway, headlights nearly smacking me in the face on the turn.

Then it's red taillights in the distance, then he's gone.

I sit back and consider the circumstances here, and it doesn't take long to decide that I'm too drunk to drive and that the best thing to do is get a room at this very motel in Old Town.

FORTY-FIVE

The man sitting behind the counter looks old enough to be the motel's original owner, and this spot has been here for as long as I can remember.

He looks up at me, stone cold, like the living dead, and waits for me to talk.

I try to sound drunk, slur my words.

"I need a room. Too much to drink, and can't make it back to DC tonight."

"Hundred dollars a night for a king. No smoking."

"Damn, hundred bucks. Better than jail, right?"

His face doesn't even twitch.

"Credit card or a hundred plus a hundred and fifty cash deposit."

"Can't put it on my card because my fiancée might find out. Damn. One hundred and fifty deposit?"

Nothing.

"Okay. Okay. I think I can do that. Got some cash."

I count out the money and put it on the counter.

"I'll need to see a driver's license."

I look at him square but throw in an innocent half smile.

"How about another fifty so I don't have to do that? I got a job where I can't let something like this come back and bite me."

He contemplates.

"Hundred."

I look in my wallet.

"All I got is eighty," I lie.

An upward nod, which I take as a yes.

"Mind making that on the bottom floor? Might not make it up your stairs."

He scans the wall that has all the keys hanging on hooks next to room numbers. He hands me the key for room 110.

I drop four twenties on the counter.

"Thank you, compadre."

"I'm not Mexican."

"I know. Just being friendly." I slur my words.

"No smoking," he orders.

I walk out and follow the same path as Diamond and Biddy. I pass Biddy's room, notice through the curtained window he's got a light on. Hear the television muffled through the front door. Walk a couple doors past his room to my room, unlock it, and enter.

Smells stale, like mold. Who knows what the fuck I'd see splattered over the bed if I had a black light? At the very least there'll be bedbugs. But I don't intend on sleeping, so who cares? I peek through the curtains and across the parking lot toward the front office. All that's visible is the office door with its four glass panels, and I don't think the old man is paying much attention anyway.

I notice a smoke alarm on the wall above the thermostat. After I put my pack down I walk to it, reach up, and remove the battery. I find a drinking glass in the bathroom, return to check the armchair cushion before I sit. Light a smoke. I try to figure how I'm going to do this, and judging by Biddy's physical stature, I know I won't have to go hard. There won't be a problem putting him down. But I don't want to go hard, maybe just nudge him a little bit.

I snort up the contents of a couple of capsules, get my mind right, find my handcuffs in the pack, and slip them through the belt at the small of my back. I pick up the pack and walk out the door.

Light's still on in his room.

I put my ear to the door. Sounds like he's still watching TV. I bow my head so he can't make me out through the peephole, take a deep breath, and knock.

Couple seconds later, I hear shuffling inside.

"Who's there?"

"Front office. Smoke detector light's blinking for your room. I need to check it out."

"I don't smoke, and there's no fire in here that I can see."

"City fire regulations, sir. I have to check. Won't be but a minute. Might be just a short or something."

"I'm telling ya there's nothing," Biddy says.

"Sir, either I check or I have to call the fire department, and they'll have to check on it. Sorry to bother you, but I have to come in."

The door opens, but only a bit.

"I'll just be a second," I say with a smile.

"I didn't see you in the front office."

"I work maintenance, stay in one of the rooms upstairs, and got a call. Smoke alarm's right there on the wall above the thermostat."

He turns his head to see, then back to me. He opens the door to let me in.

Looks like he's been lying on top of the covers. Some reality show is on cable. I smell the familiar sweet scent.

I walk to the smoke detector, look at it briefly, and reach up to remove the battery.

"Just as I thought," I say.

I take the battery and drop it in my pack, then set my pack on the armchair.

"One more thing I have to check out," I say, walking toward him.

He steps back as I pass.

In one quick move, I snatch him by the hand and twist it so he doesn't have a choice but to turn the way I want him to. He yelps, comically, as I think he meant it to be a scream. I kick him on the inside of his right knee, and he buckles and falls face-first on the bed.

"Make any noise, and you're fucked."

He turns his head so his cheek is on the mattress, his right eye trying to focus on me.

"I don't have money."

"Do I look like a burglar?"

I take out my handcuffs and cuff his right wrist.

He struggles.

"Wait, wait…"

He's double-jointed, the gangly little fuck.

"Hold on, now…hold on…what's going on here?" he squeals.

"Quit struggling or I'll snap your arm in two."

"Please…"

I manage to cuff him, but before I roll him over onto his back I say, "You scream, even talk loud, you'll regret it. Understand?"

"Yes."

"Stay just like you are."

I leave him, his legs dangling over the mattress, the tips of his toes barely touching the floor. I grab my pack and return. I pull out the duct tape and set it on the mattress where he can see it.

"Aw, c'mon. What are you going to do? Please."

I pull him up by the collar and help him turn so he's sitting on the edge of the mattress.

"Listen to me and you'll get out of this okay. Like I said, you raise your voice or try to scream, that's what the duct tape is for. Understood?"

"Yes. Yes."

I grab him under his arm to stand him up. I pat him down, but he doesn't have anything. I notice a wallet, a key ring with a couple of keys on it, and an old cell phone on the nightstand. Probably everything he has except for what I'll try to find in a second.

"Sit over here," I say as I walk him to the armchair.

He sits, falling back a bit, but then straightens himself out. I pull a chair on rollers out from a small rectangular desk and position it so I can sit to his left. Bathroom is straight ahead, the door behind me.

I look at him for a second and say, "You broke into the wrong house."

FORTY-SIX

Most of them always deny it at first. Some never give it up at all. I've also had a few who gave it up right away. Biddy's not going to give it up right away, but I can already tell it's not going to take much effort.

He's not what I imagined. He's shorter and skinnier than I thought he would be, maybe early thirties, clean-shaven. Keeps his hair tight. It's not the kind of frailty that comes with an unhealthy lifestyle, which is what I would have thought. I could see this guy on the street and wouldn't think that at all. No, it's something tenuous. Pleasant. Somehow not hardened, despite the years of criminality and abuse he's gotten himself wrapped up in.

I don't smell alcohol or tobacco on him, either, only the slightly pungent, sweet-smelling scent of smoked crack still lingering in the air. I pick up the duct tape off the mattress and lift my backpack from the floor.

"What are you going to do?" he asks.

"Don't talk or I'll tape your mouth shut."

I kneel on one knee beside his feet.

"Put your feet together."

"I'm not going to try anything. I swear."

I shove his ankles toward each other and duct-tape them together. After that I stand and walk to the place where he was resting his head before I came in. I find the remote and turn the TV off. I search the contents of his suitcase but don't find anything useful. I open his wallet; twenty bucks inside. No credit cards. He has an expired license. The name on it is Robert Graham Givens. Givens? Holy fuck, this guy's Givens? I also find fake identification showing Graham Biddy as his alias. Son of a bitch. It's the same guy. He doesn't look anything like I thought Givens would. Ray made him out to be much more. Like a cold-blooded murderer. I find that hard to believe, looking at him now sitting in that chair, scared to death. I'll keep this to myself for the moment. Fucking Robert Givens.

I open the nightstand drawer, find a baggie that contains at least an ounce of nice yellowish rock, a razor blade, a glass rose pipe, and a lighter. I look back toward him. His head now bowed, shaking it slowly from side to side.

"This has gotta be at least an ounce. Shit, what is that in DC now—seven, eight hundred bucks?"

No reply.

I grab everything and take it to the chair where I was sitting. I set everything but the blade on a round table beside the armchair. I turn on a small lamp that sits on the round table. It shows off the goods better. I go to the bathroom, drop the blade in the toilet, and flush.

I return and look down at him.

"Well, Robby—no, Biddy. I like that name better. You must have worked hard for this here." I lift the baggie. "How long will this last you?"

No answer.

"I'll ask one more time. You'd better damn well answer."

He finally looks up. "Couple days."

"Well, I've seen worse. You're probably wanting some about now. Am I right?"

I can tell he's trying to figure out if he should answer that.

"Maybe later. You took a bunch of stereo equipment from my house. Remember that?"

That gets a good reaction.

"Got some of it back from Thrift World, though."

I grab the sport bottle from my pack, take a good swig.

"It ain't Gatorade, if that's what you're thinking."

I set it on the table near the baggie.

"I will go hard on you if I have to, Bid. I don't want to, but I will. See, my life got really fucked up with the burglary. And the poor boy murdered in my kitchen."

He knows the house I'm talking about now. Even though he tries hard not to react, I can still see it in his eyes. Fear.

"Please, sir. You have the wrong person here."

I walk back to the nightstand, grab the fake identification out of his wallet, and bring it back. Put it in his face.

"This is all I need to have you put away for life. But I don't make you for the murdering type."

"I'm not. I'm not...I don't even know what you're talking about."

I bitch-slap him hard on the side of the face. Maybe too hard. I'm worried I snapped his neck.

He whimpers.

"And I'm pretty damn sure you won't last long in prison. So you're going to talk, tell me what I need to know." I pull out my wallet and flash my badge. "Or we'll take care of this outside of court."

"Oh, damn," he whimpers.

I see watery eyes and a few tears.

"Do you still have a job?" I ask.

"No."

"What did you do before you got messed up with this shit?"

"Building maintenance for DC public schools."

He didn't deny being messed up with any kinda shit.

"Damn. So you got fired?"

"Yeah."

"Piss test?"

"Yes."

"You had a pension, health, and all that?"

"Yeah, I did."

"How many years did you have?"

"Four."

"That's not so bad. Built up a little bit on your pension is all. You didn't lose much."

He chuckles, a nervous chuckle.

"I want the rest of my shit back. I want to know why that kid was murdered in my kitchen."

"How do I know you're not setting me up?"

What the fuck does he mean by that?

"What are you talking about, 'setting me up'?"

"That you don't work for him, and you're just testing me."

"No, I don't work for him. Who the fuck is him?"

"I'm sorry, sir. I can't get your stuff back."

"I'm not setting you up. This is my life you fucked. I want information. You don't give it to me, I'm going to turn you in right now. You're not going to get the shit kicked outta you or nothin' like that, 'cause I changed my mind. I got a good sense about people. Like I said, I don't figure you for a killer. You're just going to go to jail, and so is your uncle. And both of you will get charged with murder, with burglary, and then you'll find yourselves play-ing with the big boys in some federal prison."

"My uncle?"

"Yeah, I know your uncle Diamond, and no, he didn't give you up. I followed you both here. I know he's trying to protect you. He'd even go to prison for you. You must really mean something to him."

Head lowers, just like his uncle, and he starts shaking again. I realize I've already crossed the line. Too late to call Hurley or Millhoff. That'd fuck me no end, so I have to play this out.

"I…I…I don't…" He stops, scared, and it's something more than the predicament he's in with me.

"What is it? You tell me, Bid. You do nothing, but tell me. I do the rest. I'll even let you keep this shit in the baggie too."

"It's not that simple."

"Yeah, it's that simple."

"I can't."

"I don't know what the fuck you're hiding, but I'm going to dump the contents of this baggie in the toilet right now unless you talk."

"I'll pay you back somehow."

"How the hell are you gonna pay back a life?"

Tears stream.

"I had nothing to do with that," he says, and, judging by the look he gives me afterward, I know he regrets saying it.

"Fuck it," I say, standing.

I grab the baggie. I know for a fact this shit here means more to him right now than anything.

"No—wait. Don't do that."

See?

"You gonna talk? And I'll know if you're fuckin' playing me. No second chance."

I set the baggie back on the table and sit down. I can tell he's aching inside, his body and mind desperately needing to light up.

"Let's start here first—where'd you sell the gun?"

Hesitating again. Fear. I give him a couple of seconds.

"I'm not going to ask again."

"You're going to get me killed!"

"No. No one will know where it came from. They might put it together if you got yourself locked up, cooperated, and then whoever these people you're dealing with start getting locked up because of it. But you're not locked up, and what you tell me stays with me only."

"You're still a cop, though. I know how this shit goes for someone like me."

"Listen, though." I let him believe I'm still a cop. "I like to handle things my way, especially when it concerns my life getting jacked."

He bows his head.

"Look at me."

He does.

"Now answer the question. Who'd you sell the gun to?"

"Another police officer, just like you. Officer Jasper."

FORTY-SEVEN

"O fficer Willy Jasper."

That surprised the fuck outta me. But then again, maybe not so much. I don't know if I believe it. But I start to thinking it's more than a coincidence, me showing up at the night-club the few times I did, then the burglary and then Jeffrey being murdered at my home.

But why?

"What about the kid who was killed in my kitchen?" I ask.

"Listen, Officer, please—"

"Detective." Only because I like hearing that again, and I want the respect.

"Detective. You really are going to get me and my uncle killed. I gave you what you want."

"That doesn't explain shit."

I need a new tactic. He's fading out.

I stand up.

"Lean forward," I tell him.

"Why? What are you going to do?"

"I'm gonna take your cuffs off. Now lean forward."

He does.

I find the key on my key chain and unlock the cuffs. He stretches his arms out, starts massaging his wrists. It does look like I made them too tight.

I sit back down.

"Is your uncle going to return tomorrow?"

"No. He said he'd call me."

"How long he pay for you to stay here?"

"A week."

"How'd your uncle get involved with all this?"

"He's just trying to protect me. Like you said."

"So he helps you transport stolen property in his cab? That's helping you out?"

Biddy actually looks surprised.

"I know more than you think I know, except what you said about Jasper. Why did your uncle help you like that?"

"Officer Jasper caught me for an office burglary. I had a couple of laptops. He took them, took a photo of me with his phone, and wrote down all my information. Said that I'm his new informant and that he'd use what he had for a warrant if I didn't follow along. He, um, insisted that I let him drive me to where I was staying."

"Your uncle's house."

"Yeah. My uncle was there at the time. It was early. I wasn't lying when I said my uncle got caught up in all this to protect me. At first I did give Officer Jasper information, but then it didn't take long to figure he was dirty. He started giving me a shopping list of things he wanted to have, like flat-screens, laptops, jewelry, some of the stuff too big to carry. He got my uncle involved because as good a man as my uncle is, he's had a tough time paying bills."

"Does your uncle carry a gun?"

"No. Not him. Never. Doesn't even have a shotgun at the house."

"He seems like a good man."

"Is he going to be all right?"

"That depends on you."

"It's all my fault, not his."

"Tell me more about Officer Jasper."

"After a couple of months I was introduced to Jasper's other informants."

"You mean stable of burglars?"

"Yes."

"You do jobs together?"

"Sometimes. I mean, not always. Officer Jasper has a line on fucking *everything*. I mean, he wins both ways because we had to buy all our drugs from his people after we sold the goods. Sometimes trade certain things for it."

"Where do they live? Just give me a street." Like I don't already know.

"Riggs Street."

"You know anyone who goes by the name Ray?"

"Yes."

"What's he into?"

"He slings for Jasper on occasion."

"What does he deal?"

"Crack, powder, K2, weed."

"Where does he get it from?"

"The boys on Riggs."

"How long have you had this working relationship with Officer Jasper?"

"I don't know. Six months maybe?"

I take another swig from my sport bottle.

"You want a bit of this in a glass?" I ask.

"No, thank you. I don't drink," he says, knowing that it's some kind of liquor. Maybe the wince on my face after gave it up. It's almost funny, but I don't let him see me smile. I go to the bathroom, grab a drinking glass off the sink, return, set the glass on the table to use as an ashtray, and sit back down.

I light up a cigarette.

"There's no smoking in this room."

"Now, that's funny, considering what you've been smoking up."

"I didn't mean it like that, sir."

"And enough with that 'sir' shit."

I need a bump myself. I'm starting to fade out here. I'm not about to reveal that side of me to this guy, though, as much as I'm starting to like him, maybe even feel sorry for him. But my insides are starting to ache—like an empty stomach, but radiating through your whole body. I know he's feeling the same, or probably worse.

He looks at me, expecting more. I stamp the cigarette out on the bottom of the glass and pick up the handcuffs again.

"I have to take a piss," I say. "Lean forward."

"I'm not going to try to escape."

"I don't know you," I say, like it's a threat.

He leans forward, and I cuff his hands behind his back. I pick up my pack and enter the bathroom but leave the door open. I turn the water faucet on to muffle the noise.

"Don't turn around, 'cause I can't piss when someone's watching."

I find the medicine vial in a pocket of the pack, take out a couple of capsules, and carefully twist one open, squeeze the contents onto the back of my hand. I flush the toilet and snort. I look back to make sure he's not spying. I quickly do the same with the other capsule. Finishing, I put the capsules back together and drop them back into the vial, turn off the faucet, check my nostrils in the mirror. Sniff a couple more times.

There we go. That's what I was looking for.

FORTY-EIGHT

I t's not a coincidence you hit my house, is it? I just don't understand how the kid who was there with you got murdered in my
kitchen."

The handcuffs are off. He's rubbing his wrists again, keeps eye-
balling the baggie of crack.

"I don't understand," he says, looking a little dumber every
minute.

"You need a brain boost?"

"What do you mean?"

"You need to take a hit off some of your shit?"

He's shocked to hear me say it. And he doesn't know how to
answer, like I'm playing him.

"I'm serious," I tell him.

"I could sure use the help."

I cuff his hands at the front, give him the stem and the lighter,
and slide the baggie over so he can reach it.

"Blow that shit away from my face."

I roll the chair back so I'm not close to him. His hands are shaking, but he manages to pull out a little less than a dime rock and carefully place it in the part of the stem that has a pipe screen. Lights up, and after a big inhale, he comes back to life. Probably what I look like, but not as cartoonish. I wonder if it's a better high, though. I sure as hell don't want to find out. I don't need that gnawing on my insides.

He blows it out, away from me, quickly takes another big toke, faces me after, and says with a cough, "Thank you."

"Was it like the first time?" I ask him.

"What do you mean?"

"Smoking it just now. Does it still feel like the first time you tried it? I mean the high. Or are you still chasing it?"

He looks at me with furrowed brows. *The fuck?* I imagine he's thinking. Fact is, I really want to know. It's never like the first time for me. It just keeps me from falling back into darkness.

"I don't know. I don't think it ever really is," he says awkwardly. "Don't matter."

"Why?"

"Never will."

Damn. Still, I know the high won't last for more than a few minutes, so I don't waste it.

"Now tell me. Why did you hit my house?"

"I'm already screwed, right?"

"Not necessarily. There's always a way out. And don't you think me letting you have that hit means I'm open to letting you find a way out?"

"Yes, I guess so. I mean, I don't know any cop who'd let me do that in front of him. Not even Officer Jasper. Unless you're the one playing me."

"I told you I'm not like him. I got my way of working things, but I'm nothing like that piece of shit."

I want to tell him that I understand him more than he knows.

Tiny beads of sweat break through the skin on his forehead, even though it's cool in here. He starts grinding his teeth.

"He drove me to your house, on Twelfth, and pointed it out to me. He said he wanted me to hit it. He's pointed out places before where he knew there might be some good stuff, so that's what I figured. If I knew you were a cop, I never would have done it. I'm not crazy."

"What did he say about my house, specifically?"

"He said there might be a gun in there and to clean out the house, to take everything I could, even personal items."

"Personal items?"

"I didn't understand that, either, but I figured he meant jewelry, stuff like that. Your music."

"Why was the kid there, though?"

"You gotta believe me. My uncle and I had nothing to do with that."

"Tell me."

"He was buying powder from Ray, who was skimming from the young ones on Riggs Street."

"Why didn't you mention this when I asked if you knew Wrayburn?"

"I wasn't hiding anything. I just didn't think to. Like I said, Jasper controlled all that. He caught the college kid selling in his club, told him he had to work it off, and that meant helping me with a bigger haul. So he sent him with us."

"So Ray was skimming, and what he took he was selling to the kid who got killed in my kitchen?"

"Yes."

Shit. Did Ray kill Jeffrey?

I don't want to tell him Wrayburn is dead. That'll just scare him senseless.

"Was Ray with you at the burglary?"

"No."

"How'd you learn this about Ray skimming? I know Jasper wouldn't tell you."

"The boy who got shot in your house. He told me. He talked too much. Think he even enjoyed being a part of it all, like it was a game."

"When did he tell you?"

"When we were loading everything into my uncle's cab, on the way there."

"From my house?"

"Yes."

Fuck.

"How'd he get shot?"

"I don't know how I got caught up in all this——"

"You're not the victim here, Biddy. Now tell me how he got shot."

He bows his head. Streams of tears pour out of his eyes. He sniffles, shoulders heaving with every short sob. I can't let him get lost in those feelings. He'll shut down.

"Talk to me, Biddy."

He looks up, clear snot slithering from his nostrils. "After we loaded everything up, some other guy comes out of nowhere. In the alley behind your house. I know him because he's with Jasper sometimes. Big man. Big-ass white dude. He leaned in the cab and asked if we got a gun. I told him we did. He told the kid to take the gun we stole back in the house, that they don't want no part of that. I should've known that something was wrong, because Jasper does buy guns. Kid walks in the back door. Big guy follows. Minute later I hear two shots, and he walks out slow, hands me the gun so I have to take it with my bare hand. Then he said, 'This'll come back to you if you get stupid.' He walked away after that, like nothing ever happened. I heard the rest later. On the news."

"But why?" Ready to jump out of my skin with all this.

"I don't know why," he tells me. Sobs only once this time. "I don't."

"Do you know the big guy's name?"

"No."

"Okay. Okay. Fuck. What about my records and CDs and the laptop and flat-screen?"

"Huh?" he comes back, like *Why would you ask about that after what I just said?*

"Where did that shit go?"

"Officer Jasper took it."

"You didn't take anything to the convenience store on Fourteenth, right near Thomas Circle?"

He gives me that look again, wondering how I know all this.

"Not that time. No."

"Why would Officer Jasper want it?"

"I didn't ask, but I assume he likes records."

"Does he pay well for the goods?"

"Depends on what it is, but usually he does. You know, regular street value."

"Where did you meet up with him to sell him my flat-screen, the gun, and the other stuff?"

"My uncle drove to an alley near the club he works at. It was at night, when Officer Jasper was on his way to work."

"So he put that shit in his cruiser."

"No. It looked like his personal car."

"Where does he live?"

"I don't know. No one knows where he lives."

I grab the baggie so he won't try to take any.

"What are you going to do?"

"Relax," I tell him.

I walk to the nightstand, pick up his wallet and cell, then return.

I open his wallet again.

"These three pieces of paper with numbers." I show him the first one. "Who is this?"

"That's the cell for Repo, the one at Riggs Street."

"One of the boys you get your drugs from?"

"Yes."

"You said there's two of them. Is he the younger one or the older?"

"Younger."

I show him another number.

"That's Officer Jasper's cell."

Thought it looked familiar.

And then I show him the last one.

"That's just some old guy I met on the street who does lookout for me when I need it in exchange for a hit or two."

"Does he know Jasper?"

"No. Just an old crackhead is all."

I power on his cell, go to his settings to find his number. I take my phone and tap his number into my contacts.

"I'm gonna call you Tiny Tim," I tell him.

"What do you mean?"

"For my phone. That's your nickname. You know who Tiny Tim is, right?"

"That Christmas story."

"That's right," I say, thankful he doesn't know the "Tiptoe Through the Tulips" guy.

I tap the number to call his cell. It rings, but I answer. I add my number to his contacts.

"Putting my name in your cell as Fagin."

"That your real name?"

"Yes."

I know the only reason Diamond brought him here was to protect him from me, but I think Biddy realizes now that I'm not the threat. Jasper and his boys are. I also realize I can't sit on this information. I'll have to give Hurley a call later, fill him in as much as I can without giving up Biddy or Diamond. Yet.

"What are you going to do with me?" he asks.

"Well, I don't think I'm gonna kill ya," I say, then hand him his cell phone. "So call your uncle."

FORTY-NINE

I snap a head-shot photo of Biddy with my phone, then cut the duct tape from his legs. I uncuff him.

"You think about doing anything stupid and I'll break you like a twig."

"I know, sir. I won't."

I walk to the nightstand, grab his wallet, and take the fake ID and the expired license out. I let him see me put them in my pocket.

"I need that license."

"Insurance. I'll be holding on to it."

"I just want a way out of this."

"What—your addiction? Or out from under Jasper?"

"I guess both."

"You guess, huh?"

No response.

"What does your uncle think about all that?"

"I never smoke in front of him. He's tried to get me to quit. More than once."

"What's the longest you've gone?"

"Almost a week."

"That's good. So what brought you back?"

"My mother's death."

"Sorry to hear that."

"No need. I guess I'm what you'd call a crack baby."

That's a good excuse. Or is it really in his blood?

"Is that how your mom died?"

"It didn't help. She got pneumonia."

"Well, going a week is good," I say in an effort to change the subject. "That means you can go longer, have a better chance of quitting next time."

"Thing about this stuff? Once you start smoking? You can't stop. When I run out I sometimes don't get anything for a day. It's not that hard for a day, maybe."

"That's because you know you're going to get more. You trick your brain."

He looks at me like *How would you know that?*

"In my career I've interviewed a lot of users," I say.

"Oh. It's just that it's not that hard when it's not around. What's hard is not thinking about it."

He's got that right.

"Speaking of addiction, the first hit was on me. I want you to use the bathroom if you need another one, 'cause I don't want to see it anymore or smell it, so put the fan on or blow that shit into a wet washcloth."

"Wet washcloth. That's a good idea."

"I heard it works for weed."

"So I can pick this up?" he asks, looking at the baggie.

"No. I'll be holding on to it, too," I say.

I pick it up, open it, and pull out a nice chunk he can break some off of. Hand it to him.

"Use it wisely."

"Will I get all of it back?"

"Like I said, that depends on how this plays out."

I look at my phone for the time.

Daylight'll be creeping in soon, and so will Diamond.

FIFTY

There's a purpose in all this, but it still feels like nothing but an all-night binge with a crackhead. And now I have Diamond to grapple with. The first thing I did when he came in was pat him down. Doesn't matter what Biddy told me about his uncle. I don't know them, and I don't trust either of them.

Now Diamond is standing at the foot of the bed staring at the blank TV screen, like everything's starting to collapse around him. Well, it is, but I didn't put him in that position. If anyone should feel that way, it's me.

Biddy's in the bathroom. We both know what he's doing, but it's harder to take for Diamond.

Yeah, like I said, I don't trust him, but that doesn't mean he's not a good man. Shit, look at me.

Biddy walks out of the bathroom grinding his teeth.

"Everything just got real complicated," Diamond says to the television screen.

"Didn't have to be that way. It was simple, but I understand why you don't trust me. I wouldn't trust me."

"He could have turned me in," Biddy tells his uncle.

Diamond turns to him. A hard look.

"Yeah, you think he'd do that and get his ass locked up for kidnapping or some charge like that?"

He makes a good point, but I don't let him know.

"But he's a cop."

I'm beginning to think Biddy might be a little slow. Or maybe it's all the crack he's been smoking, speeding him up so fast on the outside that his brain doesn't have time to catch up.

"Robby, he ain't no cop no more. Shit, he's a private eye."

"You showed me a badge, said you were a cop."

"I showed you my retirement badge. I never said I was a cop."

"Showing your badge is the same thing as saying," Biddy says, almost like a child.

"I can understand how you'd assume that."

"So now we're caught up in all this, on top of everything else," Diamond says.

"Lesser of two evils," I tell him.

He looks at me direct.

"So what you plannin' on doing?" Diamond asks me.

"I don't know. Sleep for a bit and figure it out when my head is clear. I'll figure something out so Jasper and the big guy take the fall."

"We don't want any part of this here," Diamond says.

"You think I do? It was you two who brought me into this. Who am I to Jasper that he'd fuck with me like this? That he'd have..." I can't say Jeffrey's name for some reason.

Neither of them answers that.

Diamond sits at the foot of the bed, hunched over, arms resting on his knees.

"The only reason I had Biddy call you was to show you there's nothing to worry about with me. I need to know why Jasper put you on to my house."

"I told you I don't know," Biddy says.

"What about you, Uncle Diamond? You know?"

"I don't."

"I just have one warning, and it's not me you two have to worry about. If he finds out you talked to me, he'll realize you're witnesses, that you gave him up."

"We ain't stupid," Diamond says.

"I keep hearing that. I suspect you're not, but we all got an agenda. If I were you, Diamond, I'd get me another room at this motel, lay low for a while with your boy. I'm gonna figure this thing out. See if there's a way to keep you two out of it. I don't know if it's possible. I don't even know why I'm suggesting it, because I shouldn't give a fuck about you two."

I pull out the baggie of crack from my pocket and toss it underhand to Biddy.

Surprisingly, he catches it.

"You two run, and I'll give everything to the police unless I find you first, and trust me, you'll want the police to find you first."

I grab my backpack and open the front door.

"You damn well better take me seriously," I warn, then exit.

The chances of my getting into trouble are greater if I turn them in. That is, if they talk about how I came to find them. Fuck. Kidnapping while armed, assault, just to name a couple of charges I could face. I've also locked up hundreds of crackheads back when I was on the job. Turned a few of them into good CIs. Yeah, some of them ran when we got them out, but they always ran back to their neighborhood 'cause they had nowhere else to go. Diamond owns his home. They have no relations outside DC except Diamond's son. And I sure as hell don't think

Biddy's gonna take off to Afghanistan or wherever the hell Diamond's son is stationed. I'm taking a big chance, but if it works it'll lead me to Jeffrey's killer. Untie this whole fucking thing.

I check the whole house when I get home, make sure everything is secure. I lock the bedroom door once I enter, strip down to shower. Carry clean underwear and my gun into the bathroom with me. Lock the bathroom door, put the gun on the vanity, and cover it with my underwear.

After my shower, I dress in comfortable khakis and a white T-shirt, pop two Klonopins, and lie on top of the covers with my gun at my side. Despite the Klonopin, I have confidence that if someone kicks the door in, I'll still have the acuity to cap his ass. Be nice if it was Jasper. Save me a lot of trouble. Things rarely work out the way you want them to.

Damn, I don't need this in my life right now. I can't think straight. That long night with Biddy has floored me. I feel like he's the other side of me. A mini me.

Fuck, I'm nothing like him.

I don't know what the fuck I was thinking. Leaving them there. I got the guy who burglarized my house. The guy who can clear my name from the suspect list and put his own name in its place. Who the fuck am I?

The bedroom is cool. The ceiling fan helps, too. I like the feeling of the air as it pushes softly against my face.

Leslie sneaks into my head. I close my eyes, try to see her face, but it's no longer a clear image.

After a few minutes of lying still, something comes to me.

Something good that I need to do.

I have to try to get some sleep first, 'cause it has to be tonight.

FIFTY-ONE

That evening I park a block and half from Riggs. It's stuffy out. Before I exit the car, I grab the stun gun from my backpack, clip it to my belt behind the gun, and slip on my thin tactical gloves.

I shoulder my backpack when I exit. It's a little heavier than normal because it contains some other tools I might need, like a mini Halligan bar. Don't leave home without one.

I check the time. Coming up on midnight. Shouldn't take me more than twenty minutes. Saturday night near 14th Street, so there are a few people out, maybe walking home or looking for their parked cars after hitting a bar. Two young girls pass me. One smiles. I smile back. Just a normal guy in a suit here.

I walk leisurely so I can scope out Riggs Street. I notice a dim light on in their house through the closed curtains of the front window. An equally dim patio light is on. The block is quiet.

I walk up the stairs. They have a sturdy security gate. It's locked. I look around again.

I ring the doorbell.

Not a sound.

I ring it two times in a row. Wait a couple of minutes, and still nothing. The security gate would be easy to pop open with the Halligan bar, but it'll make too much noise. I walk down the stairs and east toward 13th, counting the homes between their house and the intersection. I turn left on 13th toward the alley. I don't take the cut on Riggs just in case there are prying eyes. This way it looks like I'm leaving.

After I make the turn into the alley I count the homes to the east of their house. A six-foot flimsy wooden fence surrounds the tiny backyard. I use my knife to unhinge the latch and enter. No exterior lights back here. That's good. I let my eyes adjust, then move to the back door.

No security gate, but it's a good door. Nothing that can't be pried open, though.

Hitting a home at night is far more dangerous than hitting it during the daytime. It's easier to surveil a house in the daytime before you hit it. Now I know where they are, but not for how long. And I haven't sat on the house long enough to know who else might live here. Not smart? Maybe. Desperate times and all that shit.

I peer through one of the square glass panes in the door. Looks like it opens to the kitchen. The light I saw through the curtains is coming from a hallway. Can't waste time.

I wedge the Halligan right at the dead bolt, give it a good tap with my lower palm. A little noise. Not bad, though. Without hesitation I slap the Halligan with the weight of my upper body, breaking the dead bolt out. I slip the bar back into the pack, take out my full face mask, and put it on. I shoulder the pack, then unhinge the stun gun from my belt and enter.

Feels like they got a bit of cool air going inside, but it fucking smells. Combination of skunk weed and somethin' much worse.

There's enough light coming in from the hallway for me to see without my Streamlight.

The kitchen's a disaster. Aged grease caked on pots and pans on top of dirty plates and glassware. I don't wanna know what else. The smell alone is starting to get to me. It comes damn close to some of the worst smells I've ever walked into, and that includes when I was on the job.

I close the broken rear door as best as I can. Once through the hallway and into the living room I have to use my Streamlight. It's bright as shit and can blind someone for a couple of seconds, so I keep it close to my feet and away from the windows. The living room is just as messy and the smell worse. Normal shit like pizza boxes, beer bottles, even a fucking half-empty bottle of Jameson. A flat-screen is on the floor across from a sofa. Looks like it's hooked up, and it sure as hell looks like mine, but I can't be positive. I didn't keep the serial number, and even if I did want to take it, I'm not about to lug that thing down the block. Then again, maybe I'll call Diamond and ask him to come pick me up. Ha.

Bedrooms are what I want to search. The stairs leading to the second floor are creaky. I got my stun gun ready and will drop it quick enough to unholster my weapon if I have to. Once up the stairs I find five doors. The frame of one is narrow enough to be a linen closet or something like that. One door is open, and it leads to a bathroom. Two other doors across from each other at the far end of the narrow hallway are partially open. There's only one door at the near end, and it's closed. A faint light on the inside from under the door. I go there first.

Fucking creaky floors. I'm no ninja. I'm closer to that smell. I know what a dead body smells like, and this is worse. I turn off the Streamlight and stick it back in my front pants pocket.

I try the doorknob. It turns. I open it slow, enough to get a look inside. The smell hits me like an evil spirit taking possession of my body. Fucking overwhelming is an understatement.

A dull light is cast over most of the room by a small nightstand lamp.

An old lady in the queen-size bed, under the covers, just her head poking out, rotting or sleeping—who knows?

Damn.

There's a chrome walker next to her bed, within her reach. On the floor a couple of steps from that are an orange bucket with a small toilet seat on it and a garbage bag that looks like it's full of diapers and used toilet paper.

I can see into the bucket. It's three-quarters full of watery diarrhea shit. That's what I smell, or part of it. Good God.

I need to check if she's alive. I'm stupid that way. I approach the bed to see if she's breathing. I can barely make it out, but it looks like her chest is expanding and contracting. Her breathing is a bit labored. I don't want to check her pulse. Her eyes open. I straighten up and step back.

Her thin, angular, bony face turns to me, but her head doesn't lift off the pillow.

"What the hell you want now?" she says like she knows exactly who I am.

FIFTY-TWO

I'm afraid I'm not who you think I am," I tell her.

She looks at me harder, with deep dark eyes, and I don't know if it's the lighting in here or if she really does have deep dark eyes. Not like death, because there's still glossy life in them. Something like onyx eyes. Knife-into-your-heart eyes.

"You wearing a mask," she says firmly, but without much volume. "Who are you, then? I ain't got nothin' for you here."

I lift my mask over my nose, but not enough to reveal my identity, just my mouth and chin. An odd sort of attempt to make her feel comfortable.

"I'm not here for you, but I can help you if you want."

"Help me?"

"Take you to a hospital."

She spits out a sickly laugh. Coughs a little.

"Hospital? Why?"

"It looks like you need help."

"Even if I do, ain't got no insurance."

"They'd have to admit you if you're sick."

"I ain't sick. I'm dyin'."

"How long you been dyin' for?"

"What?"

"I mean, it seems like you been in this bad environment for a while, having to use a bucket instead of a toilet. Seems you might be better off, even more comfortable, dyin' in a hospital."

"I don't know how long it's gonna take. I ain't God Almighty. I want to stay here in my home. That's all. Now go on. Get out of here. Do what you got to do with those good-for-nothin' boys and let me die in peace. All they is is trouble."

This really fucks things up. I was expecting maybe a sleeping grandma or at the least a livelier one who I'd have to comfortably restrain. Not this shit. I don't have time, and I'm sure as hell not about to pick her up and carry her out of here against her will.

"What do you want me to do about those boys?" I ask.

"Damn. I got to tell you?"

I exhale a "Hmmph" like an uncomfortable chuckle.

"They your grandsons?"

"Not by my choice."

"So this here is your home?"

"Bought and paid for by my deceased husband. You the damn tax man?"

I don't know if she's serious or if that was meant to be a joke.

"You got a phone in here? Cell phone, maybe?" I ask, scanning her nightstand and not seeing anything.

"No. Ain't nobody I got to call or even want to. If I did, you got no worries, so get out now."

"I need to make sure."

She looks up toward the ceiling, closes her eyes.

"Do what you need to do, then go."

How she can she stand the smell in here? Maybe it burned her sinuses out a long time ago.

I'm not going to do anything. I can't. I don't want to lift those covers to see what's under there. I just want to get out of this room. It's too much. I regret even being here.

I exit.

I'm an idiot. I know. If she does have a phone and calls the cops, I hope I'll see them or hear them coming. And the same goes if she calls her grandsons. Somehow I doubt the latter.

I turn on my Streamlight and head to the rooms at the other end of the hall. The one on the left first.

I enter but don't turn on the overheads. The light I carry is more than enough. Smells like lilac. Nose-piercing lilac. I don't know if this is Younger's or Older's room. Doesn't really matter. I'm going to hit both of them.

It's a small room. One closet. No bathroom. Clothes and shoes clutter the floor. I have to walk on them to get around. It does act as padding to muffle the creaky floor.

I check the nightstand first.

Nice 9mm Sig. No holster. Box of ammo, lighters, little baggie of weed, which I pocket. I leave the gun, 'cause it'll be more useful if I leave it here.

I check under the bed to find several shoe boxes, more dirty laundry, and a couple of CDs. I look at the titles. Not mine. I check the shoe boxes. Most of them are empty. Two contain brand-new sneakers, still tagged.

I move around to look under the other side of the bed. Nothing worthwhile, so I lift all sides of the mattress and find only a large chef's knife. I guess that would be the last resort if the gun doesn't work.

I tear the closet apart, find another baggie of weed, maybe an ounce. Slip that into my pack.

Sweat is starting to seep through my shirt now, beading on my forehead. He's got an air conditioner in the window, but turning it on would muffle any sounds from outside.

I pull the blinds up to look out the window. He has the view of Riggs. I don't see their car. Lot of headlights streaming along 14th, both north and south.

I go back to the closet, lift his coats off the hangers, and check the pockets before tossing them on the floor. Couple of live 9mm rounds in one, but that's it. After I go through everything on the shelf, I stand back to survey the room, see if there's anything I missed. Maybe, but I still go to the room across the hall. I can always come back if there's time. I've blown a little over twenty minutes in here already.

Oddly enough, the next room is tidy. He has two laptops with power cords beside them. I check the machines. Not mine.

He has his own bathroom and a larger closet.

I tear the room apart, but all I find is a lot of drug paraphernalia, like assorted zips of all sizes, a scale, and two more guns, one a .357 chrome revolver with duct tape wrapped around the grip and the other an old 9mm Taurus. I leave them.

Shit. Maybe downstairs in the living room, kitchen, or one of the closets. Maybe they're fucking out. I don't want to waste much more time here.

Then something comes to me. It's worth a shot, 'cause you never know. If I were executing a search warrant here with a few other guys, we'd certainly check every room out. So why not?

FIFTY-THREE

I knock lightly on the old lady's door. Nothing, so I rap harder.
Hear a faint "Huh."

I open the door and step in.

"You up, ma'am?"

"I'm never up," she says, as if taking me literally.

"I can't get outta here and deal with those good-for-nothin'
boys until I get what I came here for."

She doesn't respond.

"Do you know what they do to make their money?"

"I may be dyin', but I ain't a fool."

I'm beginning to think she's been dying for a long time.

"How often do they come in your bedroom here?"

"More than I care for."

"Where do they go in here?"

"They take care of the bucket, but not enough."

"Is there any spot they go to often?"

It seems like she's hesitating.

"You said you have no mortgage, right? Home's bought and paid for."

"I said that."

"Do they do anything for you except to empty the bucket on occasion?"

"Sometimes I have to eat."

"Doesn't seem like you eat enough."

"Not hungry most of the time."

She stares back at the ceiling.

"I'd like one of those new big television sets, the ones that look like picture frames."

Fuck, what do I say?

"That won't be a problem," I say, but I think I'm lying.

"They spend a lot of time goin' in and out of my bathroom, even when there are two other bathrooms in this house."

"You see them bringing anything in or carrying anything out?"

"Don't pay attention."

"I won't be long," I tell her, then walk toward the bathroom.

She doesn't say anything.

I step in and turn on the light. It's relatively clean. Old fixtures. Three nicely framed watercolor landscapes on the wall in front of the toilet, a large wooden cross on the wall behind it, and a pink shag bathroom carpet in the middle of the floor.

I look under the sink and see a large wooden jewelry box to one side of the drainpipe, well away from everything else under the sink—old cleaning supplies, couple other newer boxes that contain cutting agents, a small scale, and a hair dryer. I pull the jewelry box out to open it.

"Oh," I say under my breath. "Yes."

What I see has gotta be at least half a kilo of what I'm sure will test positive for cocaine base. It's tightly wrapped. And then beside it are three large rocks and several little ones that probably amount to over a hundred grams of crack.

I grab a tester from my pack. I made sure to stock up on quite a few testers before I left the department. I cut a tiny slice in the wrapper with my knife, pull out just enough on the tip to drop into the plastic testing vial. I close the vial, squeeze it so that another smaller glass vial on the inside cracks, releasing another liquid agent.

Fucking beautiful blue.

I drop the vial back in my pack, then use the knife to dip into a snort for myself.

Fucking shee-it!

Incredible, like it hasn't been stepped on once. I'm sure these boys will cut the hell out of it, though. Damn fine. In fact so damn fine I don't know what to say.

I tear off a little piece of duct tape, which I also carry in my pack, and seal the slit back up. I carefully stuff the half brick into my pack, but not the crack.

I turn the light off as I exit. The old lady looks like she's dead. Probably still awake. I tread lightly and close the door to her room after I step out.

I carry the large amount of crack into the room with a bathroom and slide it under the mattress. I'm assuming Older sleeps there. That amount of crack and the guns in both rooms should be more than enough to fuck them up when I'm done.

I'm walking down the creaky stairs back to the living room when I get another rushing neural-wave crash and, with that, a great idea. It's like a thunderclap. Sort of gives me the chills.

FIFTY-FOUR

I check the time again. Almost 2:00 a.m.

I snort some more of my own shit up, 'cause I don't want to chance spilling any of the new stuff on this filthy carpet. I've never had to resort to picking coke bits off the floor before, and I'm not about to now. So I leave it wrapped and in the backpack, where it's safe.

I find a wooden chair that I wipe off and move close to the front window so I can peek through the blinds and catch them walking toward the house. I got everything I need at the ready—stun gun, zip ties, and duct tape. I have the face mask off until they come. Too damn hot with it on. I'm still wearing my suit jacket, because I don't want to drape it over anything in this pit. Who knows what'll cling to it? I'm definitely going to have to drop the suit and shirt off at the dry cleaner first thing to-morrow, maybe even toss my shoes. Damn—it's like the smell is wrapped around me now. How can these mopes live with that? The thought of that pisses me off even more.

Can't deny that I'm a little excited, mostly because of the blow

I've been snorting. I finish what's left of the whiskey in my sport bottle, secure the top, and stick it back in the pack. I look around the living room, spot the bottle of Jameson I saw when I first came in, get up, and bring it back to the chair. I unscrew the cap to smell it. Seems okay. I click on my Streamlight, shine it into the bottle, and don't notice anything floating in there, so I take a small swig. It's good. Another swig. Better out of glass than plastic. After a couple more drinks I feel more relaxed.

I notice car headlights turning onto Riggs from 13th. The car slows, passes the house. Not them. Got my heart racing again for a second, so I take another drink. All of a sudden it comes to me—what if they bring some girls home or, even worse, a few people to party with? That'll fuck everything up.

I work it out in my head some more, how I'm going to do this. Feels good. Even better is that I have no doubts after I've run it through my head a couple of times.

After 2:30, another car rolls around from 13th.

It looks like their car.

It is their car.

It passes the house, takes a right into the cut that leads to the parking lot on the left and the alley at the rear of their house on the right. I lose sight of them.

Are they going to come through the back?

I put my face mask on, grab my pack, set it at the other end of the sofa, and move the bottle of Jameson to a cleared-off spot on the coffee table, in front of the sofa. I leave the wooden chair where it is. I got the zip ties rolled up and in my back pocket and the stun gun at the ready. I take another peek out the blinds and wait.

A few minutes later they appear from outta the cut, walking toward the house. It's just the two of them. I stand behind the door, against the wall. The door will open inward and block me. I hear one of them chuckling, then talking about some girl. "Fuckin' love to slap that ass. Yeah." Keys rattling, having a hard time getting the key into the lock. "Fuck," one of them says. Sounds like the security gate was unlocked. I hear a key go into the dead bolt. The key turns once to open the dead bolt, then again for the door handle, below it.

The door swings open. I let them enter, close the door. Older sees me first. Tries to swing. I easily knock his hand away and zap him full-strength in the gut with the stun gun, holding it there for a couple of seconds. Younger is still behind, as if he doesn't know yet what's going on. Older falls. Younger tries to run, but I grab the back of his T-shirt, swing him around so he tumbles over the coffee table and against the wall that the flat-screen is sitting in front of. When he tries to get up, I smack him hard with the heel of my hand, sending him some white light. He's out for the count. I notice Older starting to whimper, struggling to regain himself. I walk over to him. It's an effort for him to look up at me, but he does. Obviously scared and confused.

"Yeah, that's right, motherfucker," I say and zap him in the gut again.

FIFTY-FIVE

Big brother and baby brother sitting side by side on the sofa. Duct tape sealing their mouths, their hands zip-tied behind their backs, and feet zipped tightly together at the ankles. A sweet family moment.

I got about five hundred dollars in scrunched-up fives, tens, and twenties, an eight ball of blow, ten smaller quarter-gram zips of blow, a baggie of weed, and two phones out of their pockets. No crack, but then that's probably not something most of those clubbers are looking for.

The coffee table, which was in front of the sofa, is now in the middle of the living room. I'm sitting in the wooden chair facing the both of them. My pack is on the floor beside the chair.

I hit them in their closed eyes with the blinding Streamlight. Back and forth, back and forth...Older reacts to it first, comes to, quickly realizes his predicament. Maybe he's been in this position before. He opens his eyes, then closes them right away. He still struggles, but he only succeeds in knocking his brother so he falls on his side with his head resting on a cushion.

"I'm impressed," I begin. "Neither of you two shit your pants. Especially you, big brother. I double-tapped you with the stun gun."

"Hmmph, hmm, hmmph, hmm…"

I turn the Streamlight off.

"I ain't gonna take that off your mouth right now, so stop that shit or I'll give you some more voltage, but this time right in the ball sack. Got it?"

Nods several times.

"So for now, nodding up and down for yes and side to side for no will do."

No reaction.

"Is that good? Yes or no?"

Nods for yes.

"Hope your brother's okay. He is your brother, right?"

Nods.

The bottle of Jameson is almost empty. I take a nip.

"You got any more of this lying around?"

Shakes for no.

"I'm pretty fucked up anyway, so it's probably best I don't drink any more."

It's like he's almost gonna nod but decides against it.

"That's your grandma you keep up in the smelly room upstairs?"

Nod.

"What the fuck you keep her like that for? She needs to have nurse care, probably daily."

No reaction.

"You can shrug your shoulders if you don't know something."

He shrugs his shoulders.

"That's bullshit."

I stand up and smack him hard on the side of the face.

He does nothin' but blurt out a grunt and some snot with it.

"What kinda grandson are you? Don't answer that. I already know. I've seen your kind before. Sick little shits."

I look at his brother just lying there.

"I'm worried about your brother. He have a glass jaw or somethin'?"

A bit of fear in his eyes, but he shrugs.

"Look at his chest. Does it look like he's breathing?"

Older looks down, takes a couple of seconds, then turns to me again and nods.

"That's good. I don't want it to have to come to that."

I stand up, walk to the sofa, and pull Younger up to a sitting position again. He already has reddish bruising on the left side of his puffy face and a dried-up trickle of blood under his nostril. I tap him lightly with my hand on the uninjured side of his face but don't get a reaction. I tear the duct tape off his mouth so he can breathe better.

His eyes pop open, moving from side to side and up and down like a newborn getting his first look at the new environment. He lets out a gasp.

"Breathe," I tell him. "Calm down and breathe or I'm gonna put you out again. Understand?"

"What the fu—" he tries to say, but before he can I put the duct tape over his mouth again.

"You'll be all right," I tell him.

I want nothing more than to show Younger who I am so he knows I'm the one he ran away from at the record store. I want to, but I won't.

He turns to look at his older brother. Older gives him a look and a slight shake of his head, like *Just fucking shut up* or something.

"I cleaned your pockets out. Looks like you had a good night."

Blank stares.

"Let's get down to business, then."

I slide the coffee table so it's near the chair. I grab my back-pack, but before I sit back down, I slide the right side of my suit jacket back so that it reveals my holstered Glock. I tuck it behind the gun to hold it back. I want to make sure they see that.

They do.

"I know you don't care about Grandma, so I'm not going to even go there," I lie, because I never would dream of hurting her. "I did forget something, though."

I stand back up.

"You two scoot away from each other, give some space between."

They reluctantly obey.

I walk to the other side of the sofa and grab the orange bucket, minus the toilet seat, that I brought down from Grandma's room. I set it on the sofa cushion between them. After that I pick up a coffee mug that I found and set it on the coffee table.

More "Hmmph, hmmph" from both of them.

"Yeah, it stinks. Try not to move around or it'll topple. What direction I don't know."

Younger's cheeks expand outward, like he's gonna gag.

"Don't think about it. You don't wanna drown in your own vomit. Just deep breaths through your nose, hold a couple seconds, and release. That'll relax you."

Odd, but the kid listens. It's funny-looking.

I pick up the eight ball, which I took from Older, and put it on the coffee table. Grab my knife from my pants pocket and flick it open. I use the tip of the knife to pick up a bit of powder. Snort it. Sniff a couple of times.

"Damn, you stepped on that shit."

I seal the baggie back up and put it in my pack. Grab the wrapped half brick out and put it on the table.

"This, on the other hand, is some seriously good shit."

Older is scared but still looks like he's pissed.

Younger is doing his breathing exercises.

"You have any more lying around here?"

Older shakes his head.

"I'm sure you have a little more hidden somewhere, but I'm not gonna be selfish. Well, except for where you keep your money."

No reaction.

"I'm not going to fucking waste time here. Tell me where you stash the money, and I'm gone, never to be seen again. Fuck with me, and you both suffer."

I give them both a second, then stand up and lean over Younger.

"Damn, that fucking smells. I'm gonna take the tape off you, but if you say anything other than what I ask from you, I'll make you drink some of what your grandma left for you, then let you drown in your own puke. Understand?"

Nods several times.

I tear it off, taking some of his peach-fuzz whiskers with it. He whines a bit.

He turns away from the bucket and his brother and heaves thick, yellowish, chunky vomit on the cushion and on himself.

"Ah, that's worse than the bucket," I say. "What the fuck did you eat tonight?"

Couple more heaves, then he's done.

"You good now?"

"Uh-huh," he answers.

"I mean, I been around. Smelled all kinds of awful, but when I stepped into Grandma's room, I about puked, too. So don't feel like you're less of a man."

He nods.

I go into my pack and pull out a pair of latex gloves. I pull my tactical gloves off and zip them up in a side pocket of the pack. Slip the gloves on.

"I got almost five hundred cash outta your pockets and that nice new half a brick, so I know you have a good amount stashed somewhere. Where is it?"

Older turns to Younger, shakes his head several times, tries to speak through the duct tape, but it just sounds silly.

I stand up, take the coffee cup, dip it into the bucket. It's tough, but I bring it out. Some of it dripping down the cup, but I'm careful to keep it from getting on my latex gloves. They both start trying to scoot, but that only shakes up the bucket.

"Sit tight, you shits!" I command.

"C'mon, sir," Younger begs.

I dump the cup on Older's lap. He looks up and away from it. Closes his eyes for a second.

"I'm going to force-feed him the next cup," I tell Younger.

He looks at Older, who looks back down to him, nodding several times.

"In the kitchen! The fucking kitchen," Younger blurts.

"Where else?"

"Nowhere else. I fuckin' swear."

FIFTY-SIX

W here exactly?" I ask.

"You gonna get us killed," Younger tells me.

"What the fuck you think I'm gonna do?" I threaten.

"Gonna get yourself killed."

"By who, your grandma?"

"We got people. People you should be worrying yourself about."

I slap him hard on the face.

"It's you who should be worrying," I tell him.

"We got the police. You fucking can't run from them."

I wanna slap him again but don't. His brother's shaking his head, like *Shut the fuck up.*

"You got the police on your side, huh? Protecting you? You think they're gonna protect you when you're locked up and they're thinkin' you're gonna roll on them? You little moron."

I grab him by the neck, squeeze hard so he has a hard time breathing.

"This is your last chance to tell me what I need to know. This is for real, little man."

It doesn't take him long to figure out I'm telling the truth.

"Behind the stove." Younger coughs.

"Stove. That can be dangerous. Start a fire."

"We never use it."

"Still, not the best place to store your cash."

I take them one by one and put them belly down on the floor. Careful not to get any of Grandma's shit on me. I grab a few more zip ties, then secure their legs to the ties around their wrists. I stick the duct tape over Younger's mouth, walk to the kitchen, click on the Streamlight, and find the stove. I can see skid marks on the vinyl floor where it looks like the stove has been slid out several times. It's an old electric stove.

I grab it from behind and easily slide it out. It's unplugged. Grandma was probably the last one to use it way back when she could walk up and down the stairs.

Secreted inside the open back is a construction-type black trash bag. I pull it out. The opening is tied in a single knot. I open it.

"Fuck," I mumble.

I don't even know how much they have here, but it's a damn good hit. Folded and crumpled-up bills fill almost half the bag. I grab it, but before I go back to the living room I scan the kitchen area with my light. An unopened bottle of Grey Goose is on a counter near the rear door. I pick it up and bring it and the bag back to the living room. Then I set the bag next to my pack and the bottle of vodka on the coffee table.

I push the boys one by one with my foot so they roll over onto their sides, facing me. I rip the tape off Younger and Older, sit back on the wooden chair, grab the bottle, and open it.

"You lied to me, said you didn't have any more alcohol."

"No, sir, you were drinking somethin' different, so we figure…" Younger says.

"I'm kidding. Just shut the fuck up."

I down at least a three-shot swig of vodka.

I need to get more information, but doing so will alert Jasper and the rest of his crew. So the best thing is to let these two mopes think all this is about is hitting them for their stash. When I'm a bit more clearheaded I'll figure out how to get the cops here, maybe help out Grandma along the way.

"Who is your supplier?"

"I—" Younger begins.

"Shut the fuck up!" his brother says. "You already said too much."

I give big brother a swift, hard kick with the toe of my shoe. He hmmphs a release of air.

"You shut the fuck up," I warn him.

"I ain't gonna tell ya who it is, so do what you gotta do," Younger says, suddenly getting brave. "They'll come for you hard, and they'll find you."

"You don't know who you messin' with," Older begins. "We gots people lookin' out for us. People who'll find you."

"You do, now?" I say with a smile, but I believe him.

"Yeah, we do."

They're not gonna talk. I got enough, and they're gonna have to pay for what I got. I need to get the fuck outta here.

How the fuck can they treat their grandma like that, anyway, fucking shitting in a bucket, withering away in her own waste?

Down some more vodka. Bottle's almost half empty. I need another bump. I empty two of their little zips onto the back of my hand and snort it up. One is worth shit. Two almost gets me there, but not quite. I empty another one and whiff that up, too.

Younger and Older are watching, both of them breathing heavy. Such little fucks, thinking they're players, going out clubbing, and all the while their grandma is upstairs stewing in her own feces.

They deserve so much worse.

Older looks direct at me like he knows what's coming. "They even watchin' other police officers, one who lives up the street a bit. Eyes on fucking everybody," he says like he's pleading. "Even this cute little lawyer. No one be safe with them."

The fuck? Leslie?

That more than throws me. My stomach aches, and I want to heave. I want to question him about that but can't give it up that I care. That'd be giving them too much knowledge. They may look stupid, but they're not, especially Older. What the fuck have I gotten myself into?

A deep breath, then I stand up. Spin a little. Regain myself, set the bottle down on the coffee table, pull off the latex gloves, and stuff them into a side pouch of my pack. I replace them with my leather tactical gloves, down some more vodka, then just drop the bottle to the floor. The thud echoes through the room.

I walk over to them, hovering over Younger.

"C'mon, now," he begs. "You got what you came for."

"I realized there was more. And you said, 'Do what you gotta do,' right?"

I clock Younger on the same side of the face as before, but with more force. Yeah, hard as shit. I hear something crack, and I know it isn't my knuckles. He goes out. Like nothin'. Split his cheek open. Blood oozes from between the folds of skin and down, dripping off his chin and onto the side of his neck.

I drag the huffing and puffing Older by the neck of his T-shirt toward the center of the living room, away from his little brother. I kick him hard in the gut. Snot shoots out his nostrils. More of Grandma's shit spills off his lap. I don't want any of that on me, so I'm careful.

I kick him again, and again, then one more time, even harder. No other position he can put himself in 'cause of how he's zip-tied together. He has to take it like I give it. I start to punch him in the face. I don't know how many times. He's bleeding through his nose. After one more punch my head's spinning. He's out, but I kick him again. I straighten myself up and feel the house tip. My damn heart's trying to beat its way through my chest. I was somewhere else for a minute.

The room steadies. I look at the both of them, walk over to Younger, and decide to kick him in the gut, too, but only twice. Still hard. I have to sit in the wooden chair to catch my breath. I notice the bottle of vodka that I dropped. At least one more swig left that didn't spill out of the bottle. I pick it up and take it, set the bottle on the coffee table.

"Fuck," I say to myself. "Oh, fuck."

Did I just kill them?

I don't want to know, so I just stand, pick up the shit bucket, and walk up the stairs to return it to the old lady.

She's sleeping. I place the bucket near her bed and put the toilet seat quietly back on it. I gotta leave it like this, the way I found it. Mostly full.

I go in the room where I stuffed the crack under the mattress and retrieve it along with one of the semiautos.

I walk back down the stairs, still feeling a bit racy. I pull my knife out of my pocket and flick it open. I try not to look at their faces as I cut the zip ties that bind their feet to their hands, then I cut the rest of them off, freeing their hands and legs. I shove the gun under Younger's body and toss the bag of crack on the sofa near the vomit.

I pick up my pack and the bag of money and exit the way I came in.

FIFTY-SEVEN

I have to get to Leslie. Fuck. I gotta get there now.

When I get in my car I turn it on for the air. I'm too fucked up to drive. Too fucked up to walk. Here I am with a backpack filled with more coke than I've seen in years and a black construction bag almost half full with dirty money. It'd be enough to get me in federal court. Still, I have to get to Leslie's house.

What did I do? What the hell did I do?

Damn. I haven't been this fucked in a long, long time. Close my eyes, and the whole world spins. Burns to keep my eyes open. I adjust the vents so the cool air hits my face. That helps.

I give myself a bump to clear my head.

I back up to wedge my way out of the space. I hit the car behind me. "Shit." I do the same to the car in front. I manage my way out, though, and drive.

Fucking autopilot.

And like time stopped, I'm on her block. How the fuck that happen? I drive by her house. Slow. Front door's not busted in.

I park alongside a fire hydrant.

Something I gotta do before I go in. Can't let too much time pass or everything I did at Riggs will go to fuck.

I call 911 on my burner.

Dispatcher answers.

I act as drunk as I really am: "I live on the thirteen hundred block of Riggs Street...Northwest...I saw two guys with guns run into the house across from me. Just now...yes..."

I give the address.

"It was too dark. An old lady lives there...no...I work nights...I heard screaming. I think the old lady is in serious trouble...no. She needs help!" I even let myself sob once I'm so crazy. I disconnect.

I think this is the drunkest I've ever been. Hope I didn't screw up just now, but I had to get the police there for that old lady's sake, and I can only pray I didn't kill one or both of those punk-ass thugs.

I down two Klonopin with what I have left of my bottled water. That should ease my mind a bit. Too late to worry now. Shit, even in the fucking messed-up state I'm in, I know I wasn't fucked up enough to leave anything on the scene that can connect to me.

They'll find the old lady. See the state she's in, and, I hope, do the right thing. I did my part.

I check the time on my phone: 5:30 a.m. Fuck.

I snatch up my pack and run to her house. I have to ring the door-bell three times before I hear her on the other side of the door.

Gotta be looking through the peephole.

She unlocks the dead bolt, then the handle. Door opens.

She's wearing a white bathrobe I bought her when we were at Greenbrier a few months ago over her pajamas. The air-conditioning feels like a godsend through the open doorway.

"What the hell, Frankie?" She looks me over. "Are you all right?"

"I needed to make sure you're okay."

"Why? What are you talking about?"

"I think I really fucked up," I say, but I meant to say, "I think I'm really fucked up." Before she can answer I spit out, "I think I'm really fucked up." And hope she's too tired to realize.

"What happened? Come in."

I walk in. She closes and dead-bolts the door behind me. Locks it.

She looks at my backpack.

"You were working?"

"Been a long night of surveillance."

"You're drunk as shit."

I'm still spinning bad, so I guess I am.

"Maybe a little. I'm...I'm sorry. I had to come over. Make sure you're okay."

"You said that. Why would you think I'm not?"

"I don't..." I try to focus, but it's impossible.

"Get in here," like an order.

I stumble in and follow her to the living room.

"You smell terrible. Did you soil yourself?"

I check with my hand.

"No."

"Maybe you should take a shower."

"Don't think that's possible right now. I got clean clothes in my pack." I don't know why I said that, because I don't.

"You take the sofa, then. I'll get you covers. Don't go on the sofa until I get the sheets. And try not to pass out."

I don't even know what she said.

She walks toward the hallway and the linen closet, and I fall into a reclining position on the sofa, dropping my pack and the bag beside my feet. I close my eyes and concentrate hard on trying to control the spins.

FIFTY-EIGHT

Feels like a faucet running in my head. Maybe tinna…what the fuck's it called?

"Frank!" I hear but can't place it.

Eyes feel glued shut.

Try to open them.

See red through eyelids.

Light.

Tinnitus.

"Frank!" Again.

Leslie?

Eyes open.

She's standing over me.

I must have fucking blacked out. I don't remember shit or how I got here.

Leslie is fully dressed. What the fuck?

I'm on her sofa, covered with a soft blanket, and my head is on a pillow. Shoes off.

"Frank, it's time for you to get up."

There's firmness in her voice. Not something pleasant.

I remember where I was before here.

Fuck.

Did I say that out loud?

"Leslie."

I push myself up to a sitting position. Still a bit light-headed. Pants are still on, and I'm wearing the T-shirt that was under my regular shirt. My belt is off, along with my gun, mags, and handcuffs. I turn to notice they're on the end table. The blanket is over my legs. Faucet turned off in my head, but left me with a throbbing headache.

"What time is it?"

"It's almost four in the afternoon."

"Damn. Are you kidding me? I slept that hard?"

"I let you sleep because I've been trying to figure out how to approach this."

Approach?

"Approach what?" I say, still groggy. "Oh, last night. I don't even know how I got here. Sure as hell hope I didn't drive."

I have to cup my hands over my face, rub my eyes. I look at her after.

"A tough night on surveillance. Must have gotten stupid with what I had left in a bottle of Jameson. So much going on."

"Yes."

"I don't remember the last time I got that drunk. I think I blacked out." I shoot her my best playing-dumb look.

I got a feeling that won't help, because I finally notice my backpack on the floor at the other end of her coffee table, not where I left it, and the cocaine test vial that I used at the house on Riggs—still filled with bright blue liquid—also on the coffee table along with the white shirt I wore, now spread out as if to display the blood that's heavily soaked the right sleeve, and the bloodied tactical gloves. Then, on the floor between the sofa and the coffee table, my brown shoes, the right one with dried-up spots of blood soaked into the fine leather. *Displaying evidence?*

What can I say other than "I can explain"?

FIFTY-NINE

I didn't dare handle all the other contraband I found," Leslie says.

Feels like a large-gauge bit drilling through my frontal lobe now. I need Advil——coffee at the least. I don't ask her, though. I pull the blanket off my legs and straighten myself up on the sofa. I notice my socks. I wore the black ones with yellow polka dots. Happy socks. I feel embarrassed.

"Will you let me explain?"

"Sure. Why not? Is it going to be a good story?"

"It's all related to the case I've been working."

"The blood on your clothing, the weed—oh, and the nearly half a kilo of cocaine? I know I'm just a defense attorney now, but I used to be a cop like you, so I remember what coke looks and smells like."

"You said you were going to let me explain."

Her lips tighten. She backs up and sits on the armchair to my left. She lifts her hands, palms up, like *Let's go*.

I bow my head for a second but realize that's what guilty people do, so I look up at her directly.

"I'm sorry I lied, but I have been looking into my cousin's homicide and burglary at my house."

She's giving me that look you get from defense attorneys when you're on the stand and they don't believe a word you're saying.

"Actually, Frankie? I don't want to hear this. I can't—"

"I got a possible suspect for the burglary, maybe even Jeffrey's homicide, and was able to identify one of the fencing locations where the burglar went to trade stolen property for narcotics, and so, you know, I...I went there."

"What do you mean, 'went there'? And why wouldn't you take that information to the police?"

"C'mon, Leslie. Do you really want to know that?"

"Did you hurt them? Wait—what am I thinking? Don't tell me. In fact I don't want to hear any more about this."

"I didn't kill anybody, if that's what you're getting at," I say with all optimism. "That's what matters, right? I just wasn't thinking straight. Jeffrey, dead in my kitchen. I got information that you might be in danger. I got emotional. I took their shit is all and got in a little fight with one of them. I'm gonna turn it over to Hurley. Face the consequences." I was telling the truth until then. Why'd I have to go there?

"Emotional? Took their shit? And why would I be in danger unless you put me there?"

"I need to clear my head, then I can explain better."

"You burglarized someone's house. Like some vigilante. Are you kidding me?"

"It's not like that."

I want to tell her about the grandma. Bring some humanity into it. She doesn't give me a chance.

"You're not rational. It's like we're having the same conversation we had months ago when you brought the kidnapped girl to my office instead of to the police. But this is far worse, Frank. You brought this shit into my *house*."

"I'm going to take it to Hurley. Don't worry."

"I said I don't want to hear any more. Good God, Frankie." She cradles her head, and I wonder if she's going to break down and cry. She looks back at me. No tears. "I've noticed a change in your behavior over the past few months. I mean, is it the alcohol or is it something more, like that shit in your backpack? I've had my suspicions. I'm not stupid. I mean, cocaine test kits? Why the hell would you need those? You're retired. You don't work narcotics anymore."

"I've had those vials forever."

"Really? So why did you feel it was necessary to test that coke?"

"Force of habit."

"Fuck you."

I hesitate before saying, "Give me a break." Which is all those defense-attorney ex-cop eyes have to see. Hesitation. I know it. I know she knows it, but still, I can't admit that to her. Ever. "Why the hell would you search through my shit anyway?"

"You said you had clean clothes in the bag. You smelled bad, so I was going to get them out for you. I didn't expect that kind of laundry."

"You might be in danger, Leslie."

"That's bullshit, Frank, and you know it. Right now, you're the only one who makes me feel threatened. Besides, I can take care of myself, whatever it is you got yourself—and maybe me—into."

I know she can, probably better than I could.

"Damn. I'm sorry, Leslie. Really. I mean it. It's not what you think, though. Stupid drunk is all. I blacked out. I'm not some low-life criminal. Fuck. I don't even know if you're in danger or if I dreamed it."

"You need to leave, Frank. Turn that shit over to the police. Dump it. I really don't care, but you have to take it now and go."

"I can't leave like this, Les. I..." I want to say I love her, but I can't. But I do. Love her.

"Get dressed and go. Please."

"Can we talk later? When my head is more together and I can explain it better? I can't even remember all that happened."

"No. I don't see how. You're not who...you're dangerous, Frank. Stay away."

"What are you going to do?" I ask like a paranoid dope. It's the last thing I should ask her.

"You don't have to worry."

"I didn't mean it like that, Les."

"This never happened, Frank, because we never happened."

Shit.

SIXTY

Fuck, is this broken. All of it.

I don't know where my car is, so I use the key fob, here it chirp up the street. I drag myself there.

Ticket on the windshield.

I see the black bag of money in the backseat. What an opportunity for a theft from an auto. Would have made some fucking mope's year.

At home, I can't dump the shit, much as I want to. Instead I scrape a few grams off the good coke, wrap the big one up again, and stash it along with the money and weed in my stash wall. I have to press all the air out of the garbage bag and tie it tight to get it to fit. I clean the speckles of blood off my leather shoes and wash my tactical gloves. I squirt the white shirt with stain remover and drop it in the washer.

I know Leslie won't call the police. That is, she won't unless she sees something on the news about two young drug dealers who were killed during the course of a home invasion.

Fuck, I hope I didn't kill them.

I check the local news app on my phone. Don't find anything related to Riggs, so I google it. Nothing. That's a relief.

I snort some of the good blow. It makes this body right and fine. But not what's going on in my head. It can't be over with Leslie. I convince myself that all she needs is time, but then I realize how naive that sounds, given what she discovered and what I told her.

Damn fucking damn damn. So stupid.

I need a drink. Never vodka, though. Never again.

SIXTY-ONE

I wake up to the sound of intermittent tapping on my bedroom window. I grab hold of my gun and walk toward it. Listen.

Another tap. Makes me jump back a little. Just a little. My bedroom is on the second floor, and there's no way someone can scale up the wall, so I'm thinking someone's tossing something like acorns at it.

Another tap.

Pistol held to my thigh, I move forward and peek out but don't see anything.

That is, until a large cicada smacks into my window, making the same sound.

Blunt-headed dope.

I let the curtain fall back to a closed position, return to my bed, and set the gun back on the nightstand.

No sense in trying to fall back asleep, so I go downstairs and make coffee. Take my gun with me.

Stomach aches raw with emptiness and worry, but I'll need something more than damn grapefruit to satisfy it. The acidity will tear me apart. I drop a couple pieces of wheat bread in the toaster. I use honey instead of butter. That'll do me for the remainder of the morning.

I dress down; lightweight khakis and a T-shirt that's large enough to conceal my firearm and the magazine pouch attached to my belt.

I need to do something. I can't sit around all day and mope, 'cause that'll just send me on a bad binge.

After I recover, I get in the car and drive to Riggs Street.

I pass the alley north of Riggs, rear of Grandma's house, and notice a marked cruiser parked behind it, blocking the alley. I make the right on Riggs and see another cruiser parked along the curb in front. They've secured the residence.

I slide the passenger window down while pulling out my wallet. So I don't spook him, I roll up beside him with my wallet extended toward the window, opened to reveal the badge. He takes notice, rolls down his window. I slip my wallet back in my pocket and lean toward the passenger window.

"Hey, Officer. Frank Marr. I'm a retired DC police detective."

"You look too young—"

"Took an early out. Better opportunities, you know."

"I get that. Wait—I heard of you," he says with a smile.

"That can't be good," I say jokingly, but not really.

"No. I was in the academy with Joe Hurley."

"Hurley. Of course."

Why would he talk about me?

"We were at the FOP a couple of days ago. He mentioned you because of all that went down at your house, and a stolen gun."

"Fuck. So now everyone knows?"

"Naw, it ain't like that. He was just putting the word out is all. Had some possible suspect named."

"Graham Biddy."

"That's right."

"You know him?"

"Never heard of him."

"They recovered the gun, you know."

"That's a good thing," the officer says.

"Not for the guy whose body it was found on."

"Shit."

"No worries. Just another mope. By the way, the reason I stopped is I was passing by on my way to work and noticed the unit in the alley rear of this house, and now you in front. Anything in the neighborhood I need to worry about?"

"Home invasion gone bad. Drug-related. Back door was pried open, so we have to secure the scene until it gets fixed."

"Man, I worked narcotics when I was on the job and never had anything come up for this block on the radar."

"Fuck, man, every block in this city's got something."

"You said gone bad, though."

"Huh?"

"You mentioned it was a home invasion gone bad."

"Bad enough for the two fucking brothers to get the holy shit kicked outta them. Unfortunately, they're still breathing."

I chuckle.

"Damn, that is unfortunate," I say, feeling just the opposite. "So now I suppose they're in the hospital taking taxpayers' money 'cause they're not insured."

"Got that right. Fucking waste of my time, too."

"Sometimes I think it'd be easier if we just sat back and let them kill themselves off. Save this city a hell of a lot of money."

"Hmmph" is his odd way of chuckling.

"Doesn't look like a drug house."

"It really wasn't. Some old lady owns it. The house was taken over by her grandsons. Pretty sure it was her grandsons, anyway.

I sure as hell wouldn't want to live in there now, though. They lived like animals in there. Worst scene I been on in a long time. Poor old lady was forced to live in her own shit. Smells worse than death."

"Damn. Well, at least she's in a better place," I say, fishing.

"Well, yeah. The hospital. That is, if you consider Howard Hospital a better place."

This time I spit out a "Hmmph."

SIXTY-TWO

I feel good about the old lady now that she's getting care. It doesn't justify what I did—and I mean beating the shit outta those hog-tied brothers, nothing else. I don't need to defend the things I do because of necessity, especially when the only ones made to suffer are the bad guys. And it's not like I've never beaten the shit—or sometimes, usually by accident, something worse—outta anybody before this. It's just that I rarely lose control like that. Doesn't make sense. It has to be the fucking vodka on top of everything else I had. I'll know soon how bad I made things, and I'm talking for the police.

That's enough.

I ain't gonna rip myself over this shit anymore. It's done. Not with Leslie, though. I won't accept that. I don't care if she said what she said, that "we never happened." She didn't mean it. I know she didn't. She probably meant it then, but she won't hold on to it.

I've known Leslie for going on eighteen years. We went through the academy together before she got her law degree and quit the department. We stayed in touch even after that. It took years, but we stepped up to something more than a cozy friendship. We go back. She'd never give me up. And I know that for a fact.

I grab my phone, hit Leslie's name in the recent calls. It rings, goes into voice mail.

I say, "I know there's nothing I can say right now, but I need you to know I had my reasons and it goes beyond what happened at my house." I want to tell her about the old lady, but I don't want something like that recorded.

Instead I lie. "I've already taken care of everything. I turned it over. Lot of explaining to do." It's almost as if I expect her to pick up, but this is her cell, and I know she saw my name as the caller and let it ring through. I simply say, "I always run to you, Les. I'm so sorry." Then I disconnect.

I gotta get my head right, get back in the game or just give it up altogether. That's the smart thing to do. Give it up and get the fuck outta town. But I don't work like that. Never have. I got this far.

I light a smoke, try to figure my next move. Halfway through the cigarette I remember Younger and Older's cells. I find them in my pack and hope they have enough power left so I can search their contacts, texts, and whatever else looks good. One's an iPhone, and the other looks like a prepaid cell. Really simple. Probably their burner. Of course the iPhone is locked. No way I'm gonna find my way through that. Only problem with a burner is that most of the smart guys use them once or twice and then toss them.

I power it up. Still has some juice left, and it's not locked. No contact names are saved. Just numbers. I scroll through them. Most have a 202 area code, and a few of them have an area code for Maryland. I count twenty-five numbers, so it's a relatively new phone.

I get my notebook and a pen out of my pack, set the notebook on the end table.

I start at the top and tap the number to call it. Not in service. I continue. The answers I get are either "Yeah" and "Talk to me" or the numbers aren't in service and there's no answer. Not looking so good, but maybe I can get my girl Tamie Darling, one of my old CIs and someone I still work with on occasion, to call some of these numbers and try to get in a conversation with whoever answers. Never know. It might lead to something.

I dial another 202 number. It rings.

"Jasper," a familiar voice answers. I hang up in a hurry.

Fuck. I think I just made my day.

SIXTY-THREE

How the hell do I give all this information up without implicating myself in the home invasion at Riggs Street?

I can't. I won't.

I decide to go fishing, so I give Hurley a call.

"What's up, Frank?" he answers.

"I met a friend of yours earlier. Didn't catch his name, but he was sitting on a house on Riggs, and he told me that you talked to him about my case."

"Valdez. Good dude. He knows that area well, so I was hoping he might help get Biddy identified. That invasion on Riggs was on a whole other level. What brought you there?"

"Going south on Thirteenth, headed downtown, and saw a cruiser in back and your boy in front. Thought maybe it was a burglary and maybe they had a suspect. As you know, I only live a few blocks from there."

"Yeah, one burglar is usually good for dozens of hits within a few blocks, but unfortunately that was something else. Some sort of retaliation or drug-related home-invasion."

"That's what I heard."

"I ended up with that case, too."

"You're a one-man unit."

"Until my body can't take it anymore."

"You have a ways to go. By the way, you and Millhoff get a chance to go clubbing yet?"

"Clubbing?" He doesn't get it right away. "Oh, right. Yeah, we've been there more than once."

"What about Jasper?"

"You mean we going to turn him in for working his part-time?"

"Something like that."

"Hell, no. I could care less. Neither could Millhoff. Besides, he's good to have there because of the two decedents who're connected to that place."

"I have a source who said you might want to look into Jasper and that big guy he works there with. Said they had a little something going on the side in that club."

"Seriously? Like what?"

"Like drugs, maybe getting a cut. Maybe more. Could be a connection to the body on Rhode Island and my cousin."

"Damn. Can I meet with your source?"

"I'll ask."

"Okay. You hear anything else, you call. You're still one of us first."

"I know that, brother. You don't have to keep saying it."

Okay, now what?

Sixty-Four

I pick Tamie Darling up at the usual spot, a vacant lot near Howard University, where I park behind two detached semi-trailers. Darling is one of the best CIs I've worked with. When I was partnered with Al Luna at Narcotics we signed her up as a special employee. That had to be ten years ago. Doesn't matter that she smokes crack. That's something we never talk about, but it's obvious. The cigarettes and the crack have a way of sticking to the body like perfume. Biddy ain't there yet, but he will be. For Tamie, it's all you can smell.

She walks toward my car from the front, carrying a large, probably fake Gucci purse and wearing a summer dress with floral patterns that falls to her knees. It's a larger size than she needs so it'll hide her narrow, bony figure. She lifts the strap that falls from her shoulder, drops and snuffs out a cigarette before entering the front door and gliding in.

I greet her with "What's up, sweetheart?"

"Same ol', same ol'," she says with a sweet voice. That's why I use her often and pay her so well. She is *good* on the phone, and I have to do these sort of okeydokes a lot in my line of work. More when I was a cop.

I light a cigarette. She does the same. We both crack the windows a bit.

"Stifling out there," she says.

"That's why most of my work is in the car or at home these days."

After a deep drag she turns to me, blows the smoke toward the roof of the car. Doesn't matter. It still bounces off and curves down to hit me in the face. I hold my breath, but in a way so she can't tell.

"Why doesn't your boy Luna call me no more? He find him a new girl?"

"Seriously doubt that. There's no one like you."

She has a deep-throated smoker's laugh.

"Department's probably got him caught up on quick buy busts, shit like that. I'm sure he'll get in touch with you, though."

"Damn hope so. I need that money. I got expenses."

"I understand that. I'll take care of you well for a short one today." I realize how that sounds after I say it. So does she.

"That sounds good, baby," she says in her sexiest voice.

It does sound sexy, but she sure doesn't look the way she sounds. Doesn't matter if she did. Nothing would ever come of it. I'd never allow myself to carry that kind of extra baggage.

"You just tell Luna to call me, honey, or I'll have to start looking other places."

"I'll do that, Tamie."

I take another drag and flick the cigarette out the window before it's finished. I grab the burner cell that has Jasper's number on it. I use my throwaway cell for the call.

"So this is easy stuff," I begin. "All I want you to do is call this number, and if a man answers, just say, "Willy?" like you know him really well. That's all. I want to know if his first name is Willy."

"Simple enough."

"Let me fill you in on a couple of details."

"Okay."

"He works at a club."

"What club?"

"Come on now, Darling. You know better than to ask that."

"Just testing."

"Right. He works at a DC club. You don't have to remember the name of it, only that he runs the door and that's how you met. It was on a Thursday a few weeks ago. He gave you his card. If you get him in a conversation, just keep it going."

I hand her a clean yellow notepad and a pen.

"Write down any questions you might need to know, like about the club or something. Don't go fishing. I just want to know if his first name is Willy. That's all. No drug talk or anything like that. Once you get that, just hang up."

"What if he gets to really talkin'?"

"Like what, wanting to get together with you?"

"Something like that."

"I don't give a shit about that. Just hang up. I wanna rattle him."

"Well, that's easy enough, then."

I tap in the number and hand her the phone.

I hear a male voice answer after a couple of rings.

"Hi, Willy," she says in her best voice.

I lean toward Darling to see if I can hear him, but I can't.

"Tamie...you gave me your card, Willy, a few weeks ago. I think it was a Thursday...yes, Tamie, sweetie. I know you remember. Don't play hard to get."

Darling turns toward me, shakes her head like it's not looking good, then I don't hear him talking at the other end. She disconnects.

"Hung up on me," she says.

"Well, what'd he say?"

"He asked for my name, said he doesn't remember giving his card to any girls at the club. Then he said 'I don't know you' and hung up."

"So he never told you his name wasn't Willy?"

"No, not once. In fact it sounded to me like I was talking to this Willy guy."

"That's good enough for me."

I reach for my wallet, pull out eight twenties, which is way more than she should get, but I know she needs it.

I hand it to her, then say, "You're good to go, then. Thanks."

She takes the money. Doesn't count it, just slips it into her big purse.

"Can you help me out just a little more, Frankie? I really do got bills."

"Not gonna go anywhere else, is it?" I ask, even though I know it probably is.

"No, sweetie. I swear."

I count out another hundred, add an extra twenty. Hand it to her.

"I'll make it up to you. Don't worry."

"I ain't worried, Tamie. I'll call Luna for you."

She opens the door, smiles at me before stepping out and shutting the door. I watch her walk away, her tiny ass moving right to left like she's trying to impress. Makes me smile.

SIXTY-FIVE

On the way home I stop at a corner where an old Hispanic guy is selling fresh mangoes from a cart.

"Buenas tardes," I say.

"Buenas tardes, señor."

"Un mango, por favor."

He grabs one from a basket, lightly squeezes it for freshness, expertly peels the skin, and carves it into slices with a large knife.

He drops the slices in a Ziploc bag, squirts hot sauce on them. Seals it and shakes it up.

"Three dollar, please."

I pay him. He hands it over to me.

"Gracias," I say.

When I get home I drop my pack on the sofa and head to the kitchen, where I sit at the breakfast table and enjoy the spicy-sweet mango. Gotta put something in this stomach. Latinos know about spice. It's actually good on a hot day like this. Cools down your body temperature. Works for me, at least, and the mango has nutritional value. Lord knows I need as much of that as I can get.

Now I have to figure out what the hell to do. I don't like keeping this information from my friends on the department. It's valuable. How can I reveal it without giving myself up? I'm not ready to do that. Don't think I'll ever be ready to do that. I've grown accustomed to this life. Hell, even enjoy it. Most of it. The ups, not the downs.

Leslie.

Shit. That crept right into my head. I have to let it go. I have to finish this. Figure how to play it out. After that, I'll think about how to fix what I fucked up.

I decide to give Diamond a call, but it goes straight to an automated message. I don't leave one back. Is that fuck avoiding me? Damn well better not be.

I know now that I can't keep the police out of this. The easy thing to do would be to kill Jasper, but I can't do that. I certainly can have fun thinking about it, though.

The academy always said that drugs, money, and women are the most common things that take a cop down. I can attest to one of them, but only because I like it for myself. I don't deal, but I do steal. So I guess I got two—drugs and money. Leslie is a good person, so she doesn't fall into the academy's category of the wrong woman.

What's Jasper's jones?

I'm betting it's as simple as money—and mental illness.

Cell rings.

Hurley.

"What's up?"

"I need to talk to your source."

Shit.

"Not that easy. Tryin' to find him, see if he's willing."

"Can you tell me how involved he is?"

"Heavily."

"Can you tell the source, without making promises, that we might be able to help him if he cooperates?"

"Wait—what? So you know Jasper's dirty?"

"That's the information we're getting, too."

"How'd you find that out? I mean, I know you're a great detective and all—"

"Let's just say I had an enlightening hospital interview."

Damn, he got Repo or his older brother or both to roll. I don't remember much of that night, but I know I went right to the edge with it. Maybe softened them up a bit for Hurley. Literally. From the outside in.

"How did you find this source, Frank?"

"Hoofing it, just like the old days."

"Is he a burglar? Is it *your* burglar?"

"No," I lie, as usual.

"It would be really helpful if we had another cooperator."

So he only got one of the brothers to talk. And yes, when you're working something like this, the assistant US attorney always likes two independent sources of information. Not that he can't work it with one. It just makes the information more reliable having two.

"I can talk to him and see, but it's going to be tough. Why can't you just put a wire on whoever you have?"

"That's something we might do, but he's going to be in the hospital for at least another week."

Damn. I really did lose control.

"I need your source, Frank. This involves some heavy shit."

I think that's the first time I ever heard Hurley cuss.

"Please tell me you got something good on my cousin's homicide," I say.

"We'll know soon enough. Got a couple of guns out of the house on Riggs. One is the same caliber used in the shooting on Rhode Island Avenue. Firearms Examination is on it."

That's probably why the kid is rolling. He knows that gun and possibly the other one are gonna come back on him.

Fuck. Do something really stupid like I did that night, and it looks like it might pay off. I don't want to jinx it, so I stop thinking about it.

May as well cast the line all the way out, see what bites.

"What about me?" I ask, sighing. "I'm getting a feeling that in some weird way I'm tangled up in all this shit. Something having to do with Jasper. Maybe I was just in the wrong place at the right time."

"What do you mean?"

"When I went to surveil my cousin at the club. I don't know. It's crazy."

"We're keeping the file on your house in the same case jacket as these boys on Riggs now. Does Jasper know where you live?"

"I don't know. I think so. He pulled some off-the-wall stunt using his rookie to stop me near my house a couple nights ago. Told his rookie I might be a robbery suspect, but Jasper stayed in the car. Let's just say I had some words with him about his training methods."

"You did something to piss Jasper off."

"Wait—why? No."

"Frankie, I know you."

"I would have told you if I did. In fact I've been struggling to figure that out. Only conversation I had with him was at the nightclub he works, and that was just casual. He even bought me a drink."

"He's buying stolen property," Hurley begins. "That's what the kid in the hospital says. Who knows? Maybe he did have your house hit because he knew there'd be a gun in there. Maybe it *is* coincidence you were surveilling your cousin and all the time he was doing business with Jasper, too. Maybe he thought you were nipping at him."

"Wouldn't that be something? Listen, I'll talk to my source again, see if I can persuade him to do the right thing."

"Let me know. I'm always here."

"Later, Joe," I say.

"Later."

I disconnect.

Jasper's a big guy. Bigger than I am, but he's take-out-food big. Still, he's intimidating enough to dissuade me from going hand to hand with him if it ever comes to that. Wyatt is bigger, though, and it ain't from takeout. He's the one I have to worry about. When it comes to dirty cops, it's not something I want to handle alone. As much as I might want to, there's just too much that can go wrong. It's not like those books or shows.

I feel better that Hurley is on it now. My head is clearing up a bit, and some blow will help even more. After I snort one up, it's clear to me that I have to convince Biddy and Diamond that the only way they're going to get out from under this mess is to co-operate with the police. That means making another trip to Old Town.

Sixty-Six

I park in a space on the street and walk a couple of blocks to the motel. The streets are well lit in this area. The continuous shrill of the cicadas is starting to drive me crazy. Day after day, night after night. I know it's supposed to be some kinda love song, but all I hear in it is frenzy.

I don't see Diamond's cab in the lot.

There's a light on in Biddy's room, though. I knock on the door.

Knock again. Harder. No response.

I listen for movement or anything else, maybe the TV, but nothing. I wait a couple minutes just in case he's in the bathroom, knock again.

I call him on my phone, but it goes straight to voice mail. Call Diamond and get the same thing.

I walk to the motel office, peek through the window before I enter. It's not the old man. Some young twentysomething guy with a disturbing hair bun, if that's what you even call it. I enter.

He looks up from his iPhone.

"Can I help you?"

"I hope so," I say. "A friend of mine is supposed to be staying here for a week. I came here to take him to dinner, but there's no answer at the door. I hope I was knocking on the right door. If I give you his name, can you tell me if he's still here? Maybe he went to another motel."

"I can tell you if someone is here but not give out the room number."

"Well, I guess that's good enough. His name is Robert Givens, but he also might be checked in under his uncle's name, Robert Diamond."

He checks the computer.

"Yes, he's still checked in."

"Both of them?"

"No. Just Mr. Givens."

"Appreciate it. Thanks," I say, then exit.

It's gonna be a lot of driving tonight, but I decide to head to Diamond's house. It's late enough on a weekday for him to be home, which would mean he didn't take my advice and get outta Dodge City for a while.

Traffic isn't fighting me. The heat index, along with the humidity, is probably keeping most people indoors.

I get to his house in reasonable time.

No cab in front, but he usually parks in back. I take the cut and the alley that leads to the rear of his home.

His cab is parked in the small space behind his house. I make my way back to his street and have to drive a block up to park.

I take my pack, because the way things have been going, I'll probably end up a theft-from-auto victim if I leave it.

A few steps to his stoop. It's clean, well kept. Looks like there's a lamp on, maybe in the living room area. I ring the doorbell, rap on the door several times after.

Again, nothing. I try one more time, and when there's no answer, I decide to walk around to the back.

Lighting on this block is not like it is in Old Town. Certainly not in the alley. I walk carefully so I don't run into anything and don't get run into. Don't want to attract unnecessary attention by using my Streamlight. But once I get behind the house, I take out my Streamlight to light up the interior of the cab. I check the driver's-side door. It's locked.

I move toward the wooden stairs that lead to a back deck and the rear door. Before my foot lands on the first step, I see a shoe, toes up, sticking out from under the stairs. I already know when I step back what I'm gonna find.

Training has a way of kicking in at moments like this.

I step back slowly, around to the side of the stairs, and light the area under the deck, careful of what might be behind me or in the darkness near the corner of the house.

The light shines on a body.

It's Diamond.

His eyes are partly open, like he submitted to the inevitable. Throat's cut. Clean, all the way across. Opens up just under his chin a bit. Thin red lips with a wide smile. Fuck. Moist blood soaked into the shirt from the chest down. Bled out fast. I still kneel down, see if his chest expands. I check his carotid.

Damn. He's dead, but I already knew that standing over him.

Son of a bitch. Where's Biddy?

I light the area behind me, make sure I didn't mess up the crime scene. No signs of a struggle.

I can't stop looking at his face.

Fuck, old man.

"What the fuck did you do, Diamond?" I say quietly.

SIXTY-SEVEN

Why didn't Diamond listen to me?

First unit on the scene is an old-timer I know from back in the day. Has to have more than thirty years on by now. Sam O'Connell. Second responder is a female officer who I don't know, but she must have a little time on to be working midnights 10-99.

Blue, red, and white strobing lights pulse through the alley. The two cruisers' spotlights are directed at Diamond's backyard and the crime scene. Everything is visible. From where I'm standing in the alley, I don't see signs of a struggle.

Some neighbors have stepped out to their back patios and yards to watch.

The EMT on the scene already confirmed his death. It was obvious at first sight, but the boy still has to follow procedure. The EMT steps back into the ambulance with his partner.

"Homicide should be arriving any minute," O'Connell tells me.

"I'm going to call Joe Hurley. He's working with Millhoff at Homicide, but this is something they need to know about."

"What the fuck you get yourself into, Marr?"

"More than I bargained for, that's for sure."

"Damn. And I thought you retired early to get away from all this."

If only he knew.

"You have the front secured, right?" I ask.

"Who the hell you think you're talking to, some rookie?"

"Never know. You mighta got lazy."

"When that happens, it'll be time to go. But I sure as hell won't get myself caught up in something like this."

"You'll have a nice boat with your name on it, huh?" I say.

"Got that right."

"I gotta make a call."

O'Connell throws me a nod and walks to stand beside the female officer.

It takes more rings than normal for Hurley to answer.

"I know you're not working now," I say.

"Sleep," he mumbles with a groggy voice. "What's going on? What time is it?"

I say, "I found my source"—who was actually supposed to be Biddy, but it'll make it more serious if it's Diamond. Besides, I'm only bending the truth a little, because Diamond was a source, too. "He's been murdered."

"Damn," he says.

After I give him the location, he says, "I'll call Millhoff."

I'm worrying about Biddy. Wanna get out of here, go to the motel, but I can't.

Another marked unit shows up, parks behind the ambulance. Based on the unit's number on the front fender, I'm assuming it's the watch commander. Two men step out. I can tell that the passenger is a sergeant. The driver is a tall, lanky man, looks young, maybe early thirties. O'Connell walks over to him. The female officer stands by the scene to make sure no one steps in. The sergeant walks up to me.

Introduces himself as Sergeant John Handle.

"Frank Marr," I return.

"How'd you happen onto this?"

I know O'Connell filled him in, but he wants to make himself useful, so I oblige.

"I'm sure Officer O'Connell told you I'm a retired detective."

"Yes."

"Well, I'm a private investigator now, and I was checking in on a source because I hadn't been able to get in touch with him."

"What are you working that you'd need a source?"

"All due respect, sergeant, I don't have to tell you that."

He's taken by surprise. I don't want to piss him off.

"I will tell you it's a burglary investigation—well, and a murder investigation, too." All I say. I'll let Hurley or Millhoff fill him in on the rest.

"You mean the one that occurred at your home?"

"I don't know where you're going with this, Sergeant, but I got a man who was a decent man and a good source of information who had his throat cut. I think that's what's important. If his murder has anything to do with what I'm investigating, then I'll give it direct to Detectives Joe Hurley and Tim Millhoff."

"This is why we don't like you people working our city, pretending you're still the police. You best watch your step from here on." And with that he turns to walk back to the lanky commander.

Fuck you. A good man just died.

I look back at the crime scene, pissed to hell.

"I'm going to kill the son of a bitch who did this, Diamond," I mutter.

SIXTY-EIGHT

The only blessing in that whole shit storm was that Deputy Chief Wightman didn't show to the scene. I still feel the same way about him—I despise him—but I don't blame him for what he did. It was in the department's interest to force me into early retirement. If word ever got out that a top narcotics detective who put some major players away was, and still is, snorting up cocaine, not only the media but also all the defense attorneys would have a field day. Best do it quietly, let me have my measly 40 percent, and send me on my way. I deserved worse, so like I said, I don't blame him. I just don't like the man.

Diamond's murder was picked up by another homicide detective, but he told me Millhoff and Hurley will be kept in the loop, just in case everything is connected.

It's late, but I try to call Biddy again when I'm sitting in the air-conditioned car. Still goes straight to voice mail.

I make my way back to the motel.

No traffic, but it still feels like it took too long to get there. I pull into the parking lot, find the first space available.

Light's on in his room, dim through the closed curtain. I knock on the door, lightly at first, then harder when I don't get an answer.

"Biddy, it's Frank. Open up."

Nothing.

"Biddy, open the door."

I knock harder.

I hear a door open, then close, down the walkway to the side of me.

Fucking night manager. Different man from before. Younger, but still looks like he might be part of the family that owns this place. It's a certain look. Old Virginia.

He's clutching a cell phone in his right hand, probably ready to make that 911 call.

I take out my wallet and flash my badge.

"You have a man named Givens staying in there. I don't have time to explain, but I need to make sure he's safe."

"I can't just open the door," he says quietly.

"Yes, you can, and you will. Call Alexandria PD if you have to, but you're opening this door. Better now, though, in case he's hurt."

He thinks about it.

"I can't let you in."

"Don't need to go in. You just check, see if he's in there."

"Let me see your badge again?"

"Showed it already. He could be in danger, so either open the door or call the police here. Now."

He digs through his right pants pocket, pulls out a key ring with a lot of keys attached to it, searches for the right one.

He unlocks the door.

"Just open it and stand back."

"I said you can't go in."

"You want to go in, then go ahead, but it might not be safe."

He steps to the side.

I push the door open, look inside. His suitcase is still there. He isn't.

I walk in slowly, hand on the grip of my gun. I scan the small room, walk to the bathroom.

It's clean, no sign of a struggle. Everything as it was.

I exit.

"You can lock the door," I tell him.

"Is there something I need to worry about here?" he says while locking it.

"No, not you, but if you see him return, you tell him to call Frank. He's got my number. You see anybody else going up to this door, you call nine one one."

"You got a card or something?"

"No."

I quickly walk to my car, leaving him standing there wondering, *What the hell just happened?*

SIXTY-NINE

When I park near my house, I check out my surroundings before I exit, see if I can spot any moving heads in parked vehicles. I tuck the right side of my T-shirt behind my holstered weapon so I have quicker access.

I cross W Street and walk the block to my house. I lock the door behind me when I enter, drop my pack near the sofa. The tabletop lamp in the living room is on. I always keep it on, even when I'm in bed. I walk back to the hall to go to the laundry room and my stash.

Before I enter, I'm surprised by "Put your hands up!" It's coming from behind me, near the hallway entry to the kitchen. I immediately recognize it as Biddy's voice. Unsubstantial, but trying hard to sound tough. I resist the natural temptation to dive behind the wall of the laundry room and go for my gun. I slowly raise my hands.

"Can I turn?" I ask.

"Slowly. I swear you make a move and I'll shoot you."

Those threats hardly sound like threats coming from him.

"Don't worry, Robby, that'd be the last thing we both want."

I turn around, arms still in the air.

He's wearing the same clothes he had on at the motel, but he has dried blood on the front of his shirt and his forearms. Beads of sweat are dripping now, not seeping, down his forehead. His hands are shaking, and his finger's on the trigger of a semiauto, looks like a Beretta. His eyes are wide as hell, too, but not like fear. He's flying high on crack. Maybe a bit too high.

"Are you injured?" I ask.

Looks confused, then remembers the blood on him.

"No. No, that's not my blood."

"Did you hurt somebody?"

"No!"

"Could I ask you to take your finger off the trigger? 'Cause you're shaking so hard you might accidentally pull it."

"I plan on pulling it."

Sounds like he means it, but he's got to work himself up to it.

"All the same, you take your finger off the trigger, you can still pull it just as fast as you can with it on, but there'll be no accidents."

"No. Just get on your knees!"

"What the fuck's this about, Robby?"

It's not like it's the first time I've had guns pointed at me, but they weren't pointed by men like Biddy, who looks like he smoked up the rest of his shit. He wouldn't have this kind of courage otherwise. I don't consider myself the tough-guy type, but I've managed to either talk or fight my way out of these kinds of situations. I do feel fear but try not to sound like I do.

"Get on your knees, I said!"

"If you're gonna kill me, I'd rather be standing."

What the fuck did I just say?

"I know you have a gun on your belt, so take off your belt and let it drop, then kick it to me."

"Okay."

I unlatch my belt without lifting my T-shirt up, slide the belt out of the leather loops that secure my in-the-pants holster, then pull it all the way out. My gun won't drop because it's in a concealment holster and tucked in my pants. My cuffs drop first, then my magazine pouch, which holds two mags.

"Where's your gun?"

"I keep it in my backpack when I'm driving. Easier to get to that way."

"Where's your backpack?"

"In the living room."

"Kick that stuff carefully to me."

I obey. First the mags, then the cuffs slide toward his feet. Still hoping he doesn't ask me to lift my T-shirt.

"Your belt, too."

I step back and give it a slight kick.

"Tell me what this is about. I was just at the motel looking for you. Wanted to make sure you were safe."

"Safe?" Like a joke.

"Yes, of course. I'm on your side, Robby."

He chuckles nervously. "I'm going to kill you, then I'm going to kill Officer Jasper."

"You're so high right now, Robby. Please."

"My uncle's dead!"

"I know. I'm the one who called the police and an ambulance to the scene. So why are you at my house with a gun to my chest?"

"My uncle's dead. You said that everything would be okay."

I only remember advising them both to lay low, stay away from all this shit. I've had enough. I won't tell him that, though, because he's too emotional.

"Why did your uncle leave the motel?"

"We both left. He said he was going to pack up a few things at his house, then we'd return."

"Where were you when your uncle was attacked?"

"Waiting in the cab. He was supposed to just go in and pack a suitcase."

"So you saw who killed him?"

"It was dark. That's why the guy didn't see me. I was going to jump out when the man grabbed Uncle, but it was too fast, so I just ducked down, waited for the man to leave."

"You didn't see his face?"

"No."

"What was he wearing?"

"I don't know!" he yelps. "I was fucking scared."

"It's okay, Robby, but I still don't understand why you broke into my house again, and now with a gun pointed at me."

Tears build up, slide down the side of his nose.

"I'm not the one you want to kill. We both know where this is coming from, but for the life of me I don't know why I'm involved. He sent you to burglarize my home, remember? That's how I got caught up in this."

"Get on your fucking knees."

"Did you smoke all your crack up?" I ask.

"Don't try to screw with me."

His hands are shaking so hard that he really might accidentally pull the trigger. He's too high to try to talk out of this. It wouldn't be hard to take that gun away from him if he were closer. Too dangerous at this distance. Even with his hands shaking like they are, it'd be pretty hard to miss me. If I go to my knees I won't have a chance.

"*Everything* is messed up," he says, like he already forgot he wanted me to go on my knees.

"Put the gun down, and let's figure it out. It's messed up for both of us. Neither of us is safe."

He's clearly confused at this point, and being as tweaked out as he is doesn't help.

"Give me the gun, Robby."

"I can't trust you. You're a liar. I can't trust anyone."

"You have to. I have to trust you, too."

Shaking his head.

"Or just put the safety on, and let's go in the living room, where it's more comfortable, and think this through."

He looks at the gun.

"It's above your thumb. Carefully flip it up."

"No. I said I can't trust you."

"Then let's try this. You can keep the gun pointed at me, but take your finger off the trigger. Follow me into the living room."

I don't give him a chance to think about it. I start to slowly put my hands down.

"I swear—"

I turn around and walk down the hall toward the living room. Big fucking chance, but I have to break the stalemate.

Near the front door he says, "Stay right there."

I turn to look at him. His finger is off the trigger. He gets closer so he can see me walk into the living room. I'd have a good chance of disarming him, but I can't risk it. Last thing I want is to get shot or to shoot him.

"Okay, go. Sit away from your dang backpack at the end of the couch."

"No problem."

I sit down.

He sits on the armchair to the left of me, near the end table, an arm's length from my backpack. Let's hope he doesn't ask to search it.

From where he's sitting he can't see the right side of my body. I act like I'm positioning myself on the sofa but manage to remove my gun from the holster and tuck it under my thigh. Just in case.

"I'm far enough away; you don't have to point the gun at me. If you rest it on your lap you'll be able to cap my ass before I get a chance to stand. I need to feel safe, okay? If we're going to talk?"

He rests the gun on his lap, but he still has a grip on it.

"Thank you. I feel like I can breathe now," I say. "Can you toss my pack of cigarettes and the lighter this way? I really need a smoke."

He looks at them on the end table, tosses the cigarettes first, then the lighter. They land on the sofa, but I have to stretch a bit to get the lighter.

"Thanks."

I light a smoke. There's a tumbler on the end table at my side that used to have whiskey in it. I use it for an ashtray.

"Damn, that feels good. I got a little something that'll help you out if you want," I tell him.

"What do you mean?"

"I have a little weed."

"What? You're kidding me, right?"

"No. I'm retired. It helps me sleep at night."

"No. I'd have to say no."

"You're pretty wired, Robby. Might help you think straight."

"You gonna smoke some, too?"

"Sure."

"Don't tell me you need your backpack."

"No. It's inside the end-table drawer right next to you."

He uses his left hand to open it.

"I use a pipe, but there's some rolling papers in there, too."

"Looks like some good bud," he says, like we're having a regular conversation now.

"It is."

"What kind of ex-cop are you?"

"Weed's legal in the District. You know that."

"I guess, but still."

He pulls out the baggie, tosses it to me, then the pipe.

"You don't mind sharing a pipe with a crackhead, do you?" he asks me.

Shake my head. "Doesn't look like you got blisters, you know, on your lips. I'm good."

He almost smiles but pulls it back.

I grab the pipe, open the baggie, pick a nice bit off one of the buds, and pack it in the chamber. I snuff out my smoke in the tumbler and light the pipe. It's a nice hit. I hold it in while I lean toward Biddy, stretching my arm to hand it to him. His right hand is still gripping the gun, but at least his finger is off the trigger.

He takes a good hit.

I exhale. Comes on quick. I let him finish it up.

He straightens up in the armchair. The weed working to cut the edge off the crack high. Only a little.

"Good weed," I say again.

Such an odd moment.

"Is it my fault?" he asks softly.

Of course it's his fault.

"It's not your fault."

SEVENTY

Y ou mind if I check the time on my phone?" I ask.

He lifts the gun.

"Finger off the trigger, please."

He does.

I pull my phone out of my pants pocket.

"What time is it?" Biddy asks.

I notice on the screen that there's a message from Aunt Linda.
Why didn't I hear the phone ring?

"Four twenty in the morning," I tell him.

I set the phone on the coffee table. I need a little something to level out this loopy high, straighten my head out again. Can't reveal that side of me, though.

He lowers the gun back to his lap.

I can tell he's starting to fade, maybe feeling double what I feel right now because his drug of choice is more powerful than mine. He's not asking to smoke, so I'm thinking he's out.

"Did you smoke up all your shit?"

"Yes."

"That's hell of a lot in just a few hours."

"I had a purpose."

"Well, it brought you here. Can't say I like how you went about it, though. I didn't see any sign of forced entry. How'd you get in?"

"Scaled the drainpipe to the second-floor window, busted it out."

"Damn. You must be light as a feather and have strong arms."

"I can get into most places if I want to."

"Well, I forgive you for the window, and even for wanting to kill me, so let's end this. You're not going to shoot."

"I don't know what to do. I came at you with a gun. That's a serious charge. I can't go to fucking prison."

"You didn't come at me with a gun. You didn't even break into my house. This time, I mean."

Looks up at me, confused.

"You're scared. Your uncle's been murdered. We both know Jasper's probably behind it. You can't trust going to the police because of that. You found out I'm a PI and an ex-cop through your uncle, who I was working with. So you turn yourself in to me for the burglary of my residence, and you need protection. That's a good story to go with."

"You kidding? I told you I can't catch a charge."

"Just listen. I know it's difficult, but I have a way out of this for you—and for me, 'cause it'll get Jasper out of both of our lives. I think that's why you came here anyway. If you weren't so high, I believe you would have done it differently. You weren't thinking straight. Do what I say, but don't mention anything about the motel. If you do, I'll make sure you get fucked."

"I'm still not thinking straight."

I can say the same.

"Hear me out. Detective Joe Hurley is a good friend of mine."

"No."

"He'll tell you the same thing I'm going to. Cops can never make promises, but you can believe this: I've been through this kinda talk, and so has Hurley, more times than I can remember. I can tell you based on all those experiences that it has worked out for everyone else we've talked to, but that's only if they don't fuck up during the process."

"What are you talking about?"

"You turn yourself in through me—"

"No."

"Just shut up," I say to a man with a gun. "You turn yourself in through me to Detective Hurley. He's already investigating Officer Jasper, so he needs someone like you really bad. I can tell you you'll probably get a sweet deal, maybe even just a slap on the back of your hand, 'cause you've got a clean record. So we arrange for you to turn yourself in, and you confess to my burglary only, but say that you were directed to commit the burglary by Jasper. Outta fear, you obeyed. You still with me?"

Nods once.

"You tell him you'll cooperate. I'll tell him how much danger you're in and that you can't go into general population."

"Prison?!"

"You won't be in there for more than two or three days. Max. Really. When you get to arraignment—which, if we do this now, might be later this morning—they'll give you a lawyer pro bono."

I wish it could be Leslie, but that's a definite conflict of interest for her.

"What's that really mean?"

"Means free. On the people. You make sure your lawyer knows everything, especially about Jasper, your uncle, the burglary of my home, and what you witnessed after. You're the only one who can identify the man who killed that kid in my kitchen.

You're also the only one who can connect all this to Jasper. You tell her you already confessed and you want a debriefing with Detective Hurley. Hurley will take care of things on his end, so it'll be quick."

"What if doesn't work?"

"I told you, I've been through this tons of times, and most of the guys I was working with had serious criminal records, and even they got out. It'll work, Robby. Take the couple of days you'll have alone in a cell to get your head straight, otherwise they won't work with you. You're not going to do time unless you fuck up. You fuck up by using again. Do it for your uncle."

"I have to think."

"This will give us both closure."

He's not sold.

"Hurley will make it clear, too. It's the only way, Robby."

The gun is on his lap, his hand off the grip. He's gotten too comfortable. Maybe the good weed had a little to do with it.

I take my gun from under my thigh, point it at him. It takes him a second to notice. He straightens up when he does, but he doesn't think to grab his gun right away.

"I'm not like you. I'm trained, and I'll cap you right between the eyes without a thought."

"I knew I couldn't trust you," he says like his heart's been broken.

"Take the butt of the gun with your thumb and your index finger and set it on the coffee table."

"Just shoot me."

"I really should, but we both don't want that. So do what I say."

He grabs it with two fingers by the barrel. I don't bother to tell him that's not the butt, because the barrel is pointing up and away from me. He sets it on the coffee table.

"Slide it toward me using the tip of your finger."

He does, then looks down, shattered.

I pick the gun up and set it closer to the edge of the coffee table, closer to me.

"Where'd you get this gun?"

"Some other house. I think it's clean because it was in a gun box."

"Why didn't you give it to Jasper?"

"Fuck. Security. You won't turn it over to the police, will you?"

Worried about his prints.

"No, but I'll hold on to it for a bit."

"I'm going to get fucked."

"Look at me," I tell him.

He does.

I set my gun on the coffee table near his and lean back on the sofa.

"We're going to work this out now, got it? I'll take care of this gun of yours. No one will find it unless you fuck with me. Now, let's go over everything one more time."

SEVENTY-ONE

I'm treating Biddy like a client who needs special handling. Hurley doesn't need to know everything. That'll only complicate matters or get me in trouble.

Hurley doesn't have a life nowadays because of me. He didn't have a life before, but probably it wasn't as bad as it is now, with me in it. I owe him a nice dinner, at the very least.

Biddy's hands are cuffed behind his back. I disposed of the paraphernalia he was carrying, and he gave me the keys to the motel so I could secure his property. Told me there would be nothing in the suitcase to surprise me, like further evidence of a crime. I will turn that over to Hurley if I find it, and Biddy knows it. So I'm confident the motel will be clean. I also put his stolen gun in my stash wall. It's a weapon I think I'll hold on to for a while, just in case.

"Take him to Three Hundred, not 3D," Hurley tells the officer.

I walk up to Biddy before he's escorted out.

"Can I have a second?" I ask the officer, who turns and looks at Hurley for the answer.

Hurley nods.

"I need to talk to him privately," I say.

The officer moves out of earshot.

I get close to speak confidentially. "You give up everything to Hurley. Remember not to mention what went down in the motel room, or I'll mention how it really went down here. I'll have the gun with your prints on it. You got it?"

"Yes."

"You do everything like we talked about, and you'll come out okay. We'll both come out okay."

He looks at me with a crooked, awkward half smile. A trusting smile. I smile back like I mean it, because I do, then move away.

"You'll get my belongings from the motel?"

"Yes, as long as there's nothing illegal in there."

"There's not."

The uniformed officer escorts him out. Biddy looks over his shoulder to me before stepping into the hallway toward the front door.

"It'll be okay. Just tell Detective Hurley the truth."

They exit, leaving the front door open.

It's bright outside, cloudless, with a big sun.

"What did you have to say to him that you couldn't say out loud?" Hurley asks.

"Words of comfort."

"Give me a break."

"I didn't want the officer to hear. All I said was to trust you. You're going to personally paper the case, right?"

"Of course. I'll get with the AUSA I always work with and see if we can set up a debriefing in B One at the US attorney's office within a day or two. Let's hope it works out the way it's supposed to. He'll be good for a strong case against Jasper. We have to keep this quiet, get him processed at Three Hundred and papered so no one knows."

"What about the officer who's transporting him?"

"He's good, Marr. He's on the task force. Plainclothes, tactical guy, and uniform when he has to. He'll escort him up the stairs to the third floor from the garage. No one will see. I can't figure why the guy who burglarized your home would give himself up to you."

"It's complicated."

"In a nutshell, then."

"I told you—his uncle was my source. Biddy told you the rest. What's so hard to understand?"

"How did you manage to find his uncle?"

"Because I'm good at what I do, Joe."

"I'm going to need to know, but I don't feel like writing up more than I have to right now, so I'll wait. You will have to come in."

"Fine."

"This guy Biddy, or Robby. He's smarter than your average crackhead. Looks cleaner, too. Be hard to find if he ran."

"So you're wondering why he didn't run?"

"Yes."

"Because he knows it's a matter of time before he ends up in jail or like his uncle. He's scared, and he doesn't trust the police."

"But he trusts you."

I shrug.

"You had any sleep?" Hurley asks.

"Sleep? I was up all night with him."

"You smell like weed."

"I let him smoke what he had. Calmed his nerves."

"Calm your nerves, too, Frank?"

"You know how that shit sticks to your clothing."

"You mention you let him get high, it'll screw my whole case," he says.

"What do I look like, a moron?"

"Kinda. You should get some sleep, though, because you're in it now."

Unfortunately, I know that, and I'm not talking about the tired part.

SEVENTY-TWO

Before I can sleep, I go to the shed in the backyard and grab some of the extra plywood I have left over after fixing the back door. I take a hammer and a box of nails to the guest room on the second floor, where Biddy busted out the window. After cleaning up the glass, I board up the window. Two things I'll have to buy now—a window and a door. I'll find the time one day.

When I turn to exit I notice a cicada clinging to the door frame. Got in through the broken window.

I gently pinch it between two fingers, look at it for a second.

"You won't find a mate in here."

Probably the one knocking at my window that night. I open the second window, the one closer to the guest bed.

"Go. Find the love of your life, cause you ain't gonna live that long."

I toss the cicada out. It falls, but then regains itself and flies away, like a clumsy drunk. I close and lock the window. Not that it matters, locking the window. Like Biddy said, he can get in anywhere. Nothing's ever secure.

I go to my bedroom and lock the door.

My phone wakes me up. I don't remember falling asleep.

Hurley.

Fuck, is this bad news? I notice the time. I did sleep. It's almost 5:00 p.m.

"What's up, Hurley?" I answer.

"Sounds like I woke you."

"It's all good. I woke you enough times. Please don't tell me you got bad news."

"That depends on what you consider bad."

"What happened?"

"Everything went well. AUSA is on board. Had your boy Givens in the box for a while, so he won't go before a judge until tomorrow."

"Sounds good."

"He's going to debrief."

"Good interview and interrogation technique, right? So what's the so-called bad news?"

"Your connection to Jasper."

"What the fuck are you talking about? I don't have a connection with that good-for-nothin' SLAP."

"Maybe not one you remember, but that drive-by shooting you got caught up in a year or so back, the one where the officer got killed?"

"The Cordell Holm case. The girl. What the hell does that have to do with anything?"

"The officer who got killed. Tommy Woodrow. He was Jasper's nephew."

SEVENTY-THREE

D irty blood runs in Jasper's family," I tell Hurley.
"Yeah. They both snuck onto the department, which we know is not that hard to do."

Don't I know it.

"But again, what does this have to do with me? I wasn't responsible for his nephew's death," I say, even though I'm beginning to think otherwise.

I don't normally work missing persons, especially when it involves a teenage girl, but I got sucked into an investigation a little over a year ago, mostly by my own doing. I eventually found the girl, but the boys who had her first decided they wanted her back. She worked the brothel they were running. Hell, she even wanted to go back. Those boys backed off, though, but not for long. Enter Officer Tommy Woodrow. He rolled up to the scene at 17th and Euclid while I was holding on tightly to the struggling girl and trying to get her to my car. Couple of the boys came back, but this time in a car. The passenger opened up on us with a TEC-9 or some shit. Officer Tommy was in the line of fire. He took a couple in the chest.

Tommy supplied information to the crew who killed him, even had an ongoing affair with one of the other teen girls at the brothel. So maybe they wanted him dead. I know they wanted me dead. Nearly got me, too, but luck was on my side that day.

Can that be the reason for all this now? I can't figure it—except, like I said, maybe my showing up to the club all that time later opened old wounds for Jasper. Maybe he wanted to take it out on me or actually does blame me, because if I hadn't taken the case, and if I hadn't found the girl at that moment, Officer Tommy, his nephew, might still be alive. Silly kind of vengeance, if you ask me, because most of the people truly answerable for the crime are in prison.

"One of the special agents on the task force did a full background on Jasper," Hurley begins. "That's how we found out Woodrow was his nephew. And Biddy, or Givens, said Jasper had your house targeted, so he's definitely got it in for you. I don't know. That's all we got right now. Too much to be coincidental."

That word's coming up a lot.

"That's ridiculous."

But then I've seen a lot of ridiculousness in my time.

"You have the kid from the hospital, and now Biddy, so it's looking good, right?" I ask.

"Yeah, but you know how an investigation like this can go. It's not something immediate."

"But Jasper doesn't have a clue, right?" I ask.

"No. Unless our other source is playing both sides."

"You know those boys on Riggs work for Jasper?"

"I'm beginning to think you got a bug on me. How do you know all this?"

"From Biddy or Robby or Graham. Whatever you want to call him. But he's not my bug; he's your bug now."

"I know they work for him. But Jasper is still working the

part-time at the club, so it doesn't look like he's worried about anything."

"If he finds out Biddy's been locked up, he will be," I say.

"We don't even have IA involved in this. That's the benefit of working with the feds. They'll be notified when and if we get a warrant for Jasper. It's totally in-house."

"If?"

"You know what I mean," he says.

SEVENTY-FOUR

More than anything, I want to take care of this shit myself. Go
sit on the club when I know he's working, follow him home
after. Bust into his home when he leaves for work and get my music
and laptop back, put the hurt on him for having Jeffrey killed—and
Diamond. I'm a fucking liar, but this guy's a psychopath.

Yeah, I'm gonna fuck up a federal investigation and get myself
arrested in the process. I'm not stupid. I've said that a thousand
times before, but I mean it this time. I'm sure the task force Hurley's on already has a car or two sitting on him.

So take it easy, and slow the fuck down.

I can dream, though, can't I?

I park my car on the street again, a couple of blocks from the motel. Biddy only has the one suitcase, so I can manage the walk back.

Evening is setting in, the remaining light made dimmer by
steam in the air. It's like I have to cut my way through it. I walk
the sidewalk on the other side of the office, an effort to lessen the
possibility of prying eyes.

Looks like Biddy turned the lights off in the room before he left. I open the door, double-lock it behind me. Turn the overhead light on. I pick up his suitcase and open it on the bed to search the contents. Despite what he said, I want to make sure I won't be transporting something I shouldn't be. Looks good. Clean underwear, pants, shirts, and some fucking self-help book about finding peace. I zip up the suitcase after I clear it.

I see the crack stem on the nightstand and pick it up so I can flush it down the toilet.

I enter the bathroom and am startled by a very large older man in a suit standing against the bathroom wall across from the toilet. I recognize him. Wyatt from the club. I drop the stem on the bathroom floor and unholster my gun, but he's already holding a small canister of police-grade Mace. It streams out and hits me on the left side of my face.

"Fuck!" is all I can get out.

I tuck my gun to shoot blindly. But before I can, and out of nowhere, he slaps it from my hand so hard it feels like my hand went with it.

I hear it land somewhere with an echo.

The tub?

Feels like I swallowed hot embers. My left eye burns like shit, too, and I tear up right away. Immediately he's on top of me. I stumble back and get knocked off my feet by the corner of the mattress. I swing blindly with my right hand, and it hits something hard. *His head?* He grips the wrist of my left arm like it's going to break, then forces some wrestling move on me, and I'm flat on my back. He pins me down. Mace didn't hit me direct, mostly in the left eye and on the side of my face, so despite the burn I can see a bit. His knees pin my arms down, and his weight on my torso keeps me in place. His left hand squeezes the right side of my neck. I see him raise a folding tactical knife with his right hand.

I can see the gun holstered on his right side, but he wants to keep things quiet.

Fuck! I'm a big guy, but I don't have the weight on him.

"Where's Robby Givens?" he asks too calmly.

"Who?" I return.

"Graham Biddy!"

"I don't know who the fuck——" Realizing how bad that sounds 'cause I'm in his motel room.

He strikes down with the knife, then searing hot pain rips into my left shoulder. I kick blindly with my right foot to try to get him off balance.

"You know who I'm talking about. Where is he?"

"I'll take you to him."

"Do I look like an idiot?"

My right hand is pinned down hard by the wrist, so the palm is facing up. I thrust my body up one more time, trying to buck him off, and manage to slide my hand back, get my thumb under his thumb. With everything I can muster I twist, hear his thumb snap out of place. He yelps, jerks back, taking the tactical knife out of my shoulder at the same time. I hit him hard on the left chin with the butt of my right hand. Stuns him a bit, but that's about it.

He has years on me, but he's built like a linebacker.

A punch I didn't see coming lands on the right side of my chin, throws me back, and he drops me down with his weight so I'm completely on my back, his left knee pinning my right arm down again. I struggle to hold his right hand back, gripping him by the wrist, fighting the searing pain in my shoulder, like the knife hit bone.

He smacks me hard on the chin again with the side of his right hand. Almost see white light. Nearly gone. His right hand, holding the knife, breaks free of my grip, and he lunges it toward my chest, but I block it with the open palm of my left hand.

A sacrifice.

The blade penetrates through the palm of my hand, and I see it cut through the top, near my knuckles.

Weird.

I grip the knife's handle between the fingers of my punctured hand. At this point the pain means nothing compared to wanting to live. I clench the handle hard.

He's forcing my knife-stuck hand down, trying to get me to stab myself in the chest. My own hand over my heart. So fucking strong. I can't get my right hand free from under his knee. I grip the handle of the knife through my hand, move a bit to my left side.

Fuck if I'm going to die here!

I throw my upper body up this time, land my forehead into his nose. He loses his grip on the knife, and his knee lifts up from my right hand. Before he can regain himself, I squeeze the knife handle tighter into my palm to prevent the blade from pulling out. Another jolt of adrenaline flushes through me.

Surges.

I swing up hard with the back of my hand, the knife point piercing the left side of his neck just under the jaw. I cut in and slice out. When I remove the blade, blood ratchets out of his neck in a series of pulsating spurts, high enough to arc over the side of the bed, and some of it hits me on the feet.

Carotid.

I scramble up from under his massive legs. He tries to put pressure on his neck with his left hand and at the same time reach for what I have to assume is his sidearm with his other hand.

The movements seem strange, comical. He gives me a look like I should help him.

I step on his hand hard, preventing him from getting his sidearm. He throws silly-looking punches toward me, hitting my thigh once or twice, and allowing the blood to spurt out with more force.

Then it's like he realizes. He knows.

I step back and kick him hard with the sole of my shoe. The kick lands under his chin, sending him out of his misery.

Part of his neck is opened up, like a second mouth spitting blood. He bleeds out fast. Heart pumping fast, but so is mine. Side of the mattress above his head is soaked, blood dripping down off the bed frame back onto him.

I lean down, lift his suit jacket, and remove the weapon from the holster attached to his belt.

Glock 17.

I back away from him, call 911.

SEVENTY-FIVE

I'm in the back of an ambulance parked in the motel's lot, not cuffed but being watched closely by two uniforms from the Alexandria PD. Left side of my face is swollen. The ice pack they gave me helps. My shirt was cut off by the EMTs and replaced by a light blanket over my shoulders. There's a second ambulance for the big man, though he won't be needing it. His body's still inside the motel room, being checked out by homicide detectives and the coroner. Several marked cruisers here, too, and a couple unmarked. The chief himself responded. It's a small department, and most of them are solid workers. It's a city that has its share of crime, so something like this isn't a surprise. But it is to me.

Should have turned Biddy and Diamond in right away. Diamond would probably still be alive right now, and, most important, I wouldn't have had to kill someone. I've seen people die, mostly when I was on the job. It all stays with you, even the sweet smell of fresh blood. Worse, the look on his face is gonna stay with me.

The EMT bandaged my hand and my shoulder. They want to

transport me, but I refuse. I still got my right hand and shoulder. I'd rather take myself to the hospital, but the detective on the scene, Earl Campos, insists on driving me himself. I guess they've got too many questions, none of them really answered yet.

I hate to do it again, but Millhoff and Hurley need to be notified. Likely this is the man who murdered Diamond. I give Detective Campos their contact information. I'm sure I won't be getting any favors from them soon. Campos moves away from me to notify them, then comes back a few minutes later and says, "Both of them are on the way."

He slips his police notebook in his rear pants pocket.

"Neither of them knew anything about this motel room, though. Got the impression they were upset. Good thing you still have friends on the department."

"I'd be pissed at me, too, if I were in their shoes." I look back at the motel, lit up with police lights. "Thing is, I'm taking Robert Givens on as a client, so I didn't have to tell them. Of course, being the ex-cop I am, I would've turned over evidence if I'd found it. Givens assured me that all he had was clothing and other personal items. I was just going to secure them for him. I did see a crack pipe on the floor and picked it up, but I dropped it after the big man jumped me."

They'll probably find a partial print on the stem, so I had to tell them. Most cops don't give a shit about something like that. Hurley knows that Givens is a crackhead.

"I should take you to the hospital. We can talk more there."

"It's a good hospital? I don't want to get my left hand or shoulder fucked up for a lifetime."

"Inova Fairfax. It's one of the best."

"I know that hospital. Appreciate it."

I drop the ice pack in the back of the ambulance. I don't want to carry it through the crowd.

We get to his unmarked cruiser.

I notice a couple of news vans, cameras on tripods on the sidewalk. Pointed at me again.

"Is this related to the homicide at your house, Mr. Marr?" one reporter asks, a little too loud.

I don't answer.

"I'll sit in back with you," Campos tells me.

I see how it is now.

His partner is already in the driver's seat. Older guy, clean-cut, wearing a tucked-in polo shirt with an embroidered badge on it.

Campos opens the rear door for me. I scoot in.

He walks behind the car to the other side, where he sits in the back behind his partner.

"My weapon?" I remember to ask.

"The Glock nineteen on the floor in the room?"

"Yeah."

"We'll take care of it. Everything clears we'll give it back, but it'll be a few days."

"Robert Givens's belongings, too. I told him I'd secure them for him."

"We got it," Campos advises me.

I slide in the backseat with a few grunts when my shoulder hits the back of the seat.

"That's my partner, Gibbs," he tells me.

"Avoid the potholes if you can," I say.

"This is Old Town, man. We don't have potholes," Gibbs says.

"So you said you don't know this big boy Wyatt, but you've seen him before?"

"Yes. He works the door for a nightclub on Connecticut Avenue. I forget the name. Millhoff or Hurley can fill you in."

"What were you doing at the nightclub?"

"Having a drink, like most of the other customers. Listen, I don't know that man at all, and he didn't belong in that room. Did he have a key?"

"Why?" Campos asks.

"Because you should ask Detective Millhoff if the stabbing victim in DC, who was Biddy's—I mean Givens's uncle, had a motel key on him. I'm pretty sure he'll say he didn't."

"We'll do that. And who is Biddy?"

"That's Givens's alias, what I like to call him. But listen, more than likely this guy was there to do the same to Biddy but found me instead."

"So let me get this straight," Campos begins. "You're working the homicide-burglary that occurred at your house?"

"Which I have every right to do."

"Well, only if you don't take certain matters into your own hands, right?"

"Of course."

"But you're working it, and you end up finding the burglar—"

"Biddy found me."

"Okay, but then this crackhead burglar agrees to turn himself in through you. Why the hell would he do that?"

"I answered that exact question from Detective Hurley. That information would be up to Millhoff or Hurley to share with you guys, not me."

"You're retired. What are you doing acting like you're still on the job?" Gibbs asks from the front seat.

"I'm working as a PI. I follow those rules now."

Yeah, right.

"Like never working with us," Campos returns.

"Not true. I don't want to fuck up anything Millhoff and Hurley are working on is all."

I'm starting to get pissed off. I need a drink and more. At the very least a smoke.

"But you just did," Campos says.

"Just did what?"

"Fuck up their investigation."

"Fuck that. I probably got them their murder suspect. Also, I only went in there for Biddy's personal property. If I would've found any evidence, I would've turned it over. I even told Biddy that. And remember I entered that motel room on Biddy's behalf, so there's no crime there. That man had no right to be in there. The rest was self-defense. Where are you going with all this?"

"Trying to get to the bottom of everything is all," Campos says.

"I'm not a suspect, or you'd have me in cuffs."

"Not necessarily," Gibbs says. "We can go two ways with this. Lock you up for murder and let the prosecutor sort it all out after we do the investigation, or do our investigation and give it to the prosecutor, who will present it to the grand jury. Let them sort it all out."

"Oh, I like that. My life dependent on civilians."

"We can put cuffs on you now if you want," Gibbs says again.

"Naw, that's okay. You'll find it was self-defense. So will the prosecutor."

"Pretty damn good weapon you were given to use against him, though."

"Thank Wyatt for that."

Gibbs chuckles.

"You could say it was handmade," I add.

Both of them chuckle now.

"Fuck, I don't feel so good," I say suddenly.

"What do you mean you don't feel so good?" Campos asks.

"Think I'm going to puke. Pull the car over. Quick."

Gibbs drives fast, makes a right turn on some small road, and pulls to the curb.

I open the door, lean out.

I hurl everything I got inside, which is hardly anything, so it's like dry heaves with occasional bile.

Can't catch my breath, and with every heave, pain radiates throughout my shoulder.

I spit a few times, notice a couple cars pass and pedestrians on the other side of the road quickly walking by.

"Here," Campos says, handing me a paper towel.

I close the door, take it, and wipe my mouth. That was the second time I've vomited in——how long? I don't want there to be a third time.

"Damn," I say. "That came out of nowhere."

"Nerves, buddy," Gibbs says. "Means you're human."

I grunt a laugh, but it hurts.

SEVENTY-SIX

"Mind if I smoke?" I ask.

"Go ahead. We smoke cigars on occasion," Campos says.

"Appreciate it."

I grab my pack out of my pants pocket. It's smooshed up, but I find a cigarette that's not all bent out of shape.

"Let me," Campos says.

"Thanks."

He takes one out of the pack, offers to light it with his own lighter.

I inhale. Eases the tension. Mouth is damn dry, though.

Before I can finish, we pull into the parking lot next to the emergency entrance.

Campos and Gibbs walk me to the emergency room. They follow as a nurse escorts me to one of the curtained enclosures.

The nurse picks up a hospital gown, and before handing it to me she asks, "Do you need help changing into this?"

"I can manage. Thanks."

She hands it to me, exits, and closes the curtain for privacy.

"You two wanna watch?"

"Nothing we haven't seen before," Gibbs says.

I drop the blanket on the floor, have to use my left hand to take my belt off. A uniform officer took my handcuffs and the pouch with the two mags in it.

I drop my pants, sit on the gurney bed, and use my feet to kick my pants off. I leave my boxers and socks on. I unfold the gown, try to figure out how it goes.

"You want me to get the nurse?" Gibbs says.

The old guy's starting to bother me, but that's what cops do. Trying to get under your skin is a natural part of their nature.

"I'm good."

I have a hard time slipping my left arm through, mostly the shoulder. Could definitely use a couple Oxys right about now, or at least a Percocet. But I manage the painful maneuver, except I can't tie the gown because I can't reach the string that wraps around.

Campos walks over, takes the string between two fingers, like he's afraid he might accidently touch my ass.

"Thanks. You have a nurse's touch," I say.

His partner chuckles.

Campos blows it off.

I grab my pants. I notice blood on the legs. Don't think it's my blood. I still have my wallet, phone, keys, and the container with the capsules in my pants. Told them that was my medication. Partly true. It does state that Vyvanse is prescribed to me, but I keep those capsules somewhere else and use these bigger ones for the blow. A doctor or a good narcotics officer would be the only ones who could figure out these capsules don't belong to the prescribed medication.

"These pants are going into evidence?" I ask.

"Yeah. We're going to have to bag them. We know what you have inside, so you can secure those," Campos says.

I take everything out and set it on the gurney.

"One of you mind getting me one of those hospital bags for my belongings?"

"I got it," Gibbs says.

He leaves.

I drop the pants back on the floor, put my wallet, phone, keys, and container near the pillow.

I recline on the gurney bed.

Gibbs returns with a plastic bag.

I take it and drop everything inside the bag except the phone. I fold the top over and set the bag on the floor near the head of the gurney.

The younger cop's cell rings. "Campos," he answers. "Yeah. Yeah. Good thing. Got it. Right. At the hospital with him now. Yeah. Copy that." He disconnects, slips it back in the inner pocket of his jacket.

"Do I check out?"

"Yeah, you do, but we knew you would."

"I appreciate the confidence. So you don't have to babysit me anymore."

"We're going to stick around, wait for your two detective buddies, and maybe ask a couple more questions."

"Then why don't you pull up a couple of chairs, make yourselves comfortable? It's a pretty good story."

SEVENTY-SEVEN

X-rays looked fine for the shoulder, but there's possible nerve damage in my left hand. I'll have to wait and see. So much for the tolerance for pain I thought I had. Damn. When they stuck a needle around and in the stab wounds to numb up the area, I wanted to cry like a baby. The wrap around my left hand looks like a boxing glove. My shoulder's taped up, and my left arm's in a sling.

Hurley and Millhoff are in the room talking to the Alexandria duo when I'm wheeled in.

I can tell Millhoff is pissed. Hurley not so much. He's not easy to read. They allow me to get comfortable on the gurney before the interrogation.

"What the hell were you thinking?" Millhoff demands. "I should charge you with obstruction."

Now I see a reaction from Hurley. Don't think he expected that.

"Obstruction?" I begin. "For what, securing personal property?"

"Hell, you know there could've been evidence in that room.

You don't make that decision. We would've obtained a search warrant," Millhoff advises me.

"I told Biddy if I found anything illegal or anything that might be evidence I'd turn it over."

"And you believed him? That there was no evidence there?"

"Why the fuck would he give me his key if there was? All he wanted was whatever damn clothing he has left in the world and probably his fucking toothbrush."

"Hurley locks up the guy who committed the burglary at your residence, and you don't tell us he has a motel room in Virginia and that he might have evidence related to the burglary or even something more?" Millhoff says with a harder tone.

Because he's talking about evidence that might be related to Jasper or the homicides.

Never apologize, even though I know I was wrong, especially to a cop.

Alexandria boys slide out, not wanting to get caught up in whatever might happen.

"And now we all know that Biddy—Givens—is telling the truth, because that man was there for him, not me. No way to keep this from Jasper now," I say.

"He'll find out, but I have a feeling he'll keep doing his thing, patrol, but maybe drop out of the club. He'll never seem worried about anything else," Millhoff says. "But I'm not going to belabor the damn point. We both know what you did was bullshit, but still, I'm glad you're okay."

"Well, I appreciate that. Don't think I'm going to feel too safe once Jasper finds out I killed his boy."

"Pretty sure he's not the type to do the dirty work."

"That makes me feel better. Maybe he'll send another retired big boy to do it. Piece of shit. How can he still be walking free right now?"

"Because we can't connect him to anything except his unsanctioned part-time, thanks to you. That'll just get him a suspension, if that," Millhoff says.

"Once the AUSA and the defense attorney sign off on the plea agreement, we'll get rolling with Biddy and the other cooperator," Hurley says.

Nurse comes in at the right time. Numbness is starting to wear off. She's holding a paper cup with water and a fat pill.

"Take this. It will help with the pain."

"Motrin?" I question.

"Eight hundred milligrams."

"I don't have a headache," I tell her.

"If it doesn't help in thirty minutes we'll try something else."

She hands me the water. I down the pill. I have what I need at home.

"You'll be discharged soon. These gentlemen here to give you a ride home?"

"Are you?" I ask.

"Of course," Millhoff says, voice still tight as shit.

"Do you have hospital pants and a top I can have? I don't feel comfortable walking out in just my shorts."

"Of course we do. Let me get you those."

I give her a smile.

When I'm okayed to leave, we walk out and find Campos outside waiting.

"Where's your partner?" I ask.

"In the car waiting. Wanted to let you know you'll probably be called in real soon."

"So get an attorney?"

"I would."

"It was self-defense."

"Looks like it to us, but still. It has to be presented."

"I understand. And when it's all done, I'll get my gun back?"

"You really love that gun, don't you?" Campos asks.

"We go back."

"We know it's registered to you legally, but it still has to go through Firearms."

"I'll expect to get it back, then."

"If there's no body on it."

"You can be assured there isn't."

I have a .40-caliber Glock at home to keep me safe, so as much as I like the 19, they can take their time.

I convince both Hurley and Millhoff that I can drive, so they drop me off in Old Town, where I parked my car.

"We'll follow you home," Millhoff says.

SEVENTY-EIGHT

What day is it?

Damn. I don't even know what day it is.

Couple of Oxys and I'm all loopy. Feeling good, but still loopy. I'm more of an up man, but I enjoy the combination of the two on occasion, especially when I'm hurting.

I look at my phone for the time.

Almost 9:00 a.m.

Did I sleep?

I had to have slept. I don't remember anything.

No call from Leslie, either. Why should she call? She has to know what happened. It had to have hit the news. Still, why wouldn't she call? I realize what I did was awful, but I was almost killed. Have I ruined it this bad?

I check out my shoulder. Blood's seeping through the gauze. I'm supposed to change it, keep it clean. I grab my .40, go downstairs to make coffee. I keep the gun with me wherever I go now, even in the house. Wasn't like that before all this shit. Now it's more of a friend than it ever was. I have to remember to pick up my gun from the Alexandria PD when the time comes. It's an easier conceal-carry, and I'm more accurate with it than with the .40-cal.

After a couple of cups of coffee, I take off the bandaging and replace it with fresh gauze and tape. It's awkward to do because my hand is still bandaged, but I manage.

Wound is stapled up and looks clean enough, so I don't need to cleanse it. Damn sore, though.

I swallow a couple more Oxys. I got them from a previous hit. Have more coffee after. Coffee's useless. Has been for a long time, but I like the taste, and I'm addicted to the caffeine. Get a headache without it.

I always feel like I have to be doing something, but I think I'll force myself to stay home, loaf around, be a good-for-nothing for a day or two. I need to heal. Not only that, I need to hide from those fucking reporters.

I think about Leslie again, and that keeps me from using for a little while, until I get this hollow feeling inside, along with anxiety, and I break it out—the good stuff I picked up from the boys on Riggs.

Damn good stuff. Might be the best I ever had.

Turns into a binge. A binge isn't so fun without television or music. I fall back into the sofa and surf the Internet on my phone. Nothing specific. World news, local news, fucking me, latest presidential fuckup, fucking me again, and that's how it goes. I decide to play Boggle. A good word game'll free my mind from this shit.

I get bored after an hour, so I get the bag of crumpled-up money out of the stash wall, dump it all on the living-room floor. I find my plastic bag of rubber bands, then start straightening out the bills and making stacks of ones, fives, tens, and twenties.

I'm taking my time, with several breaks, so it takes a while.

When it's all done, I have a floor covered with fifty-dollar stacks of ones, hundred-dollar stacks of fives, and five-hundred-dollar stacks of tens and twenties. All in all, I have twenty-three thousand dollars, which is a hell of a lot more than I thought it would be.

I stack the money neatly on the third shelf in the stash wall, stuff the filthy garbage bag in the trash, and wash my hands thoroughly.

My phone rings. It's a DC jail prefix.

I hesitate to answer, but decide to risk it. "Marr."

"This is Robby."

"You shouldn't be calling me" is all I know to say, but then, "Everything good?" Because I sense something in his voice. Something not so good.

"I just don't know what the hell I'm doing. I really need something about now. I don't know if I can handle it like this."

I want to tell him this is being recorded, but I don't want to make it sound like I have something to hide.

"You can do it. You have to. That urge will pass. You cooperate, and you'll be out soon enough."

"It's just…"

"Just what, Robby?"

"I just fucking hate myself like this. I can't…too much going on in my head."

I know that feeling well. It's not like he's having the shakes or anything you get coming off of heroin. It's just a mental need. Something to ease all the shit. Self-medication. Something you're fucking used to. Your body and mind don't know anything else. I want to tell him I understand, but for obvious reasons…

"They'll debrief you tomorrow, Robby. And your attorney will work out a good deal. I'm sure you'll get probation and be released soon. You'll start feeling better every day. You'll be clean."

"I don't know. I'm not…I have to get out of here."

"You will. You're valuable, Robby. Your attorney knows that. The prosecutor knows that."

"They have to take me back now. I just wanted…I don't know. You're probably right."

"You'll get through this, Robby. Stay strong, my friend."

I don't know what else I could've said. But I'd hate to be in his position.

I could be you, Biddy.

What separates us, and keeps me from where you are now, is my meager pension, my skill, and my drug of choice.

Damn.

"Okay. Have to go." And he disconnects.

I call Hurley, but it goes to voice mail. I leave him a detailed message about the call and tell him that maybe he should look into it.

SEVENTY-NINE

I didn't expect Monday when I woke. The phone ringing snapped me out, but I'm not sure it was out of sleep.

Monday. It somehow slipped in without my knowledge. I don't know what happened to the weekend.

The only reason I answer the phone is because it's Hurley. It's late morning, so maybe he got finished with the debriefing or is finally responding to my message.

"How's it going, Joe?"

"I catch you sleeping?"

"Naw, I'm good. How's everything?"

"Not so good, Frank."

"What?" I'm afraid to ask.

"Got a call earlier from DC jail. That's where we are now."

"So you got my message?"

"Yes. But I'm afraid Givens hanged himself. He's dead."

"What the fuck! No. How? How could that happen?" I ask, even though I know of several ways it can happen. And does.

All the time.

"He was separated from general population for his own safety..."

Pauses after realizing how stupid that sounds.

"Guard found him in the cell. He tore up a pants leg from his prison uniform, tied it to a top bar, knotted it around his neck, and dropped hard, with his butt barely off the ground. So it probably took time, but it worked."

"And you're sure that's how it went down? Suicide?"

"No, but it doesn't look like there was a struggle. An autopsy will tell us more. Millhoff is handling it. Sorry, man."

"You didn't mention the message I left you saying that he called me."

"Yes. Sorry I didn't get back. Went to a Nats game with my kids, and you know..."

"He was calling for help, and I was fucking clueless."

"It's not your fault."

"Fuck if it isn't."

"It's no one's fault. How could you know?"

Thinking back on the conversation, I do know, I did know, but I was too fucked up at the time to realize it.

"He called for fucking help. All I did was tell him he shouldn't be calling me and that everything would be all right. Fuck. I mean, it was so easy. All he had to do was cooperate, and he'd probably get a slap on the wrist."

"Yeah. I don't know what to say, bro."

"So where does this leave you?"

"Floating, almost dead in the water."

"What do you mean? You got the kid as a cooperator, right?"

"No. Some more bad news there. His lawyer said he changed his mind and would rather take his chances in court."

"Son of a bitch! Jasper had to get to him somehow."

"I'm sure he did. More than likely through his brother. We

have plenty to work with, though, so we're not giving up yet. Wyatt's knife had what appears to be dried blood on a few parts where the blade folds into the handle. Not as fresh. Might be something."

"He's dead. How's that going to help the case against Jasper?"

"Everything is too circumstantial, Frank, not even close to enough for a warrant."

"Lean on the boys. Press 'em. The younger one will break. Trust me," I say with a bit too much familiarity.

"We got other evidence from their home. See where it leads."

He means the guns I left behind.

"If Biddy's suicide turns out to be something more, you be sure to tell me, okay?"

"I will."

I want to throw the phone, but then I'd have nothing. Nothing.

It's my fault. I should have realized. Get him on suicide watch. How could I not see that?

A couple of hours later, before I can fall into complete self-loathing, my phone rings again. This time Luna.

He's been checking in on me a lot, like the good friend he is. He wants to come over, bring me a sub from his spot off Florida Avenue, Northeast. I haven't had anything to eat since yesterday afternoon, so I accept.

It'd be nice to have a good friend to talk to. All this shit needs to find a release—at least the stuff that *can* be released.

Eighty

I straighten everything up around the house, make sure there's nothing to incriminate me. Luna has a tendency to wander, make himself at home wherever he is.

He arrives an hour or so after the call, holding a large brown bag. I haven't seen him in a while. The bags under his eyes are more evident. He's wearing tan BDU pants and a light green polo, tucked in. He gives me this *What the fuck?* look.

We shake hands but don't follow with the customary knocking shoulders because of my injury.

"Come in, bro," I say.

"Damn, Frankie. You got messed up."

"Yes, I did."

He steps in, turning down the volume on the handheld radio secured to his belt, then setting it on the coffee table so he can hear it. After time, your ears get keen to the dispatcher's voice and what she says, no matter how low the volume, especially if it's something related to you or an officer in need of assistance.

322 • David Swinson

I sit on the sofa, and Luna sets the bag on the coffee table and sits on the armchair.

"You be sure to get yourself a lawyer. Better yet, a good-looking lawyer who loves you."

"Afraid we're on the skids right now."

"What the fuck happened?"

"I happened" is all I say.

"That shouldn't have been enough. She's tougher than you."

"Yes, she is, but I fucked up."

"You wanna talk about it?"

"Sorry, man, but no."

"Damn. You are being tested, my friend."

"I'll see how it goes. If it goes to a grand jury, then I'll find someone. I know a few good defense attorneys." I look at the sub. "This looks great," I say, changing the subject.

"It's an everyday thing for me," he says while rubbing his little Buddha belly.

"Better slow down there, buddy."

"Fuck you. Looks like you lost too much weight. You eating regular?"

"Nothin' but solid muscle on these bones. I eat well."

He pulls out two small bags of chips, some napkins, and the two subs.

"You want something to drink? A beer, maybe?"

"That'll just make me more tired. I got a soda in here."

He pulls that out.

"I'm going to crack a beer. Be right back."

He begins to unwrap the beast of a sub he's got. I grab a good micro out of the fridge, pop the cap, and return.

After a swig I ask, "So you hear anything with my name in it?"

"Usual shit. You keep getting yourself caught up in bad situations."

"Department doesn't have anything to come at me with, though, right?"

"You mean your PI shit?"

"Yeah. I mean that and more."

"Not that I heard. Being at NSID, I'm separated from all that political crap, except for the petty shit they're making us do now."

"What's that?"

"Same as it always is—no long-term investigations, just buy busts and quick hits. Five more years of this, and I'm outta there. Maybe come work for you."

Uh, not a good idea.

"Yeah, that'd be fun. You hear anything about Wyatt Morris?"

"Only that he's—was—a piece of shit. He came on in eighty-nine, back when the department didn't care about background checks, just bodies on the street."

"Right. Dirty Dozen and all that. Anything about my source, Robert Diamond?"

"Not really," he says, then takes a big bite out of the sub. Sauce drips on my coffee table. "Shit. Sorry."

He wipes it up with a napkin.

"Don't worry about it. This place is a disaster area."

"I mean that I don't have good information for you." Luna smiles. He looks around, notices wires.

"You gonna just put a frame around those wires up there or get around to replacing the TV?"

"I'll replace it eventually. Sort of nice not having one. Waste all my time watching cable."

"Don't know how you can live without it."

I finally break into my sub. Roast turkey with provolone, bacon, and Brie. Damn; hope my stomach can take it. I bite into it, but I have bad cotton mouth, so I have to chase it down with the beer, which isn't so good.

"So you're one lucky son of a bitch, my friend," he says.

"Yeah. I'm grateful."

"Don't know what I'd do if you weren't around to constantly ask me for favors."

"You'd be drinking alone."

"Ha."

"You know this officer at 1D, Willy Jasper?"

"He's been on scenes before, but that's about it. He's an FTO, right?"

"Yeah. Wyatt Morris also worked for him at the door for a part-time gig he has."

"No shit?"

"But there's more. Jasper is related to that officer who got killed in the drive-by at Seventeenth and Euclid. Remember? Cordell Holm's boys?"

"No shit? You know the FBI managed to connect that officer to the murder of that teenage boy in Virginia, right?"

Yeah. I was the one who made the call to them.

"I heard. Don't know how they kept that out of the news."

"C'mon, man, how long you been gone?"

"Apparently too long. Cordell and his crew get sentenced yet?"

"Everyone rolled on everyone. It's still an ongoing plea agreement. Be a waste of my time if it wasn't for all the OT I'm getting."

"You need to share some of that with me. I gave them to you on a silver platter." I take a smaller bite of the sub this time.

"And I thank you dearly, but fuck you."

"Call it payback, then, for all the favors you've given me."

"Yeah, let's call it that. So how is this Jasper involved in all this?"

"Dirty motherfucker, but no way to connect him. This is between you and me, okay?"

He nods. That's all I need.

"The guy who hit my house was cooperating and giving up Jasper for some bad deeds. Just found out he committed suicide in jail. But get this: I think Jasper's got it out for me. In some warped way he might hold me responsible for Officer Tommy's death. He's connected to all this shit that's been going on. Hurley and Millhoff even know that, but they don't have anything substantial. The one good source they had killed himself, and the other one's pulled out. So for my protection, let me know what you hear. I'm not being paranoid here."

"I can look at you and see that," he says, referring to my bandages.

"The other source they had is called Repo. He's a drug dealer associated with Jasper. I know that Repo and his brother dealt their drugs out of the club Jasper worked."

"How do you know this?"

"I still have sources."

"And you never want to share them, do you?"

"We share one."

"Tamie Darling. That's just a voice when you need it. She's never good for information."

"It's something, though."

"I'll look into it for you."

"Appreciate it."

"I know every department has its own share of dirty laundry."

"Don't I know it."

"I'm serious, brother. I don't know what's going on except what little I hear, and now all this from you. Fucking be careful."

"Always."

EIGHTY-ONE

Three days of this shit. Moping around the house. I slept hard but had too much to dream, and that can be exhausting. I keep waking up.

I'm not ready to get out of bed. Need to let this aching mind settle. I think about cocaine, how it would help about now, but then I think about Biddy, his uncle, and, oddly enough, Leslie. Maybe it's not that odd. It makes me wonder how long I can go without having to have any coke.

Damn, I liked Diamond. I liked Biddy even more. Had some weird connection with him. Can't get it out of my mind that if I wasn't so fucking hardheaded and simply left the burglary investigation up to Hurley, they'd still be alive. But then there's Jeffrey. I couldn't just sit there. Do nothing.

I should've shot Biddy in the leg when he had that gun on his lap. He would've gotten arrested, but at least he'd still be in the hospital, alive, with a cop on hospital detail to watch him.

All these people floating around in my head.

Leslie especially…

I wake up later on the sofa, a half-empty bottle of Jameson in my hand, just as the doorbell rings.

I think I smell bad.

It's past 10:00 a.m.

I push myself off the sofa, walk to the door, and check through the peephole.

Millhoff and Hurley.

Hurley's holding a manila folder.

"Hold on," I say.

I hurry back to the living room, look around. The only thing is the bottle of Oxys that isn't prescribed to me. I put it under the sofa cushion. Bottle of Jameson can stay where it is. I'm still in my boxers and T-shirt, but I open the door anyway.

They give me a quick look-over, nothing that looks like concern, more like *Didn't expect this.*

"Bad night," I say.

"Can we talk?" Hurley asks. That means I have to invite them in.

"You have a warrant for obstruction or anything else to take me away with?"

"Of course not," Hurley says.

Millhoff shakes his head.

"Do you want to get dressed?" Millhoff asks.

"I'm comfortable. Been loafing around lately."

"Yeah, we can smell that," Millhoff says.

"Sorry. Been meaning to take a shower. Come in, if you can tolerate it."

I close the door behind them and walk to the living room. I sit on the side of the sofa where the Oxys are under the cushion.

I signal with my hand for them to have a seat.

Millhoff takes the armchair and Hurley the other side of the sofa.

I light a cigarette.

Millhoff looks at the bottle of Jameson.

"All the doctor prescribed me was Motrin for this shit. You believe that? That's been my painkiller."

"You okay, Frank?"

"I'm fine. Want to get back to working, though. Good news is the doctor said I'm healing fine; he'll be taking the staples out next week. You guys want some coffee or something?"

"I'm good," Millhoff says.

"Me, too."

"What's going on?"

They look at each other like *Who should begin first?*

Millhoff does. "Sorry we haven't been in touch."

"I don't expect you to stay in touch, but thanks."

"Talked to the boys in Alexandria yesterday, and it looks like they won't be pursuing any charges."

"Good to know," I say, but I was never worried about it one way or the other.

"Want to share with you a couple of things," Millhoff says. "Not that we have to, but both Hurley and I thought you should know."

"You mean like how you're obligated to share certain things with a victim?"

"We're trying to give you some respect here, Frank."

"I know. Go on. I'm just not myself."

"Forensics took that folding knife you got stabbed with apart. Every piece. Found dried blood on the bottom edge of the tang. It wasn't your blood. It was an unknown."

"Tang?" I ask.

"A little part of a knife," Millhoff says.

I snuff out the cigarette and light another one. They got my interest.

"Your informant, Diamond—" Millhoff begins.

"You're fucking kidding me," I say right away.

"DNA was a match."

"How the hell you get it done so fast?"

"Was able to get it expedited through the feds. As you probably know, the case got seriously political the day your cousin's mom flew to DC."

"I still don't have a TV, but I've seen it all over the Internet."

"Needless to say, that gave us leverage. We were under fire with this one."

"That fuck killed the—Diamond. I knew it."

"Yeah," Millhoff says.

"What about Jeffrey?"

"Nothing yet. No prints on your gun."

"Damn."

"We're working it hard."

"Diamond was a good man. If it were just him, this would have never been expedited."

"Don't go there, man."

"He got caught up in all this shit because of his nephew, who was like a son to him. You still got that piece of shit Jasper walking free, like he's king of his world, and he's the one responsible for Diamond, for Biddy, and for fucking Jeffrey. Tell me you got him."

I can tell by the look Millhoff throws my way that they didn't.

I pour myself half a glass of Jameson. Take a swig. Burns in the morning.

"The kid nicknamed Repo," Millhoff says, "finally rolled, but not like we thought he would. The gun we got out of his room came back to the shooting on Rhode Island Avenue."

"Eugene Wrayburn, remember?" Hurley says.

"Of course."

"Once that happened," Millhoff continues, "he couldn't stop yapping. But he's putting it all on Wyatt Morris. He pulled back on Jasper having anything to do with anything."

"You know that's bullshit. I mean, it's perfect, because how's a dead man gonna defend himself?"

"We know that. You know that. We have another debriefing set up. We'll try to hit him harder with what he's looking at, which is some very serious time."

"My cousin got messed up with Wrayburn, probably buying powder from him, am I right?" Of course I already know I am.

"You're right," Millhoff says. "Your cousin started dealing more and more at the club. And the club was territory to Jasper's boys, Repo and his brother. Wrayburn started skimming from their stash to feed his buyers, your cousin being one of them. They were making some good money together. According to Repo, Morris found out about Jeffrey and took care of him."

"In my house."

"That's another story," Millhoff admits.

"What about my stolen gun on Wrayburn's chest? Right now, that's looking like it was a message from Jasper because of Officer Tommy."

"The AUSA opened a grand jury original. You willing to appear?"

Fuck no!

"Of course."

"Good. You were a witness at the club, with seeing Wrayburn and the dece—your cousin—there. Then there's your gun and your interesting connection to Jasper because of the drive-by. I'm pretty sure that everything that Biddy and Diamond told you about Jasper will be hearsay because they're not here to testify. A good defense attorney will probably get that thrown out, but then I'm not a lawyer, so maybe I'm wrong. We'll have to get with the

AUSA, but we'll definitely need you for all the other stuff when the grand jury investigation gets going."

"Whatever it takes," I say.

"But not in the shape you're in," Millhoff says.

Well, there's only one way I know of to get back to the way I was—better.

"With all this shit going on, I know there's no way certain officials didn't get word. So why didn't Jasper get suspended for the part-time?"

"We want him to feel safe. Lot of shit happening in that club."

"He may be a good-for-nothing, but he's not stupid enough to get caught up in illegal activity now," I say.

"Well, he *is* working the club," Hurley says. "His supervisors at 1D don't give a shit. They'd have to suspend half the department for doing the same thing. So they let it go, and we don't talk about it. We only deal with our command, and they let us do what we have to do to make a good case."

"Remember the phrase they would pound into our heads at investigator school—'Time is always on our side,'" Millhoff says.

I'm not that patient.

I change the subject 'cause I'm getting pissed off.

"What about Biddy? Was it a suicide?"

"Yes," Millhoff says. "Nothing suspicious. No struggle. He's the main reason we stopped by, though."

"Go on."

"You must have made a connection with him somehow, because before he committed suicide he gave a guard a message to relay to you."

"What?"

"The only family he had left was his uncle, Robert Diamond, and Diamond's son is out of the country. Probably would have asked a relative to tell you instead. But he had no one."

Hurley pulls out a white piece of paper, a photocopy of someone's handwritten notes on what looks like a pocket notebook.

"This is what the guard notebooked after Biddy told him that," Hurley says, handing it over to me.

I read it.

I don't like who I am right now. I want to apologize for breaking into your house and messing your life up.

"Guard said those may not have been his exact words," Millhoff advises me.

"I don't understand. Why would he say that?"

"Make amends, something like that," Millhoff says.

"And the CO didn't think that was a bit odd and maybe they should put a watch on him?"

"Guard took it as just another crackhead trying to get sympathy from the court. He wrote it down. It went through the right channels and finally got to us."

"I guess your burglary is officially closed." Millhoff smiles.

I don't respond to that.

All I can think of now is fuck everything. It has to change.

After they leave, I sit back and think about it, what I have to do. It doesn't take long, because I already know.

I go to the laundry room, look at all that blow on the shelf in my wall.

It looks back.

"You're the best I ever had," I tell it. "But fuck…"

EIGHTY-TWO

I find an illegal spot to park, 'cause I don't give a fuck. I step out and walk easy, because it's hot with this suit on. I got my back-pack over my good shoulder. I make my way to the rear lot of the nightclub. This is Jasper's night to work. I don't know what kind of car he drives, but I want to check out all the vehicles parked back there and look at the back entrance. I don't know which way Jasper will go when he exits at the end of the night.

One of the cars in the lot has tags with an FOP logo on them, but it could belong to someone who's working for Jasper. It's a beautifully kept old-model Cadillac DeVille. I note all the tags and return to my car.

Start it up and get that air-conditioning on high. I want to have these tags run. If one of them is his car, it'll make this a hell of a lot easier. If it doesn't pan out, then I'll have to find a new sur-veillance spot where I can make out the front and the rear. Pretty certain that the only way I'll get that kinda view is on foot.

It's still the evening shift, and I know I'm gonna piss the hell out of Luna. I call him.

"How you doing, Frankie?" he answers.

"Much better. Smaller bandage on my hand now. Stitches should come out in a few days. You on the street?"

"Naw, doing some write-up. Locked up a few buyers. Fucking waste of my time. So what's up?"

"You know, the usual."

"Fuck you, Frankie."

"No. This is important. These cars keep driving up and down my block, same cars all the time. I don't know if Hurley's task force is watching my house because of Jasper or what, but it's getting me nervous."

"Get a cruiser to go over and check it out."

"No. I don't want to waste anybody's time if it turns out to be nothing."

"Fucking give me the tags."

I do.

A couple minutes later he comes back with, "I'm going to come over now."

"What the fuck? Why?"

"One of those tags comes back to Jasper's personal vehicle."

"No shit?"

"Yeah. I'll call a cruiser to get over there, and I'm on my way, too."

"No. You have work to do, and I'm still pretty good with my gun. I'm not leaving the house, and I know he's not stupid enough to come in. He's probably just checking if cops are surveilling me."

"The other two cars come back to females, but it might be a couple of his boys in them."

"I'm serious, Al. Don't fucking come here. I'm going to call Hurley. I know they have him under surveillance, and I don't want to fuck it up for him."

"Fucking stay away from your windows, all right?"

"Don't worry, partner. We've both been through much worse."

"If I don't hear from you in thirty, I'm going there."

"I'll call you back. Stay out of this. I mean it, and don't call Hurley, because I'm not supposed to be talking to anybody about it. So which tag is it?"

"The FOP tag. It's a red Cadillac sedan."

"I got it. I'll talk to you later. And do not call anybody, Luna. You'll fuck me up."

"Shut up with that shit talk. Thirty minutes."

"Later."

"Yeah."

I slip my phone in the inner pocket of my jacket.

My night just got a whole lot easier.

EIGHTY-THREE

I call Luna back in thirty minutes and advise him that Hurley's on it. I pound it into him to not tell anyone I told him about the investigation. After a few expletives, he promises.

I grab my backpack. My big sacrifice is inside it. I cut a few grams off of the brick I got from the boys on Riggs Street, enough to wean me off. The rest—fuck, that'll make District court if Jasper gets locked up with it. And if I do it right, he will.

I feel like I'm giving up my life.

Shit. Don't think twice.

I also have the gun that I took off Biddy and five thousand dollars in denominations of fives, tens, and twenties. On the way here I stopped at a gas station near my house, where I bought a few boxes of zips, like the kind a corner dealer would use to sell anything from a quarter gram to a full gram of blow. I also bought a box containing fifty rose-glass tubes, like the kind used for crack pipes.

I sit in the car until it's after midnight. Fewer people walking around on the side streets. Most of the action is in the front of the club. I do a single hefty bump and walk back to the lot.

I'm blessed, really. The DeVille is old enough for my slim jim to work on it. I'll try not to scratch the car's finish. It's in pristine condition. The fuckhead probably has it detailed once a week.

I'm good with the slim jim. Back when I was on patrol, I was the guy they called when citizens locked their keys in their cars or when there was a search warrant. Nowadays, a slim jim is useless unless it's an old-model car.

I scan my surroundings again. On one side of the building is a small side street with zero traffic on it. I look up at the rear entrance, too. Gotta be cautious.

I get the slim jim placed just right, near the inside door handle. Move it up slowly, feel the rod, and pull up.

Lock pops up. With any luck there's no new-type alarm system. Even then I can do what I have to do very fast.

I open the door.

No alarm.

I pop the trunk, close the door quietly, move around to the rear of the car, and lift the trunk lid to look inside.

Fuck me!

I huff out a half chuckle 'cause I'm so happy. It's like Christmas.

A couple hundred records and an equal number of CDs are stacked in several piles along the large bed of the trunk. I don't even have to look through them to know they're mine. The cover edges I can see reveal the titles. Fucking Fugazi, Ramones, Funkadelic, Velvet Underground, Johnny Cash, Nick Cave and the Bad Seeds, just to name a few, and then the CDs—Spacemen 3, the Cave Singers, Pogues, and so many more. And then there's a laptop, but it isn't mine. Why would that motherfucker keep all this in the trunk of his car with everything going down around him? Arrogant asshole or just stupid. Maybe he's gonna dispose of it all.

Whatever. I feel…so vindicated. But I know I have to make another sacrifice. I can't take anything. It's a chance, because Hurley is the only one who can make the connection, so I'm hoping he gets a call if—or, I hope, when—Jasper gets nabbed.

I place the money beneath two stacks of records. I set the boxes of zips and the rose pipes in a space toward the front, then open the box of zips and scatter some around the same area. I also sprinkle a bit of cocaine on the trunk liner and on a plastic Pogues CD case. I take out five of the rose pipes so it looks like he sold a few.

I quietly close the trunk and return to the front door. I check under the seat using my Streamlight.

Nothing there. Clean dude.

I slip the wrapped cocaine under the seat so it's secured between a couple of thick metal bars, but not so far under that it's hard to see. I do the same with the gun. I lock and then close the door.

While I'm walking back to my car I notice a good spot on the side street to park.

I back my car into the parking space, keep it running, but turn off all my lights.

There are so many ways this can go bad—Jasper's on midnights in 1D, but Friday and Saturday are his days off. I'm sure every cop working 1D midnights knows him. Whoever rolls onto the scene after I make the call might let it go and clear the scene as a prank call once they find out who he is. It's a roll of the dice. But if it doesn't play out here, I'll follow him into Maryland. PG County doesn't fuck around, especially on midnight shift.

I feel good about it.

I recline the seat back to a cozy position and take a nice swig of whiskey from the sport bottle. I crack the window, too, and light up a smoke.

Cicadas aren't so annoying tonight. This part of town, I guess. Not many trees to make love on. The ones that are calling out sound a little lonely.

EIGHTY-FOUR

Oh-three-hundred hours rolls around.

Oh-four-hundred hours rolls around.

It's that special time in the morning when I used to get up to go to work because we had a search warrant. Used to love that feeling. Feels like that now.

I see a few people walk around from the front. Can't see the front door with the stairs that lead up to the club, but I see four people come around the corner. Two women first, then two men. One of them is Jasper. One of the women is the bartender who served me when I was at the club. The other guy sure as hell looks like the officer who drove by Leslie's home when we were sitting on her stairs. He gave us that odd, uncomfortable look. They're both wearing suits.

I get my burner phone, and I pray those two hotshot officers who checked me out last time I was doing surveillance here are on the job.

I call 911.

A woman answers with "Nine one one. What's your emergency?"

I disguise my voice by talking fast and in a lower pitch. I give her the location of the rear of the club.

"I'm just getting off work as a bartender, and I'm sitting in my car. I saw a skinny homeless man walk up to a large man who's sitting in a red old-model Cadillac DeVille."

"What's your emergency, sir?"

"Please listen. The homeless man gave the man in the car a gun and a laptop in exchange for something that looked like drugs. The man put the laptop in the trunk of his Cadillac but held on to the gun."

"Are those men there now?" she asks.

"Yes. Again, I saw the man from the Cadillac get a clear baggie of what looked like drugs out of the front of his car, then go to the trunk to do something."

"Where are you now?"

"I'm on the side street, just a few feet away. The man just gave the homeless guy something else that he got from out of his trunk. Maybe money, too. You have to hurry. The homeless guy is leaving. The man just carried the clear baggie back to the front. I think he's getting ready to leave."

"Describe the man, sir."

I give her a good description of Jasper as well as a description of the vehicle and its tag number.

Jasper and the other three hit the parking lot. He shakes hands with the fuckboy FTO, who gets in a late-model Camry with the bartender. The other girl sticks around to talk to Jasper.

"Hold on, sir," the dispatcher advises.

I hear her dispatch a primary and a secondary unit to the scene. No lights or sirens, so it's not a code 1. Smart dispatcher.

"And you're sure he had a gun, sir?"

"Yes. Positive."

I hear her say, "Subject might be armed, so use caution."

"I have units responding now, sir. What is your name?"

"Robert, but I don't want to get involved."

The other guy backs out and drives away with the bartender.

"The responding officers will need to interview you after they investigate."

"No. He looks really dangerous. I just got married. No."

"Please stay on the phone with me, sir."

"They have to hurry. He's talking to a woman now. I don't know what he's going to do."

The woman hugs Jasper, then enters one of the other cars, looks like a Subaru. Jasper watches her drive off, then makes his way to his car.

"He's getting ready to leave," I say.

"Units are responding. Can you give me your name, please?"

"Robert. That's all," and I disconnect.

I see two units speed down Connecticut and make the left onto the side street. I recline my seat farther down and turn off my car.

The first one on the scene is a 10-4 unit. They roll in the lot and block Jasper's car just as his rear lights turn on. The second car is a 10-99. The driver pulls behind the other cruiser.

The two officers in the first cruiser shine the car's spotlight through the rear window of the Cadillac.

They jump out, guns drawn, and shield themselves behind their car doors. The officer from the second cruiser does the same.

Boys in the first car look like the two hotshots I met.

I hear the hotshot driver of the first vehicle yelling commands.

"Turn off your car! Turn off your car!"

The Cadillac's rear lights go off.

"Let me see your hands out the front window! Palms up! Now!"

Sounds like Jasper is screaming out the window of his car. Something inaudible.

More commands.

Jasper obeys, and I think he stuck his hand out with an open wallet to reveal his badge. The officers are still cautious and shout more commands.

Jasper rises slowly from the car, yelling something like "I'm the police."

The primary officer yells more commands until Jasper complies and starts to walk backwards to the middle of the lot and appears to go down to his knees. The driver and his partner slowly approach. The officer from the second vehicle approaches the front door of the Caddy. Bright light from his Streamlight lights the area ahead of him. Everything by the book.

Couple seconds later I can see Jasper being helped up, but not in handcuffs.

Shit.

My window is up, so I can't hear. The officer who yelled all the commands gets on his handheld radio. Then he talks to Jasper, who seems to be smiling now.

It's already starting to roast in here. I'm breaking out in sweat but will have to suffer through it.

I notice the officer from the second car shine the light into the front-seat area of the Caddy because Jasper left the door open. He bends down, like he's trying to get a better view under the seat. He calmly walks over to the hotshot driver, who is still with his partner and talking to Jasper. The officer, now standing a couple of feet behind Jasper, gets the driver's attention with a hand signal that I recognize as *Need to talk*. Driver walks over to him. Jasper watches. Driver's partner stands beside Jasper, gun now holstered.

Secondary officer whispers something, then the driver walks toward the Caddy as the secondary moves easily to the other side of Jasper, but taking more of a defensive position.

Driver clicks his Streamlight on, stoops down to look under the seat.

Jasper appears upset, speaking loudly, but not worried. I can't make it out. I'm fucking boiling in this car with the window up and the engine off. I hear the driver say something about "our safety." Jasper is resistant but doesn't fight them as they cuff his hands behind his back and lean him against the rear of the first cruiser.

Partner and the secondary officer stay with Jasper while the driver returns to the front of the car. He leans in. Driver moves to the trunk and opens it with the keys.

He shakes his head, something like disbelief.

Jasper tries to look back over his shoulder, like *What the fuck is going on?*

The officer from the second car pats him down and searches him. He pulls out a gun from Jasper's right side, near his waist.

Jasper's turning, now screaming at the officers.

I can hear him yell, "Fuck, I'm one of you! What the hell is this? That's my service weapon, fuckwad!"

What is there to do but smirk and smile big, despite the sweat all over my face?

EIGHTY-FIVE

Hot morning sun. Finished all my water and starting to feel dehydrated. A lot of officials showed up, even Deputy Chief Wightman.

Wightman looked happy. Probably already had Jasper on his bad-boy list.

Crime Scene Search just cleared the scene, and Jasper's car is finally getting towed.

I'm good to go.

I start the car, get the seat back to its regular position, and blast the air.

Damn, that feels good.

I let the tow truck pull out.

I head home to take a cold shower.

After a shower, I plop on my bed wearing only my boxers. I think sleep is going to be my friend today.

I look at my phone for the time, remember the message Aunt Linda left but I never listened to.

I go to Messages, click it to play. *I'm happy that we were able to talk face-to-face. I just want you to know that I believe in you, because the smile I saw on your face when we were sitting in the car is the same one I remember you having as a little boy. Don't worry, Frankie. Every day has enough trouble of its own. We'll talk soon. I love you.*

Damn.

EIGHTY-SIX

Midday, and I step out of the car onto Riggs Street, fold up the bag, and walk up to the house. Ring the doorbell. A minute later, a young lady answers. I know she's not a relative because she's Hispanic.

"Can I help you?" she asks with a kind smile.

"I'm a neighbor. I don't really know the lady who lives here, but we all heard about what happened. Is she okay?"

"Yes, she's fine. I'm with social services and here to check up on her. She's in the living room if you'd like to say hello."

"So she's moving around?"

"A little every day, but she still has to use a walker. She can take care of herself, though."

"Those troublemaking boys aren't here, are they?"

"No. They're both in jail, but that's all I know."

"Then I think I will come in and say hello. I don't think she'll remember me. It seems like forever since I saw her walking around."

"Can you wait? I'll go see if she wants company."

"Of course."

She returns, opens the security gate to let me in.

"She's on the sofa in the living room."

"Thank you."

The social worker walks to the kitchen. It's like this is a different house. Clean. Smells fresh. She's on the sofa watching a talk show on the flat-screen, which is now mounted on the wall above the coffee table. I approach her.

She looks me over. Hard.

"You can sit down."

I sit beside her on the sofa. It's a new sofa.

"I don't know you," she says firmly.

"I live in the neighborhood, but it has been a while."

She still looks frail but not so sickly. Looks like she put on a bit of good weight, too.

She looks at me direct. "I think I remember you now."

"That's good."

"What are you doing back here?"

That throws me.

"How do you mean?"

"Yes, I remember you. You're the tax man. The one who got rid of those terrible boys for me."

Tax man? Oh, yeah. Shit.

"You're confusing me with someone else, ma'am, maybe an officer."

"No officer I know would have taken care of those boys like that."

"I'm sorry. I don't follow you, but this here is something my neighborhood collected for you. Like a fund-raiser."

I offer her the bag.

She puts it on her lap and looks in.

The social worker returns from the kitchen.

The old lady folds the bag up again and sets it on the sofa be-tween us. The social worker sits on a chair in the dining room, trying not to be a bother.

"Fund-raiser?" the old lady asks.

I've read hundreds of people's faces in my line of work, and her face is utterly unreadable.

"Yes, ma'am, and we hope it helps."

"It does indeed."

"Okay. I'll be on my way, then. I'm happy to see you home."

"Happy to still have a home."

I stand up to leave.

"You can visit again," she says.

"Okay."

I smile, shoot the social worker a wave, and walk out.

EIGHTY-SEVEN

Later that afternoon I get a call from Hurley. He wants to meet me at the 3D. It's a short drive there. I park on 17th, where a lot of the cruisers are parked.

Hurley is waiting for me in the front lobby area. He's alone. Place looks cleaner than it was last time I was here.

"What's up?" I ask as we shake hands.

"How you healing?"

"Some nerve damage in my hand, but nothing I can't handle. Stitches are coming out."

"Good to hear, but sorry about the nerve damage."

"Like I said, no big deal."

"Need to see if you can identify some items."

Oh, yeah. Please let it be . . .

"In the community room."

I follow him to a set of double doors. He swings one open.

My record and CD collection, laptop, and all the stereo equipment Hurley recovered from Thrift World are all nicely displayed on a rectangular foldout table. Everything is coated with finger-print powder.

"You're kidding me," I say with excitement.

"Sorry about the mess. They had to dust for prints."

"I can clean that up. Damn. It's all mine. All my mom's shit. Where did you find the records and the laptop?"

"Laptop on a search warrant and everything else in the trunk of a car. Obviously you know where we got the stereo equipment."

I pick up one of the records, wipe the fine powder off with the palm of my hand.

"They don't look warped," I say. "I'm assuming you got an arrest."

"Oh, yeah, bro. Willy Jasper." He smiles from ear to ear.

"You serious? Fuck. Can you talk about it?"

"You still don't have a television, huh?"

"No."

"So that's why I didn't hear from you first. It's all over the news, brother. He got arrested in the parking lot behind his club. Some anonymous call about a drug transaction. Officers get to the scene, are ready to clear it as a bad call when they find out he's an officer they know, but Jasper leaves the front door open and a curious rookie looks under the seat from a distance—plain view—and makes a sweet discovery. I mean, we got a lot of pow-der cocaine, a gun that comes back to a burglary, bunch of cash, paraphernalia, and of course all this here."

"No shit? You put your cuffs on him?"

"No. We didn't find out he was locked up until the next day. After that we took it over. We hit his home and took everything. Cleaned his house out. Put it all on the book as suspected stolen property. All I have to do with your stuff is sign it over to you. I already took photos, and the AUSA approved it. Said the photos and you would be more than enough for court."

"Joe, this is incredible news. They put a hold on him?"

"District court, baby. They held his ass. PWID while armed, receiving stolen property. Throw in the two from Riggs Street, and we'll add conspiracy. His operation connects, Frank. It connects to everything."

"Well, you are officially Supercop now."

"Yeah, right. But we're going to work it, tie him to everything else, I hope."

"Great work, man."

"We got lucky."

Lucky. Yeah.

"What about the other cop who worked for him at the club?" I ask, referring to the one who gave me and Leslie the snake eye when we were on her stoop, the one I saw walking out of the club with Jasper that morning. "I got a feeling you wanna be looking at him, too."

"We are. Don't worry about that. He's on administrative leave."

I'm confident it goes deeper than Snake Eyes.

Joe helps carry my stuff to my car. I shake his hand again and give him a bro shoulder hug. It hurts a little.

I get all my property home.

First thing I do is set up the stereo, then flip through my albums, decide on Johnny Cash because he was one of my mother's favorites. I wipe it clean with a rag I got, put it on the turntable, sit on the sofa, and light a cigarette.

I think about my mother and how she'd always listen to music in the privacy of her room. It was only meant for her. Not something she shared. I heard the songs through the closed door and always knew how she was feeling by the record she was playing.

My mind wanders, and my mother follows, until "It Ain't Me

Babe" plays, and that takes me to Leslie. Maybe after all this she'll talk to me again. Big maybe. I gotta clean up first.

I take the record off, find *Violent Femmes,* which has "Blister in the Sun" on it. I used to play it for Jeffrey all the time. Used to make him hop. Looked like a comical version of the pogo dance.

When it's over I lift the needle from the record. I need to get out of the house now, so I decide to take a drive to Alexandria to pick up my gun at the police department there.

I take the GW Parkway, the Potomac at my left. It looks inviting, like I should be out there on a johnboat.

Fishing.

Haven't been to the river for a long while. The good part of the river. There is a bad part, but that's behind me now. At least I hope it is. Don't want to even think about it.

Maybe Ohio? There're a couple of nice lakes near Aunt Linda's house. Good bass fishing, maybe walleye. A good reason to visit.

Yes, it is a good day. I got my stuff back and wrapped up that piece of shit Jasper. That alone should be enough, but it's not.

I get to Old Town and slow down as I pass the motel where Biddy stayed.

A couple of good men despite their faults. Both had real heart. Who am I to judge?

ACKNOWLEDGEMENTS

I have been blessed with having the best people in the publishing business behind the Frankie Marr series.

First, I'd like to thank my incredible agent, Jane Gelfman of Gelfman Schneider ICM Partners, for her invaluable advice, support, and patience in guiding me through this process and finding me the perfect home at Mulholland Books/Little, Brown and Company. Big, big thank you to Josh Kendall, my brilliant editor at Mulholland Books, who had faith in the first book, *The Second Girl,* and took me on. Josh helped mold these books and the character, and without him, both *The Second Girl* and *Crime Song* would not be the books they are. And thank you, Mulholland Books UK, especially my UK editor, Ruth Tross, who shares the vision. Thanks to the entire team at Mulholland and Little, Brown and Company for their unending support—specifically, Pam Brown, Katherine Myers, Sabrina Callahan, Emily Giglierano, Nicky Guerreiro, and Alyssa Persons. When I first met Josh, he told me that Mulholland Books was like a family, and he was right.

I'm grateful for all my brothers and sisters in the writing community and law enforcement. All of you are always there when I need you, and for that I thank you.

And finally, thanks to Dianne and Cheri for always being my first eyes before the manuscript goes out; my mother, Connie, and sister, Sara, for always believing; and then of course my incredible wife, Catherine, and daughter, Vivienne, for keeping me grounded and realizing what really matters in life.

ABOUT THE AUTHOR

David Swinson is a retired police detective, having served sixteen years with the Washington, DC, Metropolitan Police Department. Before joining the DC police, Swinson was a record store owner in Seal Beach, California, a punk rock–alternative concert promoter in Long Beach, California, and a music video producer and independent filmmaker in Los Angeles. He lives in Northern Virginia with his wife, daughter, bullmastiff, and Staffordshire terrier.

...AND *TRIGGER*

In this latest Frank Marr novel, Frank must choose between justice and loyalty to an old friend. In *Trigger,* he teams up with an unlikely ally to uncover the truth behind a friend from his old police days who may have shot an unarmed young man.

The following is an excerpt from the novel's opening pages.

ONE

Inever count the days. Why would I want to know how long it's been since I quit? It's only a reminder of what it is I'm trying to let go of. I loved the fucking lifestyle. I loved cocaine. Didn't want to let it go. I still have cravings. Pops in my head like it's a good thing, visit from an old friend, but all I got to do is remind myself of why it is I quit—because of all the people I hurt, even got killed. And yes, it is something I did for me, too, but not for the reasons you might think.

Sometimes what gets me through the day is doing what I'm best at.

It still gives me a rush, even more so without the cocaine high. You realize how reckless it is. Just how dangerous.

I slip on my tactical gloves, grab my suit jacket from the front seat, step out of the car. I put the suit jacket on, reach back in to take my backpack. I shoulder it and lock the car door.

The house I'm going to is up the street, second from the corner, an unattached, paint-peeled, light-blue two-story with a large patio.

I ring the doorbell. Wait. Ring again. Open the storm door and knock on the door a few times.

When enough time passes so I feel comfortable, I take the tactical pry bar out of my backpack, wedge it in between the door and the frame, about half an inch below the dead bolt. I smack the heavy flattop of the handle hard with the palm of my hand, and with one solid push inward, I pry the door open, bending the dead bolt out with the door.

I scan the area, slip the pry bar back in my pack, and enter. Once inside I stand and listen, then secure the backpack over my shoulders and quietly shut the door. There's a fold-up chair leaning against the wall beside a filthy sofa. I take the chair and prop it against the door to keep it closed.

My stun gun is clipped to my belt at the small of my back. My Glock 19 is in a holster on my right side, but I don't want to have to use it unless I find myself facing another gun. I'd figure out a good story after. That's why the stun gun is preferable. Saves me having to think up a good story.

I've known about the occupants of this house since I was a detective working narcotics. It's low-level. Detective Al Luna, my former partner at Narcotics Branch, and I hit it a couple of times. Sent a CI in to make a buy, then drafted an affidavit in support of a search warrant and rammed the door in the next day. A good quick hit, and we always got enough to make us look good when other work was slow. Luna's still on the job. Me? Well, that's another story.

Nothing has changed with how the boys in this house operate, except a couple of new faces that replaced the two who are doing a bit of time. They're working the same park area a couple blocks north of here, where some of the local drunks and junkies still hang, but not near as many as back in the day. Gentrification has seen to that, pretty much cleaned everything up. Lot of the dealers had to change up their game. These guys didn't have enough sense to. From what I've been able to learn, they haven't been hit by the police in a while. That can be good for me.

What has changed is who the boys cater to and all the homes in this neighborhood, once vacant shells, now worth a million bucks. They're dealing mostly to young clean-cut men and women who drive nice cars with Virginia tags and consider themselves social users, pulling up and making their deals without stepping out of the cars. Times change. Old street junkies die or go to jail for getting caught up in something bad. The boys gotta move up if they wanna make a living.

My cell phone vibrates inside my blazer's inner pocket. Nearly sends me through the roof. I don't pull it out. Instead I just let it go to voice mail.

This house is messy and still has that bad-breath-after-a-night-of-hard-drinking smell. A few of those empty Moet bottles on the floor and empty beer cans stuffed with cigarette butts have probably been there since Luna and I were here last. Gets me to wondering if they still keep their stash and money in the same spot.

I walk up the stairs to the room and that old spot.

Fuck. Sure enough they do. In the inner pockets of a couple of winter jackets hanging in the bedroom closet. I pull out baggies containing a good amount of zips with heroin, crack, and what looks like meth. All dimes and quarters, and a few larger. Fortunately, no cocaine. That'd be too much of a temptation. But that's why I targeted this spot. I was pretty sure they weren't selling that shit. I go through a couple more jacket pockets, and then, *oh fuck,* a baggie with about an ounce of powder. The wrong side of my brain starts to work me, and I say to myself, *Take it. Recreational purposes only. I can control it.*

Who am I kidding? I put it with the rest of the drugs. My cell vibrates again. I let it go to voice mail again. I'm not going to jinx this shit by pulling it out.

I find a wad of money in another coat pocket. Doesn't look

like more than a couple thousand. Small bills, rolled up and se-cured with one rubber band. I stuff it into my empty left pants pocket. Nice bulk there.

I search the rest of the room and find a little more cash, a cou-ple boxes of 9mm ammo, cheap rounds, only good for the range. I leave them and open the nightstand drawer. There's an older-model 9mm Taurus sitting on top of some other loose rounds.

I pick it up, drop the mag, let it land on the floor, then lock the slide back. A chambered round flips out, but I catch it, put it on the nightstand. I pull out the barrel and take the spring out. Pocket it, grab the mag, and put the gun back together. I leave the live round on the table and slip the gun in my pack.

I do a quick search of the rest of the house, but don't find shit.

I take the narcotics to the upstairs bathroom, break the baggies open, and drop the contents into the toilet, along with all the little zips. I flush, wait for the reserve tank to fill. Flush again. Wait a bit longer to make sure nothing pops up, then flush one more time. I grab the baggie of coke and quickly pour the lovely white powder into the toilet, too. Damn, that's hard, but I passed the test. Again. How many more tests before I don't have to worry about failing?

This is what I do.

TWO

Clouds are high, moving over the city slow. Smells like snow. On the way to the car, I toss the Taurus spring into a gutter drain, try to be discreet when I pull the gun out of my pack, drop it at my feet, and kick it into the drain.

After I start the car, I check the phone, see who called.

Leslie.

Damn.

Haven't talked to her in more than a year. Don't wanna think about that morning we last talked. I was so fucked up. I fucked up. I can't even remember most of what was said. She kicked me out of her house after, so it must have been bad. One of the worst days of my life. Losing her was. It's the hardest thing I've ever had to go through, even tougher than giving up blow. That shit was the reason I lost her to begin with. After I got myself four months clean, I called her and confessed and asked for forgiveness. Didn't matter. I think it made it worse 'cause I lied for all those years, even about why I had to retire from the police department—pissing dirty. According to her, I'd even jeopardized her law practice. So that was that.

What does she want now, after all this time?

She left a message on the second call. I hesitate to listen, but tap the screen, put the phone to my ear.

"I'm calling on behalf of Al Luna. It's important, so please call me back."

That's it.

On behalf of Al?

What kinda message is that, unless he's in trouble or sick? Al's still one of my closest friends, but I haven't talked to him in a few weeks. I was caught up in this bullshit domestic-violence, cheating-husband case that was resolved just yesterday. In fact, Al's busier than me, working that same Narcotics Branch assignment from when we were partnered and I went down, forced into early retirement.

Best thing to do is drive home, catch my damn breath, and call her from there.

THREE

Once inside, I lock the door behind me, hang up my jacket, and go to the kitchen to pour myself a Jameson on ice. It's still early, but for me it's never too early.

In the laundry room I slide open the secret wall panel on the side of the washer and place the wad of money from the house I hit on a shelf beside several stacks of ones, fives, tens, and twenties that're bound tight with red rubber bands. I always pocket the hundreds that I find. I'll count this wad later. Need to call Leslie back first.

Back in my armchair I consider lighting a cigarette but decide against it. Too much of a trigger. Always makes me want. I'm stronger, but weakness is always trying to find a way in.

I swear I stare at the cell phone for more than ten minutes before I decide to return Leslie's call. Then—

"Leslie Costello's office," a receptionist answers. Not the voice I remember for the woman who used to work for Leslie. And damn, Leslie didn't even call from her direct line. I go straight to the receptionist.

"Frank Marr returning Leslie's call," I advise her.

"One moment please."

I take a breath.

"Hello, Frank." She answers evenly—professionally.

Aside from the tone, she sounds like the same person, but lacking a certain once-shared familiarity. May as well have answered with "Hello, Mr. Marr."

"Hi, Leslie. Sorry it took so long. I was working something."

No response.

"I didn't want to call you," she begins matter-of-factly. "It was Al's decision."

"What's going on? Is he okay?"

"He's in some trouble—"

"What kind of trouble?"

"He was involved in a shooting. Doesn't look good."

"What the—did he get hurt?"

"No. He's on administrative leave, though. Just listen for a second. You know the police shooting—a sixteen-year-old kid in Northwest, near Howard?"

"No. I don't watch the news anymore. But damn..." Because I know what's going to come next.

"He was the cop who shot the kid."

"Fuck."

"The department determined that it was a bad shooting. No gun on the kid, but Luna swears there was. He said the kid pointed it right at him. That's why he wants you."

"Of course. Anything. So you're representing him, then?"

"Yes, and you're not my first choice for investigator."

"You sorta made that clear, Leslie. I got it a long time ago. So why didn't Luna call me himself?"

"That's something you'll have to ask him."

"Is he home?"

"I believe so. There's a lot of media attention on this, but the department has managed to keep his name out of it for now. But that won't last. We both know how it goes."

"I'm going over there now."

"I'll meet you there."

"What, I need a babysitter?"

"Yes," she says a little too firmly.

FOUR

Luna lives in Northeast DC, near Catholic University, an older home on a small one-way street off Michigan Ave. It has a large front porch. We used to sit there on rickety old rattan chairs after a hard day's work, smoking cigars and drinking good scotch. Luna liked the good stuff. Still does.

Lot of families living in his neighborhood now. Not like when he bought it in the early nineties. There were a couple of good families then, long since passed, though. It used to be a rough area, but that's why he could afford it on a cop's salary. Hell, that's why I could afford my house on 12th Street, in Northwest. We still got our problems in both neighborhoods. That's the price you gotta pay if you want to live in DC.

The shades in his front window are pulled down. The patio light is on, even though it's daytime. Can't tell if he has any lights on inside, and I don't see his car, but then he's had a take-home vehicle for as long as I can remember. I'm sure the department took that back along with his badge and gun.

When I'm about to hit the steps that lead to his front door, I notice a cab pull to the curb.

Leslie steps out, carrying an expensive-looking teal-colored briefcase and sporting a gray three-button overcoat.

Damn, she looks nice.

I wait for her by the steps. "Hello, Leslie. You look good."

"Fuck you."

I shoot her an uncomfortable smile. *Was that necessary?*

"Is this how it's going to be? 'Cause it's getting awkward, and I'm here for Al. So, can you try to forget what I can't even remember?"

"That's what the problem is. But yes, because I'm here for Al, too. And I got it out of my system with the 'Fuck you,' so that's that."

"Okay, then."

I allow her up the steps first, then follow.

She rings the doorbell. After a few seconds, she rings again.

"You sure he's home?" I ask.

"No, but like I said, I know he's been keeping a low profile. I don't know where else he could be."

I open the glass security door, knock a few times on the front door.

"Al, it's Frank and Leslie! Open up!"

A moment later I hear footsteps on a creaking wooden floor approach the front door. Then we hear the dead bolt unlock.

Door opens.

Al's wearing baggy jeans and a T-shirt it looks like he's been sleeping in for a few days. His face is a week's worth of scruff.

"Come in," he says, his voice throaty. He backs away from the door to give us room. "Good to see you, Frank."

He manages a slight smile. I can smell the alcohol on his breath. Something peaty, probably his go-to, Laphroaig.

"You too, my friend."

We enter. He closes the door. Dead-bolts it.

I notice a blanket and pillow on the sofa. Been sleeping there. Probably his comfort spot, trick the mind into thinking it's a nap and you fall asleep faster. I also spot the nearly empty bottle of Laphroaig on the end table at the pillow side of the sofa, an empty tumbler beside the bottle as well.

"Sorry about the mess," he says, tries to straighten up the sofa.

"Don't worry about that, Al," Leslie says.

He scoots the blanket in a pile by the pillow and sits beside it. I take the recliner, and Leslie sits on the cleared-off side of the sofa, next to him.

Like I said, it's an older house. It smells like an old house. Not a terrible smell. Old wood. Your grandmother's place maybe.

He starts to get up again, says, "Oh, can I get you anything? I can make coffee."

"No. Sit down," Leslie tells him, like a polite order.

He obeys.

Damn, he's looking frail. Probably hasn't been eating, just drinking. I wanna say something, but I don't.

"Well, Frank," he says, turning to me. "You want I should tell you the story?"

Have you read THE SECOND GIRL,
the first novel featuring the Frank Marr?

Frank Marr may be a decorated former cop and
an excellent private investigator, but Washington
DC doesn't know his dirty secret.

Frank has managed to keep his drug habit hidden.
But after accidentally rescuing a kidnapped
teenage girl, he's thrust into the spotlight.

Reluctantly, he agrees to investigate another – possibly
connected – disappearance, all the time knowing that
the heightened scrutiny may expose him . . .

Out now in paperback and ebook.

MULHOLLAND
BOOKS
HODDER